Jacob

Encounters with the Holy Spirit

Book 3 of the *Buddy* series

Arthur Perkins

SIGNALMAN PUBLISHING

Jacob: Encounters with the Holy Spirit
by Arthur Perkins

Signalman Publishing
www.signalmanpublishing.com
email: info@signalmanpublishing.com
Kissimmee, Florida

Scriptures are taken from the King James Version of the Bible
unless otherwise noted.

ISBN: 978-1-940145-39-6 (paperback)
978-1-940145-40-2 (ebook)

Signalman
Publishing

Printed in the United States of America

Also by Arthur Perkins

Buddy

Cathy

DEDICATION

As in my previous Christian novels, **Buddy** and **Cathy**, I dedicate this work to my wife, Carolyn, the joy of my life. We both dedicate this work, above all, to our God, and to our four daughters and their families.

INTRODUCTION

The president of the United States, accepting no bounds on his narcissistic acquisition of power, used his second term in office to further his personal agenda of integrating the country into a world community of nations with himself as ultimate leader. The process of integration required the United States to abandon its notion of capitalistic exceptionalism in favor of conformance to the international norm of highly-centralized socialism, a task made easier by the Dewey-inspired educational policy of the past several decades, which promoted self-absorption and an attitude of entitlement based on mere existence at the expense of personal responsibility. Mental and moral discipline were no longer valued as personal qualities, with predictable results that came back to bite succeeding generations of indulgent, overly tolerant teachers and indifferent parents. The ultimate result of these degeneracies was to favor the development of a population that in its own narcissism both demanded and created a president with like qualities of character. In this environment, any semblance of selfless nobility simply did not exist, which made the population as a whole ripe for the plucking away of self-determination. The current president was simply the latest in a line of like-minded leaders who allowed themselves to be manipulated by a cadre of enormously wealthy and powerful political movers and shakers who were increasingly insistent on subjugating America to their vision of world government, which, of course, would operate to their own reward.

The current president wasn't the only problem with America—not by a long shot. He wasn't the first to steer America down the path of socialism. Furthermore, he couldn't have done the things that he did without a thoroughly corrupt congress. The self-service they displayed with regard to their own unique salaries, pensions and healthcare is so self-evident that anyone who needs further proof of massive congressional felony would have to be among the most naïve persons on the planet. Even the judicial system has been infected with enough individuals of dubious character that for some time it has begged to be neutralized through threats of harm and blackmail.

Regardless of its pathetic educational system and corrupt leadership, America was ready anyway to be trashed, being in the last stage of a cycle common to all great nations of the past: from bondage to spiritual faith; from spiritual faith to great courage; from courage to liberty; from liberty to abundance; from abundance to selfishness; from selfishness to complacency; from complacency to apathy; from apathy to dependency; and from dependency back into bondage.

But this president, in keeping with America's position in the cycle of bondage, certainly was the worst of the lot. He was an overt narcissist of legendary indifference to the suffering of others, his sociopathic mind being incapable of the slightest compassion toward anyone but himself. Having been promised the ultimate crown by the behind-the-scenes world leaders, he set out with uncommon boldness to dismantle the middle class of American society, disassociate the masses from property ownership, and create a new society of indolent, handout-hungry landless serfs living continuously on the edge of poverty.

Having so thoroughly destroyed the country's economy in

his communistic wealth-distribution schemes, the president, understanding that his overzealous subordinates had erred in moving too far too quickly, sought alternative means to mitigate this economic carnage in order to present the United States to the world community of nations as a viable entity. His favorite method, which he considered to be his own unique contribution to the greening of the world, was to engage in a program of massive population reduction, which he liked to think of a separating the dross from the metal, the dross being three categories of people: the infirm, the elderly and the people of the Book, namely Christians and Jews. The remainder would constitute the most productive element of society, provided that they were kept in their place by the increasingly edgy employment and labor policies of the multinational corporations.

In both attitude and methods, the current president's governance was reminiscent of the manner in which Adolph Hitler had managed the German nation. Back in 2010, Christian historian Eric Metaxas attempted in his book *Bonhoeffer* to warn the American public that it was on the path to repeating that very dark period of world history, the rise of the Third Reich. He quoted Hitler's own words in describing his opinion of the Christian faith:

"It's been our misfortune to have the wrong religion. Why didn't we have the religion of the Japanese, who regard sacrifice for the Fatherland as the highest good? The Mohammedan religion too would have been much more compatible to us than Christianity. Why did it have to be Christianity with its meekness and flabbiness?"

It was obvious to all but the terminally naïve that Hitler, whose closest associates were anti-Christian to the core, considered the Judeo-Christian God to be irrelevant to his life and the world in general, if indeed He actually did exist. Hitler, being a sociopathic narcissist, worshiped one being alone: himself. In terms of destiny and a national standard-bearer, the hard, cruel and merciless diety of Nietzsche was far more to his liking. Nevertheless, Hitler was, if anything, a pragmatist. If it served his purpose, which it did early on in his messianic calling, he was more than willing to claim Christianity as his religion, and he had to curb his anti-Christian henchmen often in order to maintain that fiction to the public.

As Solomon lamented more than once in *Ecclesiastes*, there is indeed nothing new under the sun. The current president of the United States followed in the path of his spiritual father Hitler so closely that it often seemed that Hitler himself had been resurrected in the form of this modern leader. The stated issues were slightly different this time around, but the ultimate objective remained locked on political power. The targets were essentially the same: first the legislative and the judicial branches of government, just as Hitler first neutralized the Reichstag and the courts; and after them the least productive, most potentially rebellious or useful scapegoats of society, namely Jews, Christians, the infirm and the elderly. Like the targets, the methods were virtually identical, differing only in the state of supporting technology: relocation centers co-located with massive ovens. Universal healthcare was a deliberate disaster, softening up the masses with financial untenability to the point of docility and acceptance of a world government supported by a universal tracking system: the long-anticipated Mark of the Beast, the scanning setup as described in Revelation 13.

But this time around the situation was far worse for those who were threatened, and for a number of reasons. First, there were countries back then that were not part of the Axis powers, and which were noble enough to actively oppose the totalitarian systems. Second, technology wasn't so advanced as to be able to track every individual on the planet, to sense opposition wherever it happened to crop up, and to instantly neutralize all such threats to the regime. Third, the godless depravity had not yet become universal.

The decline of the Western World's fortunes was supported enthusiastically by a public that, like the German society before it, actually knew nothing about their God or His Word despite the apparent popularity of the Catholic and Lutheran manifestations of Christianity. And, also like their German predecessors, they consequently had left themselves open to a wide range of deceptions that led them either to want nothing to do with religion or its oppressions, or to make a do-over of their God into something that might dovetail more suitably to their growing selfishness, lack of discipline, moral degeneracy, financial irresponsibility, violence and lawlessness. Their rejection of God was accompanied by a conscious and diligent effort to ignore His warnings, which were interpreted instead as random misfortunes. As long as these incidents occurred to people other than themselves, they quickly put them out of their minds, failing to notice a pattern in the increasing frequency and intensity of devastating storms, earthquakes, crop failures, and diseases. Regional mass starvations and outbreaks of killer pestilences were attributed to local wars or governmental mismanagement—certainly not to a Deity personally involved in the affairs of man.

Survival was getting tougher for the masses, but not for everybody, at least not at first. A large and rapidly-growing class of people were content to live on the poverty line, if it meant that their lowly condition entitled them to handouts. Living lives of ease and indolence on the backs of those who found it increasingly hard to maintain their work ethic, they persisted in voting for those who promised them more, until their right to vote was taken away. In the totalitarian repression that followed, they, as non-productive members of society, were carted away to relocation centers, where they, along with the infirm, Christians and Jews, awaited their transition to more permanent quarters by way of the massive ovens. Those of society who continued to evade that fate were observed and tracked wherever they went, which was limited to short commutes to and from work with the briefest of forays to local stores stocked with the most basic of necessities. Entertainment, such as it was, ran to home-based television and video games of the most graphically violent, coarse and pornographic sort. Society at large, driven by the need to validate a freedom that didn't actually exist, was pushing hard for the legalization of inter-species marriage. The centralization of government into a cadre whose dominion spanned the globe was nearly complete, awaiting only the completion of final touches on a fully cashless economic system.

In the midst of this international descent into chaotic depravity, Earl and Joyce Cook have managed to escape certain death in their prison camp by a serendipitous earthquake. They left behind their cherished adopted daughter Cathy as well as Joyce's mother Janet and stepfather Henry and, sadly, their kind and noble boating benefactors Stephen and Cindy Miller, all of whom had died in the camp. But they brought with them a cadre of dedicated Jews, now Messianic, thanks in good measure to the Holy Spirit's use of Earl to establish an irrefutable connection between Jesus Christ and their long-awaited Messiah. Using the confusion of the devastating quake to make their getaway from the camp in a military vehicle, they entered the lifestyle of desperate fugitives. Bad as their present situation was, it was infinitely better than the hopeless misery of the death camp.

CHAPTER ONE

"Take a left up that wash!" the new leader of the small band shouted to the driver of the commandeered troop carrier. His name was Jacob Perlman and, like the rest of the people on board the lurching vehicle, he was a prisoner less than half an hour before, waiting like the others for his turn to die. His crime, like that of his great grandparents before him who were trapped under the Nazi jackboot, was that he was a Jew. Seventy years later, the evil had migrated to America, where the sick, infirm, elderly, Jew and now even the Christian were no longer welcome. As part of the revamping of society into a socialist state for its integration into a one-world system, a thorough housecleaning had taken place. Spearheaded by a self-serving president who had slowly acquired in his first term the godlike powers he chose to exercise with cruelty in his second, the increasingly repressive regime had begun to divest itself of the less productive members of society. Ironically, it was doing so under the guise of providing more efficient care of the less fortunate.

The public at large had enthusiastically bought into this fiction, but then, having grown indolent, self-absorbed and indifferent to the suffering of others, they perceived that they had much to gain and little to lose by the removal of these creatures, whom the press did its utmost to portray as less than human. The notion that they themselves might eventually join the ranks of the elderly was simply beyond the scope of their shallow mindset. As a consequence, the rejects of this new society had been rounded up and herded into a vast network of holding pens located next to death factories, their brutal efficiency inspired by the depraved minds of Hitler's and Stalin's regimes. Removed from the eyes of society, the new misfits, defined as such for the public by its corrupt and evil leadership, simply ceased to exist.

All of the ex-prisoners were wearing the uniforms of their former guards, now dead from the destructive chaos of the super-earthquake that had freed the prison inmates. Having been released by the massive killer quake, they were now grasping for a new chance at life. The commandeered truck swung left, leaving a graded dirt road to climb up a shallow bone-dry draw. The vehicle slowed and the transfer case groaned in protest as the driver engaged the front wheels. The vehicle lurched forward and jounced along the dry streambed as the driver strained to negotiate a pathway through the numerous ruts and boulders. Behind them a lengthy cloud of dust marked their passage from the main camp. So far they weren't being followed. They were too far away now to discern individuals, but they could see the buildings of the camp, or what remained of them. The metal-framed barracks had collapsed, undoubtedly trapping most of the prisoners inside. They had probably either been severely injured or died. Even that untimely end, however, was to be preferred to the living hell that each day represented under their brutal overseers. A low-lying black cloud drifted toward the ruined buildings. Something didn't seem quite right with the scene, and suddenly Earl understood why. The huge smokestacks had collapsed. One lay on the ground almost intact, but the others had been reduced to heaps of broken concrete.

Earl looked over to Joyce, thanking God again for the gift of her life and her presence beside him. She gave him a smile. The truck had crested a diminishing rise above the wash and was picking up speed as it moved cross-country over the flat high-desert grassland dotted with mesquite, ocotillo and occasional saguaro. He turned his head toward the front, observing the gradual rise of the land toward the peaks to their east. Scattered high clouds cast a patchwork pattern of shadows about the desert floor, darkening the prevailing tan color to brown. White boulders jutted out from the red-streaked gray hills ahead.

"Look at that, will you?" one of the women yelled. Earl turned his head toward the direction her shocked face was pointing. At first they looked like sticks scattered around the terrain, then, as he focused, more like pieces of rope. His mind made the identification just as the woman shouted "Snakes! Thousands of them!" The rest of the passengers got to their feet and looked rearward. Joyce clung to Earl for support. He felt her shudder in revulsion, but soon the truck had left the patch behind. She nudged his ribs for attention. "Why so many?" she asked.

"Then I guess it's really true that animals can sense an earthquake long before humans can. This area's full of them, but they're usually hidden from sight. The threat of the earthquake must have driven them out of their holes and dens."

As he continued to watch the road below and behind them, the remains came into view of the isolated guardhouse they had just avoided. Situated next to the dirt road, it marked the boundary of the reservation. The earthquake had leveled the shack; there was no sign of life. Jacob must have noticed its desolate condition, for he spoke to the driver, who angled the truck back toward the road. Once back on the roadway the driver shifted out of four-wheel drive and picked up speed. Darkness fell and the temperature dropped, but in their elation at having escaped the band's spirits remained high. They marveled at the blackness of the sky, pierced only by the headlights of their truck. The earthquake obviously had damaged the power grid. "Hey!" someone shouted, looking at his wrist theatrically. "We gotta turn around. It's chow time! We'll miss roll call!" Laughter rippled through the truck.

Presently the truck stopped, then backed up slowly as Jacob

scanned the roadway ahead. It stopped again. "All right, everyone," Jacob said. "Pit stop. Do your business and get back as quick as you can. I don't see any snakes, but be careful anyway. We've been lucky so far," he continued as the passengers scrambled out the tailgate, "but I'm guessing that it won't be very long now before some sign of life shows up. And I don't mean snakes."

When the people returned to the truck Jacob switched drivers and the vehicle took off again. They began to climb. Earl saw Joyce hugging her arms, shivering. He hugged her tightly and they sat together in a corner of the bed. Much later the truck left the roadway and wound about some huge boulders. The driver doused the lights and the truck braked to a stop. With the engine off, the racket of a helicopter somewhere above them was immediately apparent. The noise reached a crescendo as it passed overhead and began to diminish. Over thirty eyeballs followed it intently as it receded into the distance in the direction of the camp. "We're safe for now," Jacob said, the relief apparent in his voice. "They're probably doing a first recon of the camp. They probably won't start rounding up strays for another day or so. Let's take a vote. Do you want to stay here for the night?"

"No!" shouted a chorus of voices. "We're too cold to sleep," one woman said. "Let's just push on, at least until we run out of gas."

The truck moved on through the darkness, the driver peering out at the feeble illumination provided by the parking lights, which were abruptly doused when someone noticed the distant light of the returning helicopter and alerted Jacob. It roared overhead as it made a beeline for some remote destination. After its passage the silent darkness enveloped them once more and they cautiously moved on. Some time later Jacob gave the go-ahead and the driver switched the headlights back on and the truck picked up speed. Eventually it slowed to accommodate a steep grade as the road twisted up along the side of a mountain. They crested the summit and the road started back down.

Despite the cold, Earl dozed off. He awoke abruptly when the ride suddenly smoothed out, announcing to them that they had come upon a paved stretch of the road. He stood up and looked around. This area was flat, and in the dim pre-dawn twilight he saw that they were now traveling through farm land. The truck stopped again, this time next to a car that had wrapped its grille around a thick wooden power pole. It was abandoned. Hopefully, the driver hadn't been badly injured. Jacob guided the truck so that its headlights shone on the driver's door. He opened it and peered inside, then reached in and retrieved a plastic bottle of water. He tossed it over to a woman who was standing on the truck bed with outstretched hands. She took a greedy gulp and passed it on. Jacob reached in once more and emerged with a partially-eaten candy bar. He tossed it up to the same woman. "Anyone have a knife?" he asked. A number of people responded by searching the pockets of their newly-acquired uniforms. Someone hit paydirt and handed him a pocket knife. He asked for and was handed the empty plastic bottle. Opening the knife, he ducked under the abandoned car and thrust the blade into the gas tank. The truck headlights illuminated a thin stream of gasoline pouring from the tank into the small plastic bottle. "Somebody pour this into the truck!" he called, handing the bottle over and sticking his finger over the tear in the tank. He repeated the process several times until the flow of gas diminished to a dribble, then got back onto his feet at motioned everybody back into the truck.

A tall, gangly fellow wormed his way through the press of people to stand near Earl. He sat down next to him and offered his hand. "Sidney," he said. "I was there when you were speaking to us from inside your coffin. I appreciate your courage and your devotion. We all do. So I get it about Jesus' feeding of the multitudes. It's a real eye-opener, especially in how the numbers fit so well. It obviously was planned that way. And how it links Jesus with Elisha. And how it links Jesus as the Word and the Bread of Life. Beautiful, actually. Any more?"

"Say what?" Earl asked, confused.

"Any more eye-openers like that one? We Jews have had a problem, I can see why pretty clearly now. Being brought up to think of Christianity as beneath us and actually our enemy, we never bothered to look at what you call the New Testament. And so we just propagated our own ignorance."

"Well said. But you're not alone, Sidney." Earl extended his hand again in welcome. My name's Earl if you didn't know that. Glad to make your acquaintance. And yes, there are lots more where that came from. I take it you're interested."

"Call me Sid. And I am. I'd like to have as much ammo as I can get because it's my intention to make it to Israel and start spreading the Word over there."

"Okay. First thing when you get a chance to, pick up a Christian Bible. Read Genesis and the other four Gospels. Then . . ."

"Hold on. Did you just call Genesis—*our* Genesis—a Gospel? Of Jesus Christ?"

"I sure did. You'll understand that better when you read the four named Gospels, and then the Book of Acts. I'll give you a heads-up right now, though. How's your memory?"

"I don't know. I think it's okay."

"The first eighteen verses of John Chapter One is a story of Jesus' beginnings, but way before He came in the flesh. It's a majestic story, called John's Prologue. Some Christian in camp scratched it out for us to read and I've happened to memorize it. Think you can do the same?"

"Have at it."

In response, Earl recited the Prologue to Sid. He went very slowly and repeated it several times. Sid finally nodded. "I think I've got it. That's enough for now. I'm going to spend the rest of the night driving it into my brain. Thanks, I really appreciate it." He shook Earl's hand again. "By the way," he commented. "It seems to me that this Prologue and the first chapter of Genesis have the same style."

"For sure. I'm convinced it's intentional, because the two passages relate so closely to each other, with one supplying supporting information to the other. Glad that you caught that. Read Genesis 1 and 2 when you get hold of a Bible and try to integrate the two together. It will make much of the rest come clearer."

Sid waved his hand in salute and moved back toward the rear of the truck. Shortly after that the truck stopped once more, then made a gentle right turn onto a larger road. They passed beneath a major highway, which Earl guessed was Interstate 10. A sign on the right side of the roadway informed them that they were entering the town of Bowie, Arizona.

The town itself was tiny, a settlement dominated by a collection of mobile homes and defunct RVs. It obviously was isolated from the mainstream of society, and undoubtedly its residents preferred things to remain that way. Earl envied them their lifestyle, being under the radar of all but the most inquisitive of strangers and authorities. Here and there were signs of earthquake damage, but they could see that the town had escaped major catastrophe. Although most of the residents were still asleep, a couple of homes had lights on, probably from personal generators. Like the RV society, they looked to be self-sufficient.

Up ahead was a well-lighted café, but before they reached it they received the fright of their lives. The door swung open and out stepped two burly men wearing the guard uniforms of the camp they had escaped. The driver swerved down an alley, but they had been seen. Soon they were being followed by a vehicle similar to theirs. They backtracked out of town, the other truck close on their tail. Emerging from beneath the freeway, they stopped suddenly by the roadside. The other truck pulled in behind them and the passenger emerged. "Hey, guys," he said, recognizing the uniforms as theirs. "How's the camp? Why didn't you stop? Are you. . ." Suddenly he shut up, realizing that the occupants were strangers, and gaunt with an unhealthy pallor to their skin. His features displayed his comprehension of the situation and he reached for his holstered gun as the driver opened his door. Two of the ex-prisoners beat him to the draw and shot him. The driver was hit before he could close the door. "Okay, everybody," Jacob said. "Out of the truck and into the other one." He and his two drivers got out of the cab and went over to where the bodies lay. They picked them up and put them into the bed of their truck, then stepped into the cab of the other one. Their new truck turned around and went back to the café.

The proprietor welcomed them when they entered, but stepped back in shock at their faces. He'd made a good living serving the camp guards with beer and Mexican fare and saw immediately that while these newcomers were dressed as guards, they obviously weren't. Before he could speak Jacob walked up to him and confronted him. "Senor. . ."

"Hey, don't get condescending with me, pal," the proprietor replied, cutting him off. "I'm as American as you. I can see where you came from and what you are. Sit. All of you. Marie!" he shouted to the rear of the café.

"What do you want, Pablo?" a heavy-set but pretty woman said from a room in back. Eventually she came into the dining area and took instant notice of the men in the room. The proprietor turned back to Jacob. "And no jokes about the names, either," he said with a glare. "Marie, these people need to be fed. Get the eggs and toast going. And put the rice and beans on. "I hope you like Mexican food," he told Jacob, "because they way you look, you're going to do a whole lot of eating. I'm cooking up some eggs, but mostly you're going to have rice and beans because that's all we've got that'll take care of the lot of you. What, did you escape in the earthquake?"

"We're very grateful," Jacob replied. "We'll take what we get and like it, but as for me, I happen to love Mexican food anyway. Yeah, the camp was pretty much demolished by the 'quake, lucky for us. What do you know about the place?"

"Just what I've overheard from the guards. They're a brutal bunch, laughing at what they did to you guys. Their entertainment sounds pretty sick."

"It was. We're very lucky to be alive."

"What were you in for?"

"Being a Jew. We all are, except for Earl and Joyce over there. They're Christians."

Hey man, I'm a Christian too. Catholic. So's Marie. My roots are Mexican, so I'm not exactly a minority around here, but I know what it feels like. That's just over the top. How long were they going to keep you for being Jews?"

"For the rest of our lives, which they didn't plan on lasting too long."

"You gotta be kidding. We didn't know about that. Sounds like Germany. Hey, Marie! he called. Come over here and listen to this. Guy says the camp was a death camp. Like in Germany, you know." She listened, shook her head and returned to her cooking.

"It's exactly like the old Nazi regime. America has become a totalitarian state too, if you haven't noticed."

"We don't get around much. There's nothing on TV that gives us that impression, either."

"Yeah, I wouldn't expect it would. The media is pretty well controlled by the government."

The proprietor went behind the counter to help Marie. Sid came up to Earl and Joyce's table with two companions and sat down. "This here's Joseph," he said, placing a hand on Joseph's shoulder, "and this other's Irving." Both men reached out and shook Earl's hand, and then Joyce's. "They heard you back in camp," Sid told them. I told them about John's prologue. They'd like to hear more about your Jesus. Me too."

"Well, for starters, He's just as much your Jesus as ours, if not more. You worshiped Him, in fact, without knowing it."

"What?" Irving said, dumbfounded. "How can that be?"

Earl turned to Sid. "Remember the last verse of John's Prologue, that said 'No man has seen God at any time. The only begotten Son, who is in the bosom of the Father, He has declared Him.'"

"I guess I didn't make the connection," Sid replied, staring at the table with contrition.

"So are you trying to say that our God, your Old Testament God, was really Jesus?"

"That's exactly what I'm saying," Earl responded. "John spells it out more clearly in Chapter Eight of his Gospel. "The Pharisees were responding to Jesus' implication that those who listened to Him would have everlasting life, and reminded Him that Abraham, who was a pinnacle of obedience toward God, was dead. Jesus took that opportunity to tell them that Abraham had seen His day, and was glad. Getting angry, they scoffed at Him, questioning Him, who wasn't yet fifty years old, about the implication that He'd seen Abraham. Jesus reply was a classic. He said 'Verily, verily, I say unto you, Before Abraham was, I am."

"Hold on, there," Irving said, half standing. "Jesus said that? Do you know what that implies? He's almost saying that He's the Great 'I AM' who spoke to Moses out of the burning bush."

"Yes. That's exactly what Jesus said, and that's precisely what He meant. He was the Great I AM who spoke to Moses. He was your Yahweh."

Irving struggled with this notion. He didn't know whether or not to get up and walk away. In the end, the cooking reached his nostrils and his stomach told him to shut up and sit. Being a religious man, he attempted to reconcile this information with his belief system.

Sid spoke up as Irving and Joseph continued to wrestle with this unexpected thought. "I kind of get it," he began tentatively. "Which means that He pre-existed before His coming in the flesh. But then why did He wait so long? Why didn't He come right away and speak directly to Abraham?"

"He did. It's right there in your Old Testament. Remember the visitation by the three men—it's in Genesis 18—and the discussion about the destruction of Sodom? One of those men was Jesus. But for the most part Jesus refrained from appearing to us. He did that for the reason that He was allowing you Jews to fashion Him out of the noble events in your own lives, so that you'd recognize Him in love when He came in the flesh. Remember Joseph, and the salvation he gave to the brothers who had abused him so terribly? How about Abraham's attempt to sacrifice his beloved son Isaac? You have a whole host of people whom God had favored by allowing them to represent in Scripture facets of Jesus' selfless, noble character. As to His pre-existence, Genesis 1 has much to say about that, especially when it is read in the light of John's Prologue. And many of your people did know about Jesus before He came in the flesh. Are you familiar with David's Psalm 2, or Psalm 22?"

"Vaguely. I guess I didn't give Scripture as much thought as I should have. But gee, you Christians have had two thousand years to fill us in on the truth. Why did you go the other way and choose to punish us and try to force us to convert?"

"I agree about that, Sid," Earl said. "I certainly wouldn't call our behavior with respect to you anything resembling what a Christian attitude should have been. But remember, for a good portion of those two thousand years, Christianity was under the thumb of a repressive and self-serving Church system that I wouldn't call Christian. It didn't just deny helping you find your God. It denied its own laypersons access to the Bible. And when that prohibition wasn't in effect, the layperson's own indifference toward God gave him nothing but a shallow understanding of the Bible. He missed most of what it said. So we Christians turned out to be just as ignorant of the true God as you, maybe even more so. Sometimes I wonder if God didn't allow that on purpose, just to even the score between Jews and Christians."

"Thanks for that," Sid replied. His two friends were still scratching their heads, attempting to fit Earl's words into their world views. Marie came up to their table at that point, setting down huge platters of food. The men's attention was drawn to the plates before them, and their conversation was put on hold as they turned into their meals with noisy enthusiasm. When asked about his plans, Jacob told him they'd probably be better off heading northeast toward New Mexico and keeping away from population centers. He watched the proprietor draw a map giving directions from Bowie to

Duncan, showing various dirt roads that were too small to show up on the state map. When Pablo was through Jacob tried to pay him when they got up to leave, but he would have none of it. "It's not ours anyway," Jacob argued. Here- take it."

"No," Pablo said firmly. "You might need it later. Good luck and God be with you." Evidently Jacob and Pablo had had a conversation of their own while the others were busy eating, as several of the men were carrying piles of blankets in their arms. Two other men held Bibles, and Jacob stuffed the map into his pocket.

"Thanks for your lesson," Sid said to Earl as they trooped out of the café. "It's amazing. We'll be coming around for more."

"You're more than welcome. I'm just glad that you're interested."

They climbed back into the truck. "Jacob's a smart one, switching trucks like that," he said to Joyce.

"Why?" she asked.

"I'd be willing to bet that Jacob thought the real guards had filled up with gas before they went into the cafe. And I'd also be willing to bet that Jacob has already confirmed that by looking at the gas gauge."

"Pretty smart," she agreed. "Earl, I'm getting scared about the two guards we killed. They're right out in the open. Someone's going to come along soon and find them dead and with bullet holes in them."

"Yeah, and I'm also pretty sure that at least one of the guards back at the camp saw us leave and stayed alive long enough to get the word out about our escape. Either way, they're probably going to come after us. And it shouldn't be much longer."

Someone handed Joyce a blanket. She wrapped it around herself and Earl, and they sat down together. The truck started up and they moved away, full for the first time since their imprisonment and thankful to God for the blessing of the proprietor's kindness toward them.

The truck took a dirt road from Bowie, heading northeast and angling toward New Mexico. Eventually they hit a paved stretch and made good time. Jacob scanned the map Pablo had given him, and then took out the state map he'd also gotten from Pablo, spotting the little town of Duncan just on the Arizona side of the New Mexico border as their next destination. They didn't know it, of course, but a military satellite had picked up their heat signature in its infrared imager. The primary heat source was recognized as an engine. Situated as it was in an isolated location, it was further recognized as a potential fugitive vehicle. Although the bodies left behind in Bowie had not yet been found, the information supplied by the satellite was sufficient to arouse the curiosity of the authorities. The hunt was on.

The Apache gunship arrived overhead just after dark. Fully armed and equipped with night vision capability, the truck stood out in stark detail to the sensor operator of the gunship crew. Protocol suggested that the truck first be identified as friend or foe before engaging, so the pilot dropped down to within a hundred feet of the truck. A bullhorn commanded the truck to stop. The disappointed passengers knew at this point that the gunship, with its massive weaponry including its 30-mm rapid fire automatic cannon and Hellfire missiles was way over-equipped for the task of reducing them to bloody shreds. The enemy, safely ensconced within the nearly-impregnable giant insect, held all the cards. They also knew that they had nothing to lose: nobody was going to go back to that camp. To the man, they'd rather die. One of the passengers had a riot gun that once belonged to a guard, a twelve-gauge loaded with six cartridges, each containing a lead slug. In the darkness and focus on the truck, the crew missed the upraised weapon. The man fired and sparks flew off a blade of the battle-hardened tail rotor. He reloaded and fired again, which angered the pilot, who knew from the act that the truck below was definitely a foe. The giant angry bee turned to position itself and the cannon head-on just as the shotgun fired for the third time. Something happened, because instead of stabilizing in a position to bring the cannon to bear on the truck, the truck itself was almost tipped over by a strong gust of wind. The gust was so violent that it almost ripped the shotgun from the shooter's hands. What it did to the gunship was more spectacular. The ex-prisoners watched in amazement as the helicopter rocked onto its side and then went down the side of the mountain as if it had been slapped by a giant hand. The Apache wobbled as the pilot fought to regain control. The jerky motion rapidly morphed into a spin as the pilot lost control entirely, and the craft buzzed off down the mountainside, impacting on a ledge and blowing up. The astonished passengers jumped off the truck and raced over to the edge of the roadway to see the spectacle. They retreated back as cannon rounds began to cook off. Jacob hurried them back aboard the truck and commanded the driver to resume.

"What a lucky break!" Sid exulted. "I've heard of freak winds like that that come up as the coming of night changes the motion of air."

"Don't you think maybe that the timing was a bit over-the-top?" Joyce broke in. "You might call it luck, but I'm thinking that we just witnessed the Hand of God." Her assertion gave them something to chew on, and they considered it in silence.

Not long after that the truck stopped and Jacob opened the door to the cab and stood up, facing the passengers in the bed. "It won't be long before they have another go at us. They'll know who we are and the next time they won't wait to fire. We're going to have to leave the truck." The passengers dropped down from the back of the truck with reluctance, knowing that Jacob was right. After instructing the driver to set the parking brake and to keep the engine idling in neutral, Jacob emerged from the cab with the other two occupants. He led the forlorn group as they continued up the hill on foot.

They were about a mile away from the truck when they heard another Apache heading their way. Jacob instructed the people to scatter, separating from each other as much as possible in the time available to minimize the heat signature. As Jacob had anticipated, the idling truck served as a decoy beacon for the Apache, and they saw it hover momentarily and release a Hellfire, which utterly demolished the vehicle. The gunship made a half-hearted attempt afterward to look for nearby victims, but quickly gave up and departed the area.

Without the truck they were forced to resume their trek on foot. Jacob reassembled the scattered band and gave them a pep talk before they set out. "The bad news is now we have to walk," he told the group, "but there's good news too. Now that they've destroyed their target, they probably think that they killed us along with the truck. If they do think so, and I don't see any reason that they wouldn't, they won't come back after us. To be on the safe side, though, we'll move at night and stay put under cover during the daylight hours. We're not good on food, though so, we're going to have to stock up in the next town, which I expect will be Duncan. We've already come a good distance since leaving Bowie, so we should get there within a day or so. I'd like to stay on this road, but it's still about ten miles from Duncan at the intersection of this road with the highway, so we'd do best to strike out cross-country in a north-eastward direction over those mountains," he said, pointing.

"Were you a Boy Scout?" one of the men asked.

"Well, no, but. . ."

"Then how do you know to maintain a northeastward direction? I'd sure hate to march all night and find myself in this same spot."

"Yeah, and what about the snakes?" someone added.

"Good point. Let's see by a show of hands who wants to stay on the road, even if it means another ten miles of walking." The response in favor of staying on the road was unanimous. "Okay," Jacob conceded. I defer to superior wisdom. Let's go, then."

When dawn broke they were still trudging up the dirt road. The highway was still beyond their vision. They decided to risk walking for another hour, and then Jacob held up a hand. "Okay, people," he said. "Time to get under cover. You with blankets, share them with others." There weren't quite enough blankets to accommodate everyone. At this place and time of day the air was chilly, but the ones left out bravely offered to stand watch for the others. Jacob formalized the offer by establishing a roster and 3-hour guard schedule that would permit everyone to get under cover and rest for a significant period.

Earl had hoped to limit his blanket partner to Joyce, but discarded the self-serving desire and invited Sid and Irving to share their cover. After Joyce fell asleep, Sid nudged Earl. "Are you sleeping?" he whispered.

"Not now," he replied, somewhat irritably.

"Sorry, Earl, but I need to know more about your—my—Jesus. I think we didn't recognize Him when He came in the flesh because we expected our Messiah to save us from the Roman occupation. We wanted a leader who was willing to fight for our freedom."

"Think about that," Earl replied in a whisper. "Jesus wasn't interested in saving you from the Romans. He plainly said that His kingdom was not of this earth. He saved you instead from your bondage to your sin. And He didn't just offer salvation to you, but to all mankind."

"Yeah, I get it," Sid whispered back. "But there are passages in our Scripture that portray our Messiah as a man of strength, not the humble Jesus that we saw in the flesh."

"Jesus wasn't always humble. You do know the story of how He overturned the moneychangers' tables in the temple? Sometimes he was very forceful, especially when He was telling off the religious leaders. But you're right, His general nature was one of meekness. But that was foretold, too."

"How so?"

"If you read the story of Joseph in Genesis, you'll see how Joseph prefigured Jesus' love even for His enemies, those who wanted to hurt or kill Him. But I'll bet you never read Isaiah 53."

"No, I don't think I have. It's usually skipped as irrelevant in our readings of Isaiah."

"Read it. You'll be surprised at how accurately Isaiah foretold

Jesus' nature for His first coming."

"First coming? What do you mean? Are there multiple comings?"

"Yes, two. I'll get into that later. First, about Isaiah 53. I don't know all of it by memory, but a couple of phrases I do remember, and they represent the general gist of the whole chapter. To paraphrase the first, it says that He was rejected of men, a man of sorrows, and we hid our faces from Him. Again, Isaiah says of Him that He bore our griefs and carried our sorrows, but we considered Him to be smitten of God. The real clincher is the next, which I've pretty much committed to memory. It goes 'He was wounded for our transgressions, He was bruised for our iniquities; the chastisement of our peace was upon Him, and by His stripes we are healed'. When Jesus came in the flesh, He pretty much fulfilled Isaiah's description of Him and His mission. This passage perplexed your theologians, because, as you said, other passages in Scripture portrayed Him as a mighty king. In fact, they got to wondering whether there would be two Messiahs: one for the strength, the other for the selfless nobility. Actually, in a way they were right about that."

"Two Jesuses?"

"Just one, but two appearances. In the first, which already took place, Jesus demonstrated the love of God toward us by humbling Himself and dying for our iniquities, just as Isaiah foretold in Isaiah 53 and Abraham foretold in his attempted sacrifice of Isaac, and Joseph foretold in. . . well, whatever, you get the drift. I could spend all day pointing to references to Jesus in your Scriptures as the suffering Servant. In His second appearance, what we Christians call His Second Coming, he will be a king, the Lion of the tribe of Judah, reigning over the nations with a rod of iron. The closing chapters of the New Testament Book of Revelation spell out the nature of this Second Coming."

"But what did Jesus have to say about that?" Irving spoke, entering the conversation.

"Shhh. You'll wake up my wife. She needs her sleep. To answer your question, it was Jesus who gave John the imagery from which he wrote the book of Revelation. But Jesus also used Isaiah to give a not-so-subtle hint about it. When He first started out in His ministry, He was given the Book of Isaiah to read aloud in the synagogue. The account is in Luke Chapter 4. Jesus read from Isaiah 61, verses 1 and 2, saying the following:

> *The Spirit of the Lord is upon me, because he hath anointed me to preach the gospel to the poor; he hath sent me to heal the brokenhearted, to preach deliverance to the captives, and recovering of sight to the blind, to set at liberty them that are bruised, to preach the acceptable year of the Lord.*

"Having said that, He closed the book and sat back down. I can imagine a whole bunch of eyeballs facing His way. But then He compounded the commotion by saying to the congregation

> *This day is this scripture fulfilled in your ears.*

"Oh boy," Irving said in a whisper, "That's a pretty forceful statement. But what does that have to do with His Second Coming?"

"I haven't gotten there yet. The connection is in what He read out of the Scripture, and what He left out. He was reading from Isaiah 61, verses 1 and 2, but He stopped short of finishing verse 2. The rest of Isaiah 61, verse 2 reads,

> *. . . and the day of vengeance of our God; to comfort all that mourn;*

"Oh. So Jesus was reserving the fulfillment of the rest of Isaiah 61:2 for His Second Coming. That makes sense."

Earl let Sid and Irving mull over those new thoughts. Turning around, he put his arm around Joyce and fell asleep.

CHAPTER TWO

"Okay, folks, rise and shine!" Jacob shouted. Blankets stirred as the sun went down behind the mountain. Some got up and rushed off for some privacy to relieve themselves. Eventually they stood together, ready to continue up the roadway. An hour into their march, Jacob halted them for a ten-minute break. Several more people went off into the bushes and returned with more cheerful spirits. Twenty minutes into the next hour they reached the summit and saw both their destination to the east and the highway that would take them there. Duncan looked even smaller, if possible, than Bowie. Knowing where it lay, they decided to strike out cross-country to shave off a few miles.

The waitress smiled warmly at them as she filled their cups with coffee. "Hi, I'm Jane. Have you decided yet?" she asked the table. Joyce put down the menu she was holding and ordered the special. Before the others could order, she spoke up to the waitress with the intent of throwing any busy noses off the scent. Pointing to her guard uniform, she explained away their unkempt condition by telling Jane they'd been trying to round up some escapees from prison. She followed that up by asking if anybody in town had seen any suspicious people, perhaps a group who might look like fugitives. Jane responded with a data dump as if Joyce had pulled the trigger on an automatic rifle.

"If there's fugitives on the loose," Jane began, "they'd best not show up in these parts. We're all law-abiding people, just doin' our best to stand by our government."

"I hear you," Jacob replied, patting his holster for emphasis. "Those are bad dudes."

"Malcontents, that's what they are. Misfits. Probably Republicans. Maybe even Christians. Wanna rock the boat, take away our God-given right to government help. Thank God for our president, he knows the troubles we been facin'. Been five years since our minin's been shut down. We need that help, much as we can get. But the president, sir, he's been good to us. He's one of us too, I seen him on Letterman. I just wish he'd be able to run again. Matter of fact, there's been talk in that direction.

"All we had to do," she continued, "was give up our stupid guns and now we get just about as much help as we need." She inclined her head to the next table, where two sleazy men were sucking on beers. They obviously shaved, just not regularly. "Right, boys?" They nodded in assent.

"Only people want guns," she went on, "are up to no good." She peered down at Jacob's holster. "Present company excluded, of course. You got a right. It's your job and your authority. All that arguing over money," she said, reverting back to the subject of her intense interest, "why don't they just leave the man alone and let him get on with the job of governing? And I'll tell you another thing. Why shouldn't we be kind to others? I don't like my feelings hurt. I could even be tolerant to Christians, but I'd like to shut 'em up first, if you know what I mean."

Joyce was so disgusted with the rant that she was in danger of losing her appetite. Smiling sweetly, she elbowed Earl in the ribs. He responded by pointing to his menu, which seemed to get her back on track. "And what'll you be having, boys?" the waitress asked, pencil poised on her notebook. Earl couldn't help but chuckle when she left, but his mirth was cut short when one of the sleazebags at the next table turned his head to them with an offended look.

After the meal they stopped in a general store for non-perishable food, some flashlights and batteries, and eating utensils. Two of the women and two men were allowed to buy heavy coats, Jacob telling the rest that too many purchases of clothing at one time would raise eyebrows. Joyce came out with a coat for herself and an armful of underwear for several others besides her and Earl. "I couldn't help it," she explained. "We're all getting pretty gamey. We needed to do something about it."

One of the men had bought a shirt and Levi's as well as a coat. Seeing these garments gave Jacob an idea. "Put those on now, Paul," he told the man. "See that sporting-goods store?" he said, pointing down the street as Paul put on the new clothing. He reached into his pocket, pulled out the former guard's wallet and extracted some bills. "How about you go in and buy a couple of hiking packs? And maybe a couple of canteens, too. And some rope."

When Paul returned with three packs, three canteens, two sleeping bags and a package of rope, they filled the packs with the groceries they had purchased earlier and, with Jacob in the lead, continued their walk toward the northeast. They hadn't gone more than a couple of blocks when they came up to some railroad tracks, which were at the present occupied by a motionless freight train. Jacob looked both ways, seeing that they were about in the middle of the train. Annoyed, he resigned himself to going around the rear and headed in that direction. He stopped abruptly, an idea having entered his mind. *Might as well put these uniforms to work,* he thought. Turning around, he started walking in the opposite direction, toward the southeastward-facing engine. When they reached it, he called up to the cab and the engineer stuck his neck out. "We're guards from the prison down south," he called up. "We're on the lookout for some escaped fugitives. We need to get into a boxcar and ride along while we look over your train. How about the keys?"

The engineer didn't even question him. He tossed down a key.

"That's a master key. Take the third car down," he called. "That'll have to do for now. But hurry up. I'm about to get the signal to move."

Jacob unlocked the door and they climbed in, ecstatic to be riding again. They didn't care where it went; at least they'd be putting miles between them and the prison camp.

Earl guided Joyce over to the opposite side, where they sat with their backs against the wall. Jacob came over and sat next to Earl. "If you don't mind staying awake a little longer, now would be a good time for me to learn more about our God. Okay?"

"Sure," Earl agreed. How about your Torah, the words of Moses? What do you know about Noah's Flood?"

"Actually, quite a lot. You ever read Velikovsky?"

Earl laughed. "What's your take on him? A lot of people thought he was crazy."

"I don't, not at all. If you look at the details of what his opponents had to say, their arguments were shallow in the extreme. Worse than shallow. Inconsequential. What really convinced me was what happened during the two or three decades after his books and rebuttals were printed. He'd made some predictions, you know. All of which were found to be true when our technology reached the level that we could verify them. And, all of which were surprises to the scientific community."

Earl laughed again. "Now you're preaching to the choir," he said. "I'll bet you've read Homer's *Iliad* too."

"Yeah, and it scared the pants off me, knowing the events actually happened."

"Well, so much for the Flood," Earl said. "And the Exodus. And Joshua and the Hezekiah incident. You know just about exactly what I do. Actually, Jacob, I'm really tired now. Can we continue this later?"

"Of course. Good to know that we have the same mind about the

Flood." The rhythmic clatter of the train over the rails put them all to sleep within seconds of each other.

"Wake up, Earl." Joyce shook him again.

"Huh?" he said, stretching his arm. He rubbed his butt where the hard floor of the boxcar had pressed into it while he slept, and then forgot about it and stood up. The sleeping accommodations weren't that much different than his bunk back in the camp. "What's up?" he asked her.

"The train's stopped. Some of the folks are getting nervous, like maybe the engineer's gotten the word about us. Jacob has the door open and he's peeking outside." As she said this, Jacob withdrew his head and closed the door. "Hey, everyone," he said loudly. "I think we're just stopped for traffic. This is probably a busy line. Guess where we are. Lordsburg," he added before anyone could respond. "Yeah, closer to Bowie than when we boarded. But I've a feeling we're on the fast track through New Mexico and on into Texas. If we can just get started, we should be putting some fast miles between us and Arizona."

Paul fished inside his backpack and brought out some surprises —a small one-burner camp stove, a can of fuel and a metal pot. "Thought these might come in handy."

"Good thinking," Charley said, fishing among his own belongings and extracting a packet of Top Ramen. "Here, catch, Paul. This oughta hit the spot."

"Hold on," Jacob said. "Not while we're stopped. If someone came by snooping, we'd look like bums instead of guards." Disappointed, Paul nevertheless obeyed the command, stuffing the items back in his pack. The group sat around, engaging in desultory conversation, but their minds were now fixated on their stomachs. Eventually they heard a noisy bang and their car gave a lurch. A succession of bangs rippled down the line, eventually fading out. The train picked up speed. Grateful to be on the move again, Jacob signaled to the men to go back to their cooking. Soon the smell of chicken-flavored noodles made the famished group drool in anticipation. Martha retrieved her own backpack and organized an assembly line of women to make cheese sandwiches. Despite the need to ration the scant supplies, everyone had at least something.

Julia came up to Jacob. "I have a problem," she said timidly. "I have to pee and I can't hold it."

"That's okay, Julia," Jacob reassured her. "I knew that was going to happen. Wait one. Hey, you two," he called over to the men, "grab a blanket and see what you can do to tie it up over on the far corner for a bathroom." When the two finished the task, Julia hurried over and relieved herself. She was embarrassed at first, but that went away when she saw the line that had formed for the same facility. "We're gonna need pilings to stand on," the last one grumbled when he left the area.

It was obvious that the "facility" was used for more than number one. A distinct odor began to pervade the boxcar, causing Jacob to open the door. Almost within touching distance was a major freeway. The highway wasn't overly crowded, but it was far from empty. Cars in the closer westbound lanes rushed past. Most of the ones in the farther eastbound lanes also were going faster than the train, but not by much. In fact, they were nearly matching the speed of an older vehicle, which stayed even with them for several minutes. "Stay back from the doorway," Jacob cautioned. You don't know if and when a highway patrolman is going to show up and look in our direction."

"Yeah, and we've gotta get out of these guard uniforms ASAP," Sidney said. "By now they probably have an APB out for guys wearing these uniforms."

"You're right," Jacob replied. As a matter of fact, you people who bought civvies back in Duncan, better put them on now." There was a scramble to comply.

They passed a highway rest stop. The apparent elegance displayed in their fleeting view impressed Earl. His last impression of it was of a high-end motor home parked next to a casita-styled shelter. The couple were having a picnic lunch on the bench inside. The sight depressed him for a short time. Joyce noticed it and nudged his arm with a fist. "Don't let it get you down, jarhead. Remember that kind of freedom that couple is enjoying now comes from not being a Christian or a Jew. You're going to have all eternity to make up for the rough times now. Besides, you have me, don't you?"

The last comment instantly brought him out of his brief funk. "You bet I do, and I wouldn't trade you for the world." He kissed her. In the middle of their kiss, he started to laugh.

"What's up with you?" Joyce asked.

"Sorry. Something just popped into my head. That rest stop looked so clean and well-maintained. Not all rest stops are like that. I remember one time in California, I was heading south toward the Bay Area and stopped at a place near Sacramento. When I got to the urinal I discovered that I wasn't alone. There was a whole colony of cockroaches living there. Giant ones, like they were radiation mutants. They obviously were healthy. Disgusted, I peed on one, who acted like it was rain from heaven. But now I have another idea," Earl broke in on himself, changing the subject. "Hey, anybody know whether this track parallels the highway all the way into Las Cruces?"

"It doesn't," Paul said. I used to drive a semi for Schneider. That's I-10 out there. It goes into Las Cruces, then makes a sharp turn south into Texas and El Paso. About halfway between Deming and Las Cruces the train leaves I-10 and heads southeast, bypassing Las Cruces and heading directly for El Paso. Going through El Paso, I can tell you that the mother of all switching yards is down there. As a matter of fact, there's at least two of them."

"Are there any more rest stops between here and where the train parts company with the highway?"

"No. The rest stop we just passed was the last one before we get into Texas."

"Too bad. I was hoping that. . ."

"I think I know what you're getting at. I'm with you. We have to leave the train before we get into the switching yards. We may not get to a rest stop before then, but right where I-10 makes a sharp turn as it follows the bend of the Rio Grande, it's real close to the train track. And right at the bend there's a big truck stop."

"That's better yet. And the train probably slows way down at that point."

"I'd think so."

"Which way does I-10 curve?"

"To the left."

"Then if we go out the right side like we came in, the engineer wouldn't see us."

"That's right. The only problem is that it'll be daylight when we jump out. We could be seen."

"By whom? The Mexicans? If the Rio is that close, the border would be right next to us. That's Juarez over there. I'd think they'd be so busy trying to avoid bullets from their own gangs that they wouldn't give us a second thought. Especially if we had uniforms on."

"Good point. Let's talk to Jacob about it."

"It's a workable plan," Jacob agreed, "but only because Paul has experience driving big rigs." He scratched his head in wonder. "How could we be that lucky?"

"I think it's anything but luck," Earl said. "It's all about God, and it's about time that we acknowledged his help."

"Well said," Jacob replied, and firmed up the plan. "We'll wait until dark to head over to the truck stop. There the first to go in would be those dressed in civvies, who would each buy three sets of clothing and return to the diesel pump station, where some of those with nothing but guard clothing would be waiting in the shadows. These, in turn, would go into the store and buy more clothing for the remaining people who needed civvy clothes. They'd get rid of the guard clothing in a nearby field, where they'd also leave their weapons until they'd finished eating. Then they'd all go back in twos and threes and have dinner. After that they'd pick a truck with the engine running, pop the cargo doors and they'd cram into the back while Paul drove. They wouldn't get very far, but they could probably make it to the nearest rest stop off I-10.

As the plan unfolded with their purchase of civvy clothing and ridding themselves of their guard uniforms, Paul went in and looked around for an empty booth. Finding none, he went over to a table by the wall and sat down. When the waitress came over with a menu, he gave it back to her asking her for a cheeseburger and chocolate shake. As she left he looked beyond her retreating back to lock eyes with a man three tables down. He looked away quickly, for below the eyes was the uniform of a city cop. Paul attempted to collect himself. After some time, he cast a brief glance at the cop and was startled to see him still looking his way, his face registering interest. After another eternity he saw the waitress approaching with his order, and he looked up at her, using the occasion to give a quick look at the cop. He was immensely relieved to see the cop looking in a different direction, and actually enjoyed eating his burger. But when he opened the door to exit the restaurant and saw the others approach, he waved them off. "Cop's in there," he told Jacob. "If I were you, I'd wait till he leaves."

They went away into the shadows, Paul following them. When he saw the cop exit the restaurant, he gave Jacob the all-clear. They went in to eat as he remained behind, looking around the parking lot.

Paul allowed several minutes for the others to dig into their meals, and then he started scanning the lot for likely new arrivals. After several minutes where nothing useful showed up, he saw an elderly rig come in with a familiar cab. The driver took a few minutes to park and set up, and then he climbed down out of the truck and headed for the restaurant. Not more than a few minutes later the fugitives came out of the restaurant, passing the trooper on the way. Signaling them to follow him, Paul went to the rear of the truck and opened the doors. There was more than enough room to accommodate them all. When they all climbed inside, he shut the doors and walked back to the cab. He climbed up, looked at the various controls, and, satisfied, got rolling.

CHAPTER THREE

Inside the dark and airless cargo areo, Earl had a bout of claustrophobia. "We can't open the door from the inside, can we?" he asked Jacob in a small voice.

"I'm afraid not, friend," he replied. "The only thing I can say is that it's big inside here. I'd rather be here than stuffed in the trunk of a car. Not much you can do about it except take it to God."

Earl did just that, and was both surprised and relieved to get an instant answer. It just wasn't the kind of answer he expected from Wisdom.

"Deal with it, Earl," She told him. "Remember what happened the last time you got in a tight place?"

"Well, sure," he replied. "The earthquake got me out of the box."

"And out of the camp besides. By now I'd think you'd know that We're always covering your rear. Knowing that, you should be ready for anything." She left.

Having been dressed down by Wisdom, Earl felt his fear leave him, to be replaced by guilt. But then, knowing of Her love toward him, he began to relax.

As it was, not even a half hour later those in the cargo area felt the truck slow and then creep some distance, after which it came to a full stop. The engine was shut off.

"I'm scared, Earl," Joyce whispered in his ear. "What if it's the Texas Rangers and they've come after us. Whatever happens, I'm not going back to that camp. Not ever."

"I'm not so chipper myself. I think everyone here feels about the same way you do."

The rear door suddenly swung open, terrifying the occupants. But it was only Paul, and he had a smile on his face. "Okay, everybody out. We're at a rest stop and it's the end of the line for us in this rig." Jacob added a few words, urging them to hurry out before the authorities came and found them. He thanked them all for not leaving scat behind like they did in the boxcar and told them to use the facilities before they did anything else.

"Where are we?" Earl asked Paul after he'd made his own head call.

"We're just past a little town called Fabens. It's on the outskirts of El Paso."

Jacob looked around the rest stop. He came back to Earl. "See that motor home over there?" he said, pointing to a big Diesel pusher rig, obviously top-of-the-line. An elderly man waited outside for his wife. In the distance they could see a woman walking a tiny dog, guessing that she was the wife. "Well," he spoke to Earl, "guess I'm gonna have to do the dirty deed. You and Joyce stay out of sight while I tell them the bad news." He patted the pistol hidden inside his belt.

"No," Earl said. "Thanks, but if you're trying to protect me, don't bother. I happen to believe that avoiding participation in an evil deed is every bit as bad as doing the thing itself. Worse, because it's cowardly."

"I hear you, but I happen to think I can be meaner than you. At least I look it," he said, rubbing the dark stubble on his chin.

"At least let me tag along. Maybe we can play good cop, bad cop. I can reassure them no harm will come to them if they play along. Maybe it'll prevent a heart attack, who knows?"

"Okay. But let me do the talking first." He waited until the lady and her dog went inside the restroom and walked up to the man as he began to turn to the doorway, Earl following. "Hi," he said. Nice digs. Mind if we look inside?"

The man was about to usher them inside, but something about Jacob's look warned him off. "Sorry, but it's private. Go to a dealer. There are lots of them around. They'll be more than happy to . . . "

The barrel of Jacob's gun poking into his ribs shut him up. "Don't make a peep," Jacob told him. "We're desperate and I won't hesitate to shoot. Go on in and we'll follow you."

"Aw," the man wailed. "Don't hurt my wife. Please."

"We have no intention of doing you any harm," Earl said. We just need to get away from here. We'll even go where you're heading, as long as it's to the east. Where are you planning to go?"

"San Antonio, for a little while."

"What's your name?" Earl asked him.

"Jimmy."

"Mine's Earl, and this here is Jacob," he said, extending his hand. Jimmy reluctantly shook it, ignoring Jacob. "And my wife's name is Millie."

"Millie's coming back," Jacob said. "Have her come in. And do it with a smile, or you'll both be dead," he said in what he thought would be a convincing thug tone of voice. Jimmy's wife cowered in a corner, holding a hand to her mouth but the dog, knowing all about the situation, ran up to Jacob with a screeching yap and bit him in the leg. "Ow," he said, shaking the dog off. "Get control of your dog," he said to the lady, "or he's gonna be a meal for some nearby coyote."

"Puffins!" she shrieked. "Come here! Now!" The dog reluctantly obeyed and Jacob told the man to get behind the wheel and asked Earl to round up the others. Four of them were missing. "They decided to head out on their own," Paul told him as he signaled to his companions. "Said something about being cooped up in camp and the train and the truck and now. . . anyway, they pulled guns on two bikers and took off."

"Harley riders?" Earl said, surprised at their guts.

"Nah. One was a Goldwing and the other a BMW. Julia's on the back of the Goldwing like a queen on a throne."

"Still. Well, I'll pray they make it. The rest of you, come on. Our chariot awaits." He took Joyce by the arm and the rest followed him back to the motor home. There were now eighteen fugitives in their group.

Millie was weeping quietly at the dinette table as they came into the vehicle. Tense and distraught as she was, she relaxed a bit when she saw the womenfolk among them. Jimmy started the engine and pulled the rig out onto the roadway. They saw the flashing lights of three police cars as they merged into the I-10 traffic. The cops turned off, entering the rest stop.

Several of the fugitives went back into the bedroom. Paul whistled at the elegance of the rich dark wood paneling in the long hallway, peeking in to the various doors. He whistled again in appreciation when they came to the bedroom with its queen-sized bed, twin nightstands with lamps and the mirrored closet. Gratefully, they lay down on the quilted comforter, reveling in a luxury that none of them had enjoyed for months.

The thoughtless invasion of her privacy made plain by the whistling set Millie's teeth on edge. "Get away from me!" she shouted to Earl, who had guided Joyce to the dinette table where Millie sat. Puffins responded with a session of furious barking. Joyce apologized for them as they backed off, and they retreated to a corner and Earl sat on the floor. Puffins ran up to him and, snarling viciously, bit him on the ankle. "Ow!" Earl yelled, shaking his leg. Eventually Puffins let go of the leg, but continued to screech.

"Shut that dog up!" Jimmy yelled from the driver's seat. Millie refused to help, descending instead to another bout of weeping. Irving, leaning against a wall, got Puffin's attention. With a smile, he beckoned to the dog, who stopped barking and came over to investigate. With a gentle hand, he rubbed the dog's head behind the ears. The dog raised his head into the hand, his tongue lolling from his open mouth. Millie watched the betrayal in shock, but made no comment.

Jimmy saw the outbreak of pandemonium as an opportunity and initiated a pattern of erratic weaving, hoping to attract the attention of a Ranger. Jacob, sitting next to Jimmy in the front passenger seat, tiredly withdrew his gun. "Don't," he said. The gun said the rest. For several minutes after that, the vehicle was stable and quiet reigned within it.

Joyce attempted to sit beside Earl, but her prosthetic legs made the attempt awkward. Seeing her distress, Sidney was quick to give up his chair opposite the dinette table, and Joyce sat there, relieved. Millie saw the exchange and the reason for it, but again made no comment. Yet her eyes softened as she looked over to the other woman.

Sidney took Joyce's place next to Earl. "I know you'd rather have Joyce next to you, but we might as well make the best of this situation. How about another seminar?"

"Might as well," Earl replied. "So you Jews have a tradition that's around thirty-five hundred years old," he began. "As a rule, you've been very faithful to it."

"You're talking about our Pesach, the Passover, aren't you?"

"I am. We Christians read the Old Testament too. At least we should, because it all goes together." The word "Christians" caught Millie's attention, and she picked up her ears. So did Jimmy.

"As you know, the account is in Exodus 12," Earl continued. "The month Nisan was to be the first month of the year because of the greatness of the event that was to take place. Very shortly the entire people Israel were to be a nation apart, dedicated to God. They were to leave Egypt and their enslavement behind after four hundred and thirty years to the very day. In preparation for it, on the tenth of the month, each family was to take to itself a yearling lamb, without blemish of any kind, and bring it into their household. There they were to care for it as part of their family. After four days, on the fourteenth of Nisan, and after learning to love this gentle little lamb, they were to kill it and sprinkle its blood on the doorposts and lintel of their home. They would roast it in fire and eat it in haste, for that evening the Lord their God would perform the last of His plagues upon Pharaoh by killing the firstborn of every family in Egypt. But in doing so, He would pass over without harm all those homes for which the blood of the lamb had been applied to the doorposts and lintels. On the very next morning, the fifteenth, Israel would depart *en masse* from Egypt with Moses as their leader."

"You know our custom very well," Sid told Earl. "When we were free, we would observe our Passover every year."

"It's very meaningful to us also," Earl replied, "because it's all about Jesus."

"How so?" Sid asked, surprised.

"When Jesus approached John the Baptist to be baptized into His ministry, John, when he saw Him come, said 'Behold the Lamb of God who takes away the sin of the world.' Jesus is the ultimate sacrificial Lamb, and He's described that way in the Book of Revelation as well as in First Peter, where Peter describes Jesus as a Lamb without blemish. But it's in the Old Testament also. Your prophet Isaiah, in that great Messianic fifty-third chapter that you tend to overlook, described Jesus as being brought as a lamb to the slaughter."

"That may be," Sid cut in defensively, "but being called a Lamb doesn't necessarily relate to our Passover."

"There's more. Jesus was crucified on the day of preparation for the Passover at the precise time that the other Passover lambs were being slaughtered."

"I didn't know that," Sid replied meekly.

"I didn't either," Millie said, clasping her hand over her mouth at her involuntary outburst.

"There's yet more. A lot more. How about this? David's—*your* David's - Psalm 22 begins with the words *My God, My God, why have you forsaken me?* the same words that Jesus uttered on the cross. It goes on to present a detailed description of the effects of crucifixion on the body. The rub there is that crucifixion was unknown to the Jews until several centuries after David wrote that Psalm. Then there's the account in Genesis where God commands Abraham to sacrifice his beloved son Isaac, which is an obvious prefigurement of God's sorrowful sacrifice of Jesus on the cross.

"But to me," Earl went on with feeling, "the real grabber is where Jesus was born. Luke's account has Joseph and Mary turned away from the Inn at Bethlehem, because it was full. They then went to a manger where Mary gave birth to Jesus. What Luke didn't say was that the manger wasn't plan B. It was God's plan A all along. The manger, you see, was a special one. There's a hint about it in Genesis 35, that speaks of Jacob's wife Rachel being buried near the tower Edar. The same is spoken of in Micah 4:8, which foretells the coming of the kingdom from there. Migdal Edar was the watchtower over a special flock, because that was the place reserved for the birthing and rearing of the Passover lambs. It was precisely the place where God wanted Jesus to be born."

"That's big," Sid said, scratching his chin reflectively. "I'll say so," Jacob chimed in.

"Here's an added touch. To ensure that the newborn lambs didn't injure themselves, it was customary to wrap them in swaddling clothes at their birth." Sid and Jacob didn't get the connection, but Joyce noticed from her shocked expression that Millie instantly understood. Earl explained it to them. "Luke's account of Jesus' birth includes the angels telling the shepherds that they'd find their Lord wrapped in swaddling clothes."

"That's a pretty convincing argument," Jacob said. "I'd like to hear more, if you have it."

"I do. It comes from your prophet Daniel. In Chapter Nine, he speaks of sixty-nine weeks from the decree to rebuild Jerusalem until the coming of Messiah."

"I know the passage," Sid said, "but I don't know anything about what happened about it. Do you?"

"Yes. The fulfillment has gotten to be pretty common knowledge among Christians. But we learned about it only recently. If one does the math and notes that Daniel's 'weeks' are periods of seven years, and that these 'years' are prophetic years of 360 days each, one arrives at the number of 173,880 days between the decree to rebuild Jerusalem and the coming of Messiah."

"What about the decree? I suppose you're going to say it actually happened."

"Why not? It did, with precision. It's in your own Scripture. There was some confusion about it, because there actually were two decrees. The first was issued by the Persian King Cyrus, who was named by Isaiah in his Chapter 44 about a hundred and fifty years before Cyrus was born. His decree was for the rebuilding of the temple, and the account is given in the Book of Ezra. But that's not the decree that Daniel referred to. The decree prophesied by Daniel was issued by the Persian king Artaxerxes Longimanus in 445 B.C., and it was for the rebuilding of Jerusalem. The account of that decree is given in the Book of Nehemiah. Jesus made His triumphal entry into Jerusalem on the ass precisely 173,880 days after the issuance of that decree."

"To the day? The very day?" Jacob asked in astonishment.

"Yes." Silence reigned again in the vehicle. Joyce noticed the surprise on Millie's face. She asked if she could speak with her. This time Millie acquiesced. Joyce reached for Millie's hand. "I'm so sorry that we're here interrupting what seems to be a wonderful lifestyle," she began. "We'll do everything we can to minimize our presence here."

"If you're Christians, why did you barge in on us?" Millie asked sharply. "The use of force doesn't sound very Christian to me."

"These are desperate times. We all were about to be put to death. Ordinarily, we'd have accepted the martyrdom, but it appears that God has a special mission for us. You may have noticed that some of the people here are Jewish. The Holy Spirit has used Earl to feed them the Gospel of Jesus Christ. They're Christians now. They have to get back to Israel to spread the Word."

"Why didn't you Christians just go with the flow instead of becoming so—so militant and cruel? You wouldn't be in the pickle you are if you'd been a little kinder to the gays."

"It isn't a matter of kindness. It's more the necessity to be obedient to our Lord. And despite the label of hatred applied to us, our obedience to God requires us to love even those who are our enemies. We don't hate gay individuals. What we do hate is society's deceptive labeling of their state as normal. It isn't. It's an abomination to God. But most of our Churches would have welcomed gays into their worship services if such would only make an effort to see it as an abnormality and attempt to abstain from practicing the perversion."

"But you're fugitives from the law. The law declares you to be bad."

"Perhaps more of you should question whether the law itself is bad. You, too, are getting close to violating the law."

"Oh, you can't be serious," Millie scoffed.

"Oh? I won't ask you your age, but I'm willing to bet that the RV crowd has been undergoing a demographic shift over the past couple of years. In other words, Millie, did you have many friends older than you?"

Millie thought for a moment. "Yes. There were several that we used to play cards with. I've lost track of most of them."

"They aren't around any more?"

"No. I suppose they may have settled down in homes. Sometimes it can be tiring to always be moving about."

"I'll tell you where they are. They are—or were—in the camp along with us. The guards liked to abuse them, just like they do with the handicapped."

"You're trying to tell me that my friends, who are decent . . ."

". . .Law-abiding citizens," Joyce supplied for her. "Get that bias out of your mind. Look around you. All of us were decent, law-abiding citizens until the law turned bad and came after us. We had a handicapped child, a little girl named Cathy." Joyce dropped her head. "She's dead now," she said in a pinched voice.

"Why? What has that got to do with your being fugitives?"

"I've been trying to tell you that you yourselves will be fugitives in the near future. Just for being elderly. Haven't you noticed that there aren't any handicapped persons around any more? The government tried to take Cathy away from us. We took her and ran away, but they caught us and tossed us into a concentration camp, it was just like what we heard about the German camps during World War II. It was really a death camp. They killed Cathy for being a cripple, and we were next. In the meantime, they were slowly starving us."

Millie grabbed her throat in shock. "Here? America? Surely you can't mean . . ."

"Just be thankful you're still self-sufficient. When you start to need assistance or if you get sick with something that can't be cured with a pill, they'll come to you, too, and then it'll really be checkout time for you."

CHAPTER FOUR

Joyce raised her head from the dinette table. Dawn was approaching. It looked to be a clear day coming up. Judging from the view out the window, this area must be overwhelmed with clear days. Yet it had its own beauty. It had a dry appearance, but the land was dotted with mesquite shrubs, some large enough to qualify as trees. Sharp, flat buttes rose out of the desert floor, their sides painted golden by the low-hanging sun. Her bladder became insistent. She arose from the table and went over past the other sleeping forms to stand beside Jimmy, who was about to shut his eyes with his foot on the accelerator. She shook him on the shoulder. "Maybe you'd better stop and get some rest," she suggested. I need to go to the bathroom. I'd rather not use your facilities. Twenty of us are probably more than you can handle."

Jimmy looked at her appreciatively. "You're right, and thanks for the thought."

"Maybe we should be the ones thanking you. I see that Jacob

over there is sound asleep. Why didn't you pull over and flag down a cop?"

"Because the stop probably would have awakened him," Jimmy responded gruffly.

"That's not the reason, is it?" she countered. "Maybe you're beginning to think that we're not out to get you. That just maybe we might have been treated badly by an oppressive and dictatorial government. How about it?"

"Well, That might be some of it," he said with reluctance. "But don't count on it," he quickly added. If you can hold on a few minutes longer, we just passed Balmorhea. We'll be coming up to a rest stop soon."

When Jimmy pulled his rig into the rest stop he motioned them out. Sid shook Earl awake and headed for the rear to wake those on the bed. Jacob remained in his seat, staring down Jimmy.

"Don't bother with me," Jimmy told him. "Go take your leak. I'm not going anywhere."

Jacob was tempted to compel him to go with him to the restroom, but realized that this moment gave him an opportunity to establish some trust. "Thanks, Jimmy," was all he said as he arose from the seat and headed out the door. Jimmy decided to follow. When they returned, Jacob motioned for Millie to sit in the passenger seat next to her husband. She happily complied.

Sid came back and sat down next to Earl. "I know you've given us a lot of Gospel ammo to spread around, probably more than enough to make a convincing case that Christ is our Messiah. But to tell you the truth, the more you've told us, the more interested I get. I never knew that God could be so—so *exciting*."

"Oh, yeah. There's plenty more. Most of us Christians think of the Gospels—the good news about Jesus Christ—to be Matthew, Mark, Luke and John, the first four books of the New Testament. But there's at least one other Gospel in the Bible, and it's in your own Torah, our Old Testament."

"How so?"

"It's Genesis, the first book of the Bible. When you come to a mature understanding of Scripture, you'll realize that Genesis is more about Jesus than any other topic. I'm not putting you down about your understanding. It's just that you'll have to make several intricate connections before you'll come to that recognition."

"No offense taken. But I would appreciate some clues to get me started in the right direction."

"I'll be happy to oblige. I've already told you about God's commanding Abraham to sacrifice his beloved son Isaac, and how that drama, which ended up with God at the last moment providing a ram in Isaac's stead, represented the Father's sorrow at having to sacrifice His Son Jesus. And that was the real thing—there was no sacrificial substitute for Jesus. But Isaac comes back into the picture of Jesus with his marriage to Rebekah. You see, Sid, Rebekah was a type of the Church, which meant that Isaac's marriage to her represented Jesus' marriage to His Church."

"I thought Jesus was God. Christians make a big deal about that. Aren't you going off the deep end with that claim?"

"Not at all. I'm not the first to make the claim, not by a long shot. The first, in fact, was Moses, who wrote of Isaac's marriage to Rebekah. Do yourself a favor and read Genesis 24 very carefully when you get a chance. And then there's Isaiah 54, and, of course, the Apostle Paul in Ephesians 5 spelled it out directly. I'll give it to you from memory:

Husbands, love your wives, even as Christ also loved the church, and gave himself for it, that he might sanctify and cleanse it with the washing of water by the word; that he might present it to himself a glorious church, not having spot, or wrinkle, or any such thing; but that it should be holy and without blemish. So ought men to love their wives as their own bodies. He that loveth his wife loveth himself. For no man ever yet hated his own flesh, but nourisheth and cherisheth it, even as the Lord the church; for we are members of his body of his flesh, and of his bones. For this cause shall a man leave his father and mother; and shall be joined unto his wife, and they two shall be one flesh. This is a great mystery, but I speak concerning Christ and the church.

"Oh, my!" Millie exclaimed. "How beautiful!" Sid just stared at Earl, trying to absorb this new revelation.

"Back to Genesis as the first Gospel of Jesus Christ. It really starts at the very beginning, Genesis 1, where God wills the Light, which comes into existence in response to that will. To understand the significance of that act, you have to go all the way to the end of the New Testament, where in Revelation 3:14 Jesus describes Himself as the beginning of the creation of God. I'll let you digest that on your own."

"Oh boy," Sid said, rising up. "I have to tell Irving and Jacob about this."

"Wait. I'm only getting started."

"I'm gonna have to write this down, Earl. I'll never remember it all."

Millie reached for the cabinet as Jimmy glared at her. "Go ahead and open it, then," he said caustically. She extracted a pen and a notebook and passed it back to Sid. They'd obviously been listening in on the conversation. Sid wrote down the basics of what Earl had said about the Light, and then looked to him for more.

"There's more about the Light. You'll want to read John's prologue, verses one through eighteen of Chapter One. But getting back to Genesis, remember how Cain and Abel presented sacrifices before God, who accepted only Abel's?"

"Sure. But I never did understand why God turned down Cain's. After all, he did work for it. He probably worked hard. It always seemed to me that God wasn't very appreciative."

Earl smiled, knowing that another revelation was in store for his friend. "Here again, it's all about Jesus, Sid, and His work on the cross in our behalf. God turned down Cain's sacrifice for the very reason that it was from his own effort. Abel, on the other hand, knew that there was nothing he could do of himself to earn God's acceptance, so he sacrificed an animal, one of God's creations, and in so doing he pointed directly to God's sacrifice of Jesus for our redemption from sin. That act of Abel's, by the way, became formalized in your Passover many centuries later, and also pointed directly to Jesus, our eternal Passover. Even now all the world's religions, except for Judeo-Christianity, represent attempts of man to storm the gates of heaven by their own works. It won't work, since no matter what a person does, it just doesn't come up to the standard that God set. That's why our salvation is a free gift from God."

Sid remained silent, pondering what Earl had said. So did Millie, which obviously irritated Jimmy. Earl continued before Jimmy had a chance to speak. "Then there's the story of Joseph, which takes up much of the book of Genesis."

"But I thought you said that Genesis was a Gospel of Jesus Christ."

"So I did. And the story of Joseph is a big part of that Gospel. Think about it—Joseph spent much of his early life suffering after his brothers sold him into slavery in Egypt. On top of that, his loyalty to his master Potiphar earned him a ticket to jail. But through his suffering he grew into the person that God wanted him to be. I'm convinced that we are defined less by the good things that happen to us than by our adversities. Our characters are formed and exposed by the tribulations which we are forced to face and by the way that we handle them. When Joseph's character had matured enough that God was able to use him, he was given a gift of insight into dreams. The result was that through this gift he was released from prison by Pharaoh and given responsibilities. He handled his tasks well, and rose to second in command under Pharaoh of all of Egypt. When the great seven-year famine hit the region, Joseph's brothers were forced by starvation to approach the Egyptian potentate who was in charge of the grain storehouses. That high figure was, of course, Joseph their brother, who fed them and eventually brought them into his care in Egypt."

"That's a good story," Sid said. "I know, I've read it several times. But what . . .?"

". . .Does that have to do with Jesus?" Earl replied, finishing his sentence for him. "Everything. Joseph's life was a type of Jesus', in that both of them rescued those who hated them, who wanted them dead. By God's grace, Joseph understood that, and in talking to his brothers he specifically spoke to them of how God used their anger toward him for their own salvation."

"I never got that out of the story," Sid said. "But now that you've spelled it out for me, I understand. I'm very grateful, Earl. To you, but even more to God."

"And that's the way it should be," Earl replied. The same can be said of your prophet Jonah."

"Jonah? It made a good story, but sort of far-fetched."

"Not so. As recently as the twentieth century, a whaleboat was upended and its occupant swallowed by a whale. Over a day later the whale was killed. During the gutting, out popped the man. He was blind from gastric juice and was an albino for the rest of his life. But he lived. As for Jonah's relevance to Jesus, remember that Jonah was asleep in the bottom of the boat when the storm came up. After being fingered as the cause of the storm, Jonah willingly allowed himself to be tossed overboard to what appeared to be a certain death. Jesus Himself re-enacted that event."

"Say what? Where?"

"It's in Matthew 8. Jesus was asleep in the bottom of a boat when a fierce storm came up. His disciples woke Him and pleaded with Him to calm the waters, which He did. In so doing, Jesus repeated the calming of the waters enacted by His predecessor Jonah. The point is that for those with eyes to see and ears to hear, Jesus quite plainly was informing His disciples that He, too, would have to die for their salvation."

"I have another point to make about Genesis as Gospel of Jesus Christ," Earl said as his audience pondered over this new insight, "and that is about the Six Days of Creation. Your Psalm 90 equates a thousand years of the Lord to a day. Peter, in his second letter, repeats this equation and expands upon it by making the equivalence bidirectional. It's not a trivial relationship; it's a key to the interpretation of several important passages in Scripture, starting at the very beginning, at Genesis One. The creation story involves seven days, as you know. God intended us to perceive the Biblical story as playing out over seven millennia, or seven days according to Psalm 90. In that context, each year of Abraham's one hundred seventy five-year lifetime, when multiplied by the thirty-three point six-year lifetime of Jesus, results in a total period of five thousand, eight hundred eighty years. That time period involves one hundred twenty 49-year intervals. In each such 49-year period, there is an additional parallel Jubilee year that must be added into the total. Adding in those one hundred twenty Jubilees brings the total to six thousand years. That's six thousand years of mankind that culminates, according to Revelation, in a thousand-year Millennium when Jesus returns with His Church to reign on earth. The grand total, then, of the number of years that God wishes us to view as belonging to human history is seven thousand years."

"Hold on," Sid said, writing furiously in the notebook. "I have to catch up." He looked up to Earl again after several moments. "Okay," he said. "I'm ready for more."

"Jesus came on the fourth day of the Lord, or the fourth millennium," Earl continued. "In Chapter eleven of John's Gospel is the account where Jesus resurrected Lazarus from the dead. The account notes that Jesus could have acted on the news of Lazarus' death sooner, but that He waited until the fourth day to bring him back to life. In doing so, Jesus was prophesying His own resurrection, again, on the fourth day of the Lord."

"Wow." Other than that exclamation, Sid was at a loss for words. Dropping all pretense, Millie stared at Earl. He could see Jimmy's eyeballs in the rear-view mirror.

"I'm not done yet. In several Gospel passages, Luke 9:22, for instance, Jesus said that He must be slain and be raised on the third day."

"Well, even I know that that's already happened," Sid said. "According to your New Testament, He did rise again on the third day."

"Sure, but remember that we're talking about days representing thousand-year periods. Prophecies often have short-term and long-term fulfillments. The long-term fulfillment of that particular prophecy is yet to happen. But it's very, very close. In the long-term fulfillment, Jesus will come again in the third millennium after His resurrection, or on the seventh millennium of the Lord, just as foretold in Revelation. I could say more about millennia, such as the notion that each of the seven twenty-five-year intervals in Abraham's life represented a major prophetic event, but to tell you the truth, I just can't remember those events. Sorry."

"You've given me—us—more than enough to digest. It's very much appreciated."

"Don't thank me. Thank the Holy Spirit."

Sid rose up, apparently to go talk with Irving, but before he started away, Millie spoke. "About the Passover, Earl. Can you tell us any more about the connection with Jesus as the Lamb of God?"

"Yeah," Jimmy said. "That bit about the manger in Bethlehem was a humdinger." Jimmy's expression darkened after he said this. He became lost in thought.

"Well, sure, okay." Sid quickly sat back down.

"Remember, in Exodus twelve, a yearling lamb is to be selected on the tenth day of Nisan, kept in the home for four days, and then be killed on the fourteenth. Jesus was crucified on the fourteenth of Nisan. But in Chapter Twelve of John's Gospel, John relates how, six days before the Passover, or five days before the fourteenth, Jesus came to Bethany. Remember that by Jewish reckoning the days begin at evening. So that night, which would be Nisan Ten, Jesus ate with Lazarus, Martha and Mary. Martha served dinner, but Mary did something else. She took a pound of spikenard, a very expensive embalming ointment, and anointed Jesus' feet with it. Then she wiped His feet with her hair. When Judas Iscariot complained about the cost, Jesus told him to let her alone. He and Mary alone knew what she was doing, which was fulfilling the Passover Scripture by selecting Jesus as her Passover Lamb."

Silence again pervaded the vehicle. Joyce, looking over from the table, was surprised to see a tear leak down Millie's cheek. "Can you tell us more?" she asked in a small voice.

"Gladly, Millie. We'll go to Exodus Chapter 40, where Moses is setting up the Tabernacle in the wilderness. When the Tabernacle was prepared for worship, the Scripture says that a cloud covered the tent of the congregation, and the Glory of the Lord filled the tabernacle. Many Bible commentaries refer to this Glory as the Shekinah, a Hebrew term. As long as the Glory remained, the Israelites would stay put; when the Glory lifted, the Israelites would continue their journey. This same Glory filled Solomon's Temple when it was completed. The account's in First Kings Chapter Eight. The prophet Isaiah referred to this same Glory in Chapter 51. So did Paul, indirectly. What Paul said in First Corinthians Chapter 3 was that we ourselves are human temples of God. Jesus promised in John 14 that we Christians, as temples of God, would be indwelt by the Holy Spirit, which, of course, began at the first Pentecost after Jesus' resurrection. Since then, all Christians understand that they are indwelt by the Holy Spirit. This indwelling was prefigured by the Glory of God, which indwelt the Tabernacle in the wilderness and later, Solomon's Temple. This prefigurement leads one to make a natural association of the Glory with the Holy Spirit. I certainly do."

"So do I," Joyce said enthusiastically. She was followed by Sid and, surprisingly, Millie.

Earl laughed. "Well, here's the kicker. If you look up the word 'Shekinah' on the Intenet, say Wikipedia for example, you'll find that the word has an associated gender. The gender is feminine."

"That doesn't surprise me as much as you seem to think it would,"

Sid said. "I don't know that much about Christianity yet. Now that I am one, I intend to learn more as quickly as I can. But back in the camp guys would talk about it. One of their main hang-ups about Christianity was their perception that Christians think of the Holy Spirit as being either male or genderless. Most of us Jews always thought of the Holy Spirit in feminine terms anyway. Solomon's Proverbs contributes to that view, as does his Song of Songs. The most telling is the Shekinah you spoke of, the cloud of Glory who, as you said, indwelt our centers of worship. But doesn't the New Testament refer to the Holy Spirit as a 'he'?"

"Yes, but that can easily be reconciled with a functionally female Holy Spirit. Too bad the Church never bothered to do so." Anyway..."

"No way!" Jacob shouted, breaking his prolonged silence. "That explains everything!"

The raising of Jacob's voice visibly distressed Jimmy. "Keep it down, Jacob," Earl said, pointing to the frowning driver. "Explains what?"

"I had a vision," Jacob began. "In the night after I accepted Jesus as our—my—Messiah. It was frigid in the vision, snowing, bitterly cold. There was a cave in the face of a cliff. Inside the cave was a she-wolf, her eyes smarting with discomfort. But she patiently remained in her uncomfortable position, because she was feeding a bunch of hungry cubs. They were warm and comfortable nestling against her body, and they had no idea of the cold outside, or of the pain that their mother was enduring for their sakes."

"Hoo boy," Jimmy scoffed. So that's your God? A wolf?"

"I instantly recognized the cubs as us, almost completely oblivious to the cold, dark vastness of the universe surrounding us, or the epic, painful at times, of God fashioning a habitable world out of that stark blackness for our comfort and pleasure. I also recognized—instantly, too—that the wolf in that vision represented the Holy Spirit. And I said 'represented', not 'was'. I wept at the imagery. Knowing that the New Testament referred to the Holy Spirit as a 'he', I put this vision in the back of my mind as a confusing issue that I'd deal with later. Now you make it all come back and now, with the Son front and center, where a female Holy Spirit as the spiritual Mother of Jesus makes a lot more sense than a genderless union or one in which gender exists only as a personality characteristic. Where's the glue in that kind of arrangement? It's hard to picture the unity that it might produce, or the Divine Son that such sterility might bear. Actually, I think that the female *persona* of the Holy Spirit is as important as the pattern of the cross in Jesus' feeding episodes."

"I'm glad you said that, Jacob. The issue is important, because a functionally female Holy Spirit changes our awareness of the Trinitarian Godhead to a perception of a Divine Family. I'm probably taking the words out of your mouth, but what you're about to say is that it's very easy to picture the Godhead as the ultimate Family, and, of course, it would have been in this Family context that Moses was able to speak of God as One. Which, of course, is a very natural and loving way to view God. Not only that, but the New Testament itself, in Chapter 3 of John's Gospel, associates the Holy Spirit with spiritual birth, birth being an eminently female function regardless of whether it's in the spiritual realm or our own. But I'm afraid that I'm all talked out, and to do it justice would take a lot of time. . ."

"Let me, Earl," Joyce broke in. She made a concise review of all the issues associated with a female Holy Spirit that Earl had struggled with in his dialogue with Pastor Wilson so very long ago. When she had finished, Sid had filled several pages of his notebook and Millie had rather timidly asked Joyce to come near. "Joyce," she said, holding her hand, "can you show me how I can come to Christ?"

"Not so fast!" Jimmy yelled. "And get away from my wife!" he shouted to Joyce.

"Why, Jimmy, what's wrong with you?" Millie said, shocked at his outburst.

"I'll tell you what's wrong with me. These guys come in, highjack our home, kidnap us, and now you want them to convert you? You know what these Christians are like. They're misfits. Unhappy malcontents. Throwbacks from the Middle Ages. Don't you remember how we were told about them? Society's finally ridding itself of them, and now you want to join them? Where's your brains, Millie?"

"Weren't you listening?" Millie shot back. Obviously, she wasn't intimidated by her husband. "Explain to me yourself how Jesus' coming could have been predicted to the very day if it wasn't God who provided that information. Just maybe it's been us who've been brainwashed, not them."

Jimmy clamped his lips together. He was through trying to reason with her. Hearing the exchange, Jacob walked back to the bedroom, where he conferred with his companions. Presently he came back out and motioned to Earl. When the two had moved out of earshot of their driver, Jacob spoke. "We have to do something about all of us here. I think there's just too many of us for Jimmy to handle. It's too threatening. Some of the guys in the back have agreed to offload themselves when we get to the next town. At best, there'll be a bus station there. At worst, they'll have to steal a car. You can go too, you and Joyce, but I'd rather keep you with Sid and Irving and me.

"That's a good idea. I think Millie would like a little privacy, too. And then we wouldn't be putting all our eggs in one basket either. Of course we'll stay with you. I think Joyce is beginning to bond with Millie. Who knows what God has in mind in that direction?"

They sat back down. Despite Jimmy's rant and his ugly looks in her direction, Millie got up from the passenger seat sat beside Joyce at the table, where Joyce quietly led her into a saving relationship with Jesus Christ. They crested a rise and the city of Fort Stockton came into view, appearing as a tiny enclave of civilization in the middle of a vast wasteland. Jacob came over and stood beside Jimmy. "Take that next off-ramp, please," he told Jimmy, pointing to the I-10 business route. Beneath the polite request, the command was unmistakeable. Jimmy struggled with a desire to refuse to comply, but then thought better of it and pulled off onto Dickinson Street. "Turn into that Walmart lot," he commanded. When Jimmy did so and parked the vehicle, the group hiding in the bedroom trooped out and headed for the store.

"That's all you'll be seeing of them," Jacob explained to Jimmy. We'll still be here, but you'll get a little of your privacy back." Millie breathed a heartfelt sigh of relief and went back to use the bathroom. "Those of us who are staying," Jacob continued, "will be taking turns going into the store to use the bathroom there. We'll buy some provisions, too."

When they had completed their chores Jacob had Jimmy pull back out. Jacob saw the group they'd left behind walking toward a Greyhound station just down the street. They waved and the RV continued eastward, stopping briefly to fuel up and then merging back into the I-10 freeway.

Millie returned to the passenger seat next to her husband. Looking over to him, she smiled. It didn't work. His expression remained surly. She continued smiling. "What?" he asked testily.

"Don't you realize what we just accomplished?" she said. "What's happened every time we've come into Fort Stockton? Don't tell me you don't remember."

"Oh, yeah," he said. "This is the first time we didn't have a breakdown as we came into town. I'd be jumping with joy if we didn't have a more serious problem on our hands. More serious than breaking down."

"That's all in your mind," she countered. "After what I've heard from them, they're about as dangerous as toothless snakes."

"Yeah, but they're still snakes."

"Oh, go on," she said, disgusted. She sat straight in her own seat, looking at the road ahead.

Sid sat down next to Earl. "Any more time-stamped prophecies?"

Earl laughed. "Yes. Almost as amazing as Daniel's about Jesus. You'd find it extremely relevant to yourself."

"From our own Scriptures?"

"How about Hosea?"

"Sure. What've you got?"

"Hosea Chapter 6. The prophet says that after three days, God will revive Israel. In the context of Psalm 90, that would be in the third millennium after Hosea's prophecy. You know that this prophecy is accurate, because it's already happened."

"Okay, I'd say that was impressive, but not as much as Daniel. Hosea still had several hundred years to work with on that and still be right."

"I agree. But I'm just warming up. Would you rather have the same prophecy, but this time to the very day?"

"That would grab me. Sure."

"Ezekiel's still in your Scripture, just like Daniel and Hosea. Would that suit you?"

"Of course."

"Ezekiel 4 then, verses 4 through 6. God has Ezekiel lie on his left side for 390 days, counting a day for the years of Israel's iniquity. Then he was to lie on his right side for another 40 days, counting a day for the years of Judah's iniquity. A total of 430 years, like Israel's sojourn in Egypt. You'll recall that you left Egypt 430 years after coming in. According to Exodus 12, it was to the very day."

"Yeah, I know all that. So where do the 430 years come in?"

"The captivity in Babylon, from 606 B.C. until 536 B.C., was 70 years. So that took care of 70 of the 430 years."

"Which leaves 360 years remaining. Our Diaspora, the Great Dispersion, lasted a lot longer than that."

"It sure did. The late Dr. Grant Jeffrey, who, as far as I know, was the first to figure it out, had that very problem with it. I don't know how long it took him to do it, but he finally came to a passage that put it all together. It's in Leviticus 26, where God says that if, after Israel continues to refuse to listen to Him after her punishment, she will be punished seven times as long. After her 70-year punishment,

Israel did indeed refuse to listen to God."

"So that meant, you're saying, that her follow-on punishment, instead of lasting for 360 years after the end of the Babylonian captivity, actually was to last seven times that long?"

"Yes. Multiplying 360 times seven comes out to two thousand, five hundred twenty prophetic years, which amounts to 907,200 days. Which, in turn, brings us to a date for Israel's return to her land of 1948. I made quick-and-dirty calculation myself and arrived at 1948, but Jeffrey claimed that a detailed calculation showed that it was to the very day of May 14."

"Unbelievable!" Sid breathed.

"I'll say," Jacob said. Millie nodded her head in assent.

"Yeah," Jimmy cut in brusquely. "It's way too over-the-top. There's gotta be a catch somewhere."

"No, Jimmy. There's no catch. I've redone the calculation several times, and it still comes out to 1948. And when you add in Hosea's prophecy about it, and then read Ezekiel Chapters 36 and 37 that speak of Israel's rebirth out of Hitler's holocaust, it all dovetails together. Scripture itself is supernaturally written, just as it claims to be."

Jimmy frowned, then looked over at Millie. He shrugged his shoulders. "We don't need God," he said. "We never did. We're evolving quite nicely without Him or His intervention."

"Evolving?" Jacob said. "As in Evolution? That's my field. I was a microbiologist before they came after me for being a Jew. What do you know about it, Jimmy? How about DNA, and the fact that it's a molecular chain inside of which is pure information, almost a gigabyte of information about its human host. Every one of the trillions of cells in your body carries this information. A colleague of mine—a highly respected scientist, I might add—calculated the odds against a much smaller chain of information having come about by chance. The number was larger than all the known particles in the universe. That's particles, not stars."

"But think about the time involved," Jimmy blustered.

"What about it? Suppose that you had twenty million years to create a small chain of information, like for a bacterium. The number representing that time, even in miniscule units of microseconds, is puny, insignificant next to the number associated with the odds against chance accomplishing the creation of the DNA for a bacterium."

Jimmy's face reddened in embarrassment, but Jacob didn't back off. "And that didn't even take into account the chicken-and-egg problem of protein production. Some sections of DNA called genes are really software subroutines that specify the assembly of proteins out of amino acids. We haven't figured out much about the rest of the human DNA chain, but we do know a lot about the human genome. A gene tells a machine in the cell to assemble amino acids in a specified order to make a protein. Now here's the problem. The machine responsible for the assembly consists of proteins. So there's the issue of what came first—the protein-based machine or the instructions it uses to make proteins, because if the instructions came first they'd be meaningless. On the other hand, if the machine came first, it would be meaningless, having no instructions to act upon. Obviously, they had to have been operational at the same time, which increases the complexity factor by a huge amount."

"Another big issue that the odds didn't take into account is chirality," Jacob continued. "Which means that the molecular orientation of every single backbone structural element in the enormously long DNA chain must be right-handed. The problem with that is that the molecular orientation of these elements is equally likely either right- or left-handed, so there's a fifty-fifty chance of each coding element being of the wrong orientation. This is for every DNA chain in every creature. If just one such molecular component is of the wrong orientation, it will gum up the works. So what do you think that this little restriction does to the odds? But wait—there's more!" Jacob said in a quip that evoked images of a high-pressure sale, "All the amino acids associated with life have to be of a left-handed orientation, which adds even more to the complexity burden."

"What about the fossil evidence?" Jimmy said in an attempt to regain control over the conversation. "You know, the missing links between man and ape. Lucy."

"I hate to tell you this, but they're all frauds, every last one of them, including Lucy. And when I say frauds, I'm talking about rank dishonesty. If you want be to go into details, I'll be glad to do so. It'll take me some time, but I'm game."

"If that was the case, why would such a prestigious magazine like National Geographic present Lucy and her place in the evolutionary chain as an established fact. Nat Geo is just one of a whole host of sources of that kind of information. That tells me that better people than you say that evolution is a fact. Proven. Q.E.D. They're teaching the factual basis of evolution to every school child in the country."

"A terrible tragedy. So Jimmy, do you believe everything you're told? If there's something too deep or requires too much effort for you to understand for yourself, do you run to the self-proclaimed experts and accept everything they say as truth? Sure, I'll buy into the fact that there are better people than me who say evolution is a fact. But I didn't automatically accept everything they said. I searched out the issue and acquired an in-depth understanding of Darwin's thesis. Then I continued on and gained an understanding of the alternative thesis from those who were capable of effectively rebutting the evolutionary point of view. In the process I found real experts in the area, who themselves are better than the evolutionists that are better than me. What these scientists had to say opened up a new world to me—the world of molecular biology. Then I, too, became an expert in the field. All I can tell you about National Geographic, by the way, is that its staff appear to be committed naturalists, which is essentially equivalent to being committed atheists whether they perceive that identity or not. They're not stupid. They're just blind, refusing to contemplate the overwhelming evidence against evolution for the simple reason that they don't want to. Their marketing success is based entirely on a population like themselves that doesn't know God nor ever wants to."

"Shut up and leave me alone."

Seeing a sign for a rest stop ahead, Jacob made a quick calculation. With Millie opposing him, Jimmy probably wouldn't alert the authorities about them. He decided to take a chance. "We've put you folks out enough," he told Jimmy. "Thanks for your hospitality, but if you pull into that rest stop, we'll get out of your hair."

"Are you serious?" Jimmy asked.

"Yes, I am. You think we'd put a gun to your heads and shoot or something?"

Jimmy was quick to comply. When they stopped Joyce gave Millie a fierce hug. "God bless you," she said, and walked out of the vehicle. Millie watched her leave, observing her struggle down the steps on her prosthetic legs. What was left of the group walked together toward the restrooms. Jacob turned his head back to the RV and saw Millie behind their large windshield. She was speaking with Jimmy. It wasn't a pretty picture. "Well, we still have some sleeping bags between us," he told Earl. Maybe we can take turns in them come nightfall.

"Yeah," Earl said dejectedly. "At least it's not freezing."

When they returned from the restrooms Jimmy was standing at the entrance, waiting. Jacob saw him, but ignored his presence.

"What's up, Jimmy?" Earl asked.

"Come on back to the RV," he said. "Millie's convinced me that it's the right thing to do. I'm not saying I'm converted just yet, but Millie is."

Earl laughed inwardly. *Poor Jimmy*, he thought. *Millie must have given him both barrels.* "I don't know," he replied. You really want to do this thing?"

"I do," he admitted. "But just you and Joyce. We can't handle more than you two."

Earl knew that what Jimmy wanted was to sleep in his own bed tonight, with Millie beside him. He also knew that Jacob hadn't exactly endeared himself to them. This presented a problem. He didn't want to abandon Jacob and the others, but he was also concerned with Joyce's welfare above all. He decided to talk to Jacob and see how he responded. "Thanks for the offer, Jimmy, but wait one, please." he said.

"Hey guys," he called to the others as he walked over to them.

"What's up?" Jacob replied.

"Something came up that I don't know how to handle. Jimmy's just offered Joyce and me a ride farther up the road. But we're the only ones they invited."

Jacob laughed at that. "Being the bad cop does have its downside. By all means, go. It's best all around. Joyce gets to stay off her prosthetics a while longer, and with you two gone, it just might be easier for the rest of us to get a ride."

"I was hoping you'd say that. But I still feel a bit guilty leaving you behind."

"Don't. You've done enough for us already. Besides, I have a feeling that God will help us all out of the tight spots ahead, so don't worry about us. Just take care of yourself and your lovely wife."

"Thanks, Jacob. I don't know if we'll ever see you again, but know that our hearts are with you."

"As ours are with you." They clasped hands all around, and Earl gave them a last wave of the hand as he turned back to Jimmy.

"Okay, Jimmy," he said. "I guess we're on, and thanks again."

CHAPTER FIVE

J oyce was met by another fierce hug from Millie.

That day they passed through Ozona and stopped at another rest area several miles to the east of there near Sonora. As that day wore on Jimmy began to relax, showing a kinder, more fun-loving side to his personality. Nevertheless, Earl backed off from taking an insistent approach to Jimmy's salvation. He simply had no urgent call from the Holy Spirit to pursue the matter, realizing that perhaps Jimmy's own wife might do a far better job of it than he could.

The two ladies cooked a decent meal for them inside the RV and they conversed briefly, most of the time looking idly out the window at the highway traffic racing by. Earl watched a yellow school bus drive past, wishing that Jacob and his lot could have found some decent transportation like that. Everyone was tired to the core, mostly from the emotional situations they had all experienced. Earl and Joyce conversed together for a time, worried about Jacob and his bunch, and speculating on what they might be doing at that moment.

"I can't seem to get Jacob out of my mind," Earl said to no one in particular. "He's had such a hard life, he deserves some kind of break."

"Look, Earl," Jimmy started defensively, "what was I supposed to do? You can see for yourself how cramped it is in here. Not only that, but I have a wife to think of too, and. . ."

"I'm not blaming you for anything," Earl broke in. "And Joyce and I are grateful that you let us stay. Did you know that Jacob had a wife and a two-year-old baby?"

Joyce looked at him in shock. "I didn't know that. He never mentioned them. What happened to them?"

"Guess. They lost the baby the first day in camp. A guard bashed his head against a fence-post and that was that. As Jacob told it to me, the guard walked away as if nothing had happened and eventually an inmate came over and hauled off the remains. Jacob didn't see it himself. He'd been hauled off to the mens' barracks, but he did see his wife from time to time through the chain-link fence. Said that the loss took all the fight out of her. He only saw her for a month, and then she never appeared again. He supposed that she died. What else could he think?"

"Oh, that's horrible," Millie said. We had no idea, none at all, of what you people must have gone through. Sometimes I wonder why God allows such things to happen."

"Don't go there," Earl told her. "To his everlasting credit, Jacob didn't either. He saw it more as a display of God's mercy, getting her and the boy out of that hellhole. They both knew that their little boy had no future, unless they—and, eventually, the boy—were to renounce their faith in God, which just wasn't an option. Jacob saw his incarceration, and everything that happened along with it, as a strengthening process that eventually would permit him to serve his God with courage and devotion. He had an uncommon faith through all the tribulations there that came his way. He knew even before he perceived his Lord as Jesus that somehow he would be free to bring others to God. That's why he was so open to me, and why he was so eager to know about Jesus and His exploits on earth.

After accepting Jesus as his Savior and Lord, he was secure in the knowledge that Jesus had been preparing him for a mission. What caught us all off-guard was the earthquake that occurred just about the same time as Jacob became a Christian."

"Which freed you from your coffin and the rest of us from the death camp," Joyce supplied.

Jimmy remained silent, but Earl could see that he was having difficulty with his conscience. "Jacob is a very lonely man, and I know that he's still grieving inside over the loss of his family. But don't kick yourself about it. If God wanted Jacob and the others to remain with us, He would have brought it about whether you had objected or not. God obviously has other plans for Jacob. I just hope that someday he'll find another companion who he can love, like Joyce and I did."

"Oh?" Millie said. "This wasn't your first marriage?"

"No," Joyce spoke up. "Both of us were married before, and both of our spouses died prematurely. Mine from a drunk driver and Earl's from a terminal illness. Both of us, too, thought that our lives were essentially over. Not over, but you know what I mean, the good part, the joy, like we'd just be marking time for the rest of our lives. But even that isn't exactly true, because we were both Christians and we had our Lord. I guess we were just lonely, though."

"I can understand," Millie said sympathetically. "So how did you meet?"

"That's the good part," Joyce continued. "We met at work, but it was all orchestrated by God in the most beautiful way. And it was love at first sight for both of us. What made it even better was our involvement in Earl's ministry, which was really exciting. He was working with a severely handicapped fellow. He had cerebral palsy, but his mind was sharp as a tack. I helped out with the piano."

"And singing," Earl added. "She has a beautiful voice. That's where we met Cathy, our daughter." Their faces turned sad. "She was disposed of at the camp," he said grimly, his teeth set. "Her crime was that she was afflicted with cerebral palsy too."

"I wonder what happened to Buddy?" Joyce mused, attempting to get her mind off Cathy. "He was a wonderful fellow, always cheerful. We like to think that his hang gliding experience set him up for a career in the Special Olympics."

"Say what?" Millie exclaimed. "I've seen people with cerebral palsy. How did you ever get someone to take him flying?"

"Oh, that was Earl," Joyce said.

Jimmy's eyebrows shot upward as he pointedly looked at Earl's prosthesis. "With a game arm?"

"No, the accident put an end to the flying," Joyce said, displaying her own prosthetic legs. "But not to our association with Buddy. At least not then. Buddy, as a matter of fact, got Earl out of a big jam. Saved his job. I miss him. Both of them. Actually, I have a feeling that Buddy went the way of Cathy. Probably thought of as a useless burden on society, which is anything but true." She cast her eyes downward in sorrow. So did Earl.

"How about a game of cards?" Jimmy offered in an attempt to cheer them up. "That's something that the RV circuit's famous for."

"Golly, I'd like to," Joyce said, "but with everything that's happened to us over the last year or so, I'm not sure I can remember any game."

"That's all right, dear," Millie said with warmth. "We can show you. How about Mexican canasta?" she said, looking over at Jimmy.

Millie made a pot of tea and they spent a thoroughly enjoyable evening playing cards. "That was the most fun I've had in years," Joyce said to Earl after their hosts had gone into their bedroom.

The couch unfolded into a bed, rather comfortable for such a thin mattress. Of course, any bed was infinitely better than the cots back at the camp. When they tucked themselves in, Joyce let out a gasp. "What are you trying to do, Earl?" she asked, surprise on her face. "They'll hear us."

"Don't you think it's about time?" he replied. "Joyce, you're all

I can think about now. I'm going crazy with want. Think about the unbelievable providence that brought us back together. We need to celebrate. We can be quiet. . ."

"Sush," she said, grinning. Looks like you're going to have your way with me whatever, so I might as well enjoy it. Just be quiet, and take it slow."

CHAPTER SIX

As Earl and Joyce mounted the steps back into the RV's interior, Jacob and the others watched them with envy and a resurgence of fear. Nobody really wanted to sleep out in the field with no prospect of going anywhere with the troubling task before them of commandeering another RV. Jacob knew that Earl's compassionate way with people, no doubt driven by the Holy Spirit, would be sorely missed. But he collected himself like the man he was and sat everyone down on a picnic bench for a conference.

"All right, everybody, he began. "Things aren't looking too great at the moment. We seem to find ourselves homeless and rideless. If you start getting down about it, just remember where we came from. God got us out of that hellhole, so I have no doubt that He has plans for us that don't involve more jail time." He thought about his latest words and decided that an amendment was in order. "At least I hope so, for a while anyway." He looked at each face. There are five of us left. Too many to get an easy ride. . ."

"Hey boss," Sid interrupted, pointing down the parking area, "catch what just arrived." They all turned to where he was pointing.

A yellow school bus had just entered the rest stop. Except for the driver it was empty. He climbed down from the vehicle and walked over to the restroom. When he returned, he mounted the steps and took his seat without looking around, closed the door and fired up the engine. His hand was on the brake handle and about to release it when he looked in the rearview mirror and saw to his shock that he had five passengers.

The driver instantly turned off the ignition and swung around to face them. "What do you think you're doing?" he shouted. He opened the door and fumbled in his jacket for his cell phone. "Get out now, before I call the cops!"

Jacob waved a hand, palm up in supplication. "Hear us out, please. We're not criminals—we're law-abiding folk just like you. We got caught in a situation not of our own doing."

"Hey, that's not my problem, pal." The driver dialed nine. Before he got to the first one, Jacob sprang from his seat and grabbed the cell out of his hand. He got his arm around the driver's throat and started squeezing, looking furtively out of the window. Nobody was watching. "I told you we're not criminals. That doesn't mean we aren't desperate. We don't need you to drive. As a matter of fact, pal, we don't need you for anything, so if you wanted to make trouble for us you just lost out. Now what's it going to be—do you want to keep losing 'til you stop existing?

The driver stopped struggling, waving his arms to be released. Jacob complied in stages, ready to ratchet his threat back up at the slightest sign of combat. "Okay, okay," the driver said when he found his voice. "What do you want with me?"

"First off," Jacob replied, "where are you coming from, and where are you heading? Why don't you have any passengers?"

"I'm heading back home to Ozona. This bus was at the shop in Fort Stockton. The Ford agency. Had a problem with the tranny and they have the maintenance contract. I can take you to Ozona if you want."

"Do you have a map?"

The driver reached into a cubbyhole and extracted a map of Texas. "Here."

Jacob looked at it, then handed it back to Sid. He thought for a while, and then spoke up. "We're going a lot farther than Ozona. Sorry, pal, but you're going with us—all the way to Houston. I'll promise you this: don't give us any trouble, and when we get to Houston we'll tie you up and leave you in the bus. Other than that we'll leave you unharmed. Deal?"

The driver knew that he had no choice. "Okay, I guess. But I want to drive. My name's Carl, by the way."

"Glad to know you, Carl. So drive on."

Carl drove expertly, doing nothing to attract authorities, as Jacob noted with watchful eyes. They spent the day and long into the night enduring the tedious drive in silent reflection of their uncertain futures.

Jacob couldn't get Earl and Joyce out of his troubled mind. He already missed them both. Joyce's femininity had comforted them all, while Earl's knowledge of the deeper things of the Bible had given them an unexpected and life-changing excitement about God, who had used Earl in a mighty way to bring them to salvation. Continuing to think of the two, Jacob dozed off.

Light came into his head, not suddenly but softly and gently, awakening him in stages. An image formed in the center of his mind's eye, that of a spectacularly beautiful woman, so real that he felt able to touch the apparition. *Is this a dream?* He questioned.

"No, Jacob, I'm real," the vision spoke without words.

Jacob was speechless. He started to stutter a question, but the vision put a finger on his lips. "There's no need to use your voice. I can see your thoughts. As for My identity, just call Me Wisdom. And yes, I've been within you for longer than you would think - I just haven't made My presence known to you before. Jacob My darling, I know how much you miss your Gentile friends Earl and Joyce, and how you hope to see them again. That's not going to happen, but you'll have comfort with Me. You'll have perils too, but think of them in terms of adventure. Remember what Jesus said, that your every hair is numbered. I'm here with you to make certain nothing happens of which I don't approve. And We have wonderful plans for you."

"Was—is our heading to Houston in your plan?" he thought.

"Right on. I gave you the idea, to be exact. You're going back to Israel, Jacob, you and another. The attitude of the entire nation is going to get an upgrade, and you're a part of that event."

"How are we going to get there? We're already hunted fugitives. Transportation isn't our strong suit just now."

She laughed, a crystal tinkle. "When you get to Houston, go down to the docks. You'll find a boat in a roundabout sort of way. The accommodations aren't going to be pretty, but the boat will start you on a path that will take you to the Mideast, where your real adventure will begin."

"What then, and how?"

"That's all I'll say for now. But I'll be with you always. Comfort yourself with that thought. Sleep now—you're going to need it."

Carl started driving erratically in the early morning hours and Sid took over the driving as Carl lay on the rear seat snoring loudly. With a couple of bathroom breaks and a fast-food meal in-between, they skirted San Antonio and reached Houston at seven in the morning. Carl allowed himself to be trussed at a park-and-ride, and the five set out on foot.

"Got an idea, boss?" Sid asked Jacob as they walked.

"Yeah, but we'll need some big-time help from God to pull it off. Look at us—we haven't shaved in days, and we probably smell pretty ripe. About the only possibility open to us is to find a sleazy ship on the docks that's heading for the Mediterranean, and a first officer who isn't too picky about choosing his help."

There were several such ships scattered about the port, all of them in advanced states of disrepair and streaked with rust. Jacob and his men headed down to a portside tavern to seek out hiring prospects.

The darkness of the interior momentarily blinded them. What they saw when their eyes adjusted gave them cause for dismay. Five sets of eyeballs behind dark, deep red sockets confronted them with the promise of violence. Three others were at the bar looking into space, two bearded men and a tattooed blonde woman. Their studied indifference signaled that they wouldn't be of help either way. "What're you doing here, stranger?" one set of eyes challenged. "Best step right back out."

Bringing up the rear, Sid chose that moment to stumble into Paul, which initiated a domino effect that thrust Jacob toward one of the men. Sensing the move as confrontational, the man hurled a fist into Jacob's face. As he did that, another man rushed over to the pool table and grabbed two cue sticks. He kept one, poising it over his head ready to smash into one of the intruders' brains, and gave the other away.

Jacob went to his knees, but he had had it to his eyeballs with bullies. Something snapped and with an adrenaline-fueled rush, he straightened up to deliver a massive head-butt into his assailant's chin. Before the man could recover, Jacob reached over to his crotch and, grasping the man's hair and privates, slung him through the flimsy door out onto the cracked and rutted sidewalk.

The heavy end of a cue stick connected with Paul's skull, rendering him senseless. He dropped like a sack of potatoes. Sid rushed in before the goon could raise the cue again. Grabbing the blood-spattered end of the cue, he jerked back and then forward, aiming his thrust at the goon's belly. The goon caved and immediately hit the ground, lying alongside Paul's inert form. Sid held onto the stick and used it to parry the other cue from swinging into his head. He swung a glancing blow to the attacker's head. The man didn't go down but as he staggered Jacob led Frank into a rushing defense against the other two men. The tavern patrons they fought were meaner, but Jacob's men were both hardier and angrier. Jacob's people won the battle. They surveyed the room, which was eerily quiet now. Another man lay unconscious on the floor and the other ran out through the remains of the door. The last man was still lying on the sidewalk.

Paul got the worst of it. Jacob bent over him, checking his pulse. As he did so he noticed the pronounced dent in his friend's head and realized that Paul was no longer among the living. Hearing a siren in the distance, Jacob grabbed Sid's arm. "Let's go!" he shouted, heading out the doorway. Once out the door, he broke to the right and ran to the corner, where he made another right onto a narrow alley. Gasping for breath, he waited until the other three had come up. "Paul's dead," he said. "There's nothing we can do for him now except complete our mission. Follow me." He continued up the alley to the next street, where he turned left. In the middle of the next block was another tavern, this one in better condition than the last and better lighted. They walked through the door cautiously, half-expecting another confrontation, but the patrons remained on their stools. They found a table that wasn't occupied, sat and ordered burgers and chips all around. When the bartender came around with the bill, Jacob reached in his pocket and withdrew enough to cover the cost and more besides. He gave it all to the barkeep, hoping that the generous tip might open up some opportunities, and asked him if he knew where they might find some work. The man pointed to a corkboard on the wall. "That's the message board over there," he said. "You're looking for a job, you put your name over there. You're looking to hire, same thing. Either way, the info's on the board. Have at it." Phil posted their job needs and then walked outside, where the others grouped around in a huddle. "We're probably not going to get a response on that board until tomorrow at the earliest. Let's do the same thing elsewhere.

By nine o'clock they had gone to five other bars in the area and decided to bed down for the night. They walked until an eighteen-wheeler presented itself. The owner was enjoying the luxury of a bed in a nearby motel room, so Sid picked the lock and they climbed into the sleeper behind the cab. It was crowded, but they didn't mind. The proximity of their bodies made them reasonably warm. "Before we get to sleep," Jacob said, "I thought we might say a few words to our Lord about Paul. Mind if I go ahead and do it?"

They all gave Jacob the nod. "Lord," he began, "we'll surely miss our brother Paul, but we know that he's in better hands now. Please take care of him better than we did, and thanks for giving him to us. And I'd like to ask too for Your hand upon the rest of us who aren't among us now, including Earl and Joyce. Thanks. Amen."

Wisdom visited Jacob during the night while the three others continued sleeping. Again, Her beautiful face and the overwhelming warmth of Her eyes took his breath away. "Hello, Jacob," She said. "Your prayers were answered. Paul's job was done in helping get you here, and now he's enjoying himself in heaven. We're with the others, too, so don't fret about any of them. But don't you think you might have asked Us to comfort Jimmy and Millie too?"

"Oh, oh," Jacob replied in his mind. "Sorry about that. Well, then, would you please also watch over Jimmy and Millie?"

"Already done. Go back to sleep." She departed.

Sid awoke at dawn and shook the others awake. "Hey, get up," he said to nobody in particular. "We need to get out of here before the driver of this rig gets back."

"Chill out, Sid," Frank said testily. "Guy's probably bedding down a girl and getting the most out of a real mattress and central heating. He won't be getting up for a while."

"No, Sid's right," Jacob spoke up. "Maybe he's on a tight schedule. All it would take would be one phone call to bring the feds and the cops down on us like flies. Besides," he added, standing up, "I have to pee." With that, the four men got up, arranged their clothing best they could, got out of the cab, and, finding what meager privacy they could, relieved their bladders.

The second bar they entered offered breakfast burritos. They gobbled these up, ignoring the stench of old fat, and Jacob went over to look at the bulletin board where they had posted their request for work. Jacob did a double-take when he saw the responding message: "I need four able-bodied seamen on the *Rising Star* by 11 o'clock today. Report to Sam on Pier 37."

Jacob waved the others over to the message. It was all they could do not to whoop for joy or get on their knees in gratitude to God. Jacob offered a prayer of thanksgiving and made a further request: "Lord, we know that it was your hand that did this. We hope and pray this will get us near Israel."

They met Sam on time at eleven that morning. Sam was the first mate. Being of about the same social level that their own unkempt appearance suggested, he didn't have any quarrel with their beards, uncombed hair or dirty condition. In fact, as he looked them over with a furtive expression, he seemed to be pleased with them. "My regular staff's kind of under the weather," he explained to them, "so you'll be filling in for this trip to Latakia. Job's only temporary, keep in mind. More temporary than that you slack off. Any diseases?" he asked, not bothering for a reply. "All able-bodied like I asked?" He paused after this question. It was obviously more important. The four men replied in the affirmative, after which he pointed to the ship. The sight suppressed their joy, which had infected them at the mention of a destination. The *Rising Star* wouldn't be rising any time soon. If anything, it would be sinking. The rusting near-derelict was actually listing to port.

"Where's Latakia?" Jacob asked.

Sam eyed Jacob with suspicion. "What's it to you?"

"Nothing. I just thought it would be nice if. . ."

"Stow it. You don't need to know. You don't need to think, either."

"You notice that he didn't ask for credentials of any kind?" Jacob muttered to Sid. "Probably carrying a shipment of weapons or something they don't want to advertise."

"Yeah, but who's gonna worry about that?" Sid replied. "It's a boat, it's still afloat, and its destination isn't very far from Israel, even if it may be a problem getting across the border. And we don't have any credentials to show anyway, so what's to be upset about?"

"So you know where Latakia is. How about sharing the wealth?"

"It's in Syria. A seaport town not too far from Aleppo."

"Oh. Well, then, maybe the boat is carrying weapons. To Israel's enemy. I'd sure hate to think we're going to be helping out one of Israel's enemies."

"This seems to be in God's hands, if you think about what's been happening to us."

"Yeah. Maybe we should let God run the show. Actually, everything's in our favor so far," Jacob continued. "Thank you, Lord, for all of it."

Sam came after them as they boarded the ship. He showed them a single stateroom with four basic bunks and gave them duty assignments. Frank was given the task of cook, which included cleanup work and hauling the slops. Sid was assigned to the engine room. He'd work as a helper under Chief Engineer Jake Hapley. Jacob, being the most responsible-looking of the lot, was given the position of helmsman. Charlie, being the least responsible-looking of them, was assigned the task of general dogsbody, the fetchit-man. "An' we ain't on a watch system on this ship," Sam said. "Y'all 'r on duty twenty-four, seven. Ya eat when ya can. Same with sleep." He didn't bother introducing the men to the captain, or to their individual superiors. Looking at Sid, he simply pointed to his feet, indicating that Jake was to be found somewhere below in the bowels of the ship.

Sid finally found a passageway with a ladder into the engine room. At first the vast room didn't make sense. It looked like a factory floor with machinery on top of machinery in a jumble that resembled a junkyard. But then as he focused more he began to assimilate the pattern: an enormous engine filled the hold. He'd seen the diesel engines on locomotives; big as they were, they couldn't touch the size of this beast. As he focused more, he could discern an open crankshaft, its connecting rods reaching up to pistons hidden within cylinders the size of garbage cans—twelve in all. The beast was quiet now, but he wondered about the noise level when the monster came alive. He saw a man in the distance, dwarfed by the engine. He descended the ladder and approached the man, who sat on a deep canvas folding chair. He obviously was comfortable there, because Sid could hear his snoring from twenty feet away. His tongue lolled out like a dog's, and Sid could see it quiver with every intake of air. Where it wasn't covered by straggly hair, the man's face was as red as his tongue. He was a chewer, as Sid could tell from the bulging left cheek and the brown color of his chin beard. Sid was at a loss of what to do. He didn't want to wake the man out of an obviously deep sleep, but he didn't want to leave without knowing what his responsibilities were. He fidgeted in front of the sleeping man for about a quarter of an hour. Tiring of this meaningless waste of time, he finally turned around and went back toward the ladder. He heard a shout behind him just as he put his foot on the first rung. "Where d'you think you're goin'?" the man said. "Get back here!" Sid nervously complied. When he was facing the man again, the chief engineer spoke up. "You ain't Bill. What happened to Bill?"

"I think he took sick, or maybe he had an accident. A fall. I'm here to. . ."

"Aw shuddup. I know what you're here for. See that oil can over there?" he asked, pointing to an object sitting atop a little cabinet. "That's yours. You oil the bearings and the fittings every hour on the hour when we're running."

"Y-yes, sir," Sid replied, trying to process the command. *If it's every hour, when do I sleep?* he asked himself.

Jake anticipated the question. "In case you're wondering when you sleep, you don't." He laughed at his joke.

"Yessir," Sid said. He'd have to figure it out later. "Can you show me what I'm supposed to oil?"

"Hey, you dense or something? I jus' tol' you. An' no slackin'. Anything happens to that engine, I'll have your balls for breakfast. Now git. You feel the engine movin' you get back here on the double. Scram!"

Sid looked behind him. The man was asleep again before he

reached the top of the ladder.

Frank looked forlornly at the cooking utensils arrayed before him. He'd never gone so far as to cook an egg in his life. He rummaged frantically among drawers, searching for anything that might look like a cookbook, but came up empty. In desperation he looked up Charlie and begged him to switch jobs. "They'll never know we switched," Frank pleaded. Charlie grinned. He had done some cooking, and that did beat being a dogsbody. "Sure, Frank. No problem," he said, much to the other man's relief.

Standing on the bridge deck behind the helm, Jacob looked toward the bow, trying to discern shapes beyond the grimy glass. Sam stood next to him, uncomfortably close, running through the duties of the helmsman, his lecture interspersed with nautical terms, maybe half of them vaguely familiar. *This is the blind leading the blind,* Jacob thought with panic. *Lord, please,* he petitioned God in silent prayer. *At least let us not be in arctic waters when this ship goes down.* "That's all there is to it," Sam said, winding up his talk. "Relax for a while," he added with a furtive smile. "You're dismissed until we get going. Oh, by the way," he said with an attempt at indifference. "There's some mags in the saloon for your reading pleasure. You might want to check them out."

Charlie was the first to hear from the captain, who had rung up the galley demanding a pot of coffee brought to his cabin. Charlie prepared it and called for Frank, the new dogsbody, to serve it. In carrying out the task, Frank was the first of them to actually see the captain. He was still in bed, his red, bloated face portraying the chaos taking place inside his head. An immense hangover was most likely the cause. Frank couldn't see a bottle, but he suspected that a number of dead soldiers lay scattered underneath the man's bunk.

Curious, Jacob went into the saloon and searched through the magazines. *So that's his game,* he thought bleakly. *No wonder he was trying to be nice to me.* The magazines were all of the same genre: porn. Specifically, male-on-male porn. Disgusted, he left the saloon, trying to come up with a plan to bring Sam's lustful intentions to a screeching halt without jeopardizing their ability to get to Israel.

The *Rising Star* left the dock the next day and headed southeastward toward the Atlantic. Sid, of course, knew very little about this first leg of their journey, being occupied with oiling the myriad moving parts and keeping out of Jake's way, which was fairly easy as his primary occupation was sucking on a bottle of cheap rum. The first time that Jake started up the massive engine, the awesome spectacle of the enormous parts in actual motion gave him an almost uncontrollable urge to run up the ladder to escape the gigantic beast. He held the fright in check only with the sternest self-commands. The overwhelming visual impact of the monster connecting rods thrusting up and down to turn the huge crankshaft abated enough during the next few hours to allow him to make his assigned rounds with the oilcan. The threat from Jake also diminished as he descended into his daily alcoholic stupor, leaving him only the heat to contend with, a condition that he accepted gratefully.

Jacob had a far better view of the world outside the ship than Sid, but he had other problems to contend with. Sam headed the list. Sensing Jacob's reluctance for intimacy, he turned surly and retreated to a large wooden chair at the rear of the bridge. From that position he snapped steering orders to Jacob, who was forced to stay on his feet. The captain remained in his quarters.

Left with little to do, Charlie voluntarily helped Frank with the preparation of the meal, which consisted of potatoes, biscuits that turned out flat and hard, and fried chicken legs. "These spuds don't look right," Charlie said as he plucked the boiled potatoes out of the pot and set about to mash them. Looking over to what he was doing, Frank contradicted him. "I don't see anything wrong with them at all. Keep it up."

The captain saw plenty wrong with them. "This here chicken leg is bloody, and you mashed the skins in with the potatoes!" he shouted in a rage. Get this slop out of here and fix me a decent meal or I'll toss the lot of you overboard.!"

Charlie retreated out of the Captain's cabin and back to the galley, plate in hand. "We need to boil up another batch of spuds," he told his companion, "this time without the skins. Here, fry up those legs a little longer and gimme three plates right away. The rest of us shouldn't mind." He dashed down the ladder with two plates, handing them to Sid. "You take this one to Jake," he said, rushing back up the ladder. Sam remained surly when Charlie came back on the bridge with two more plates, but his beef wasn't with him. A fixed glare directed to Jacob remained on his face as he took the plate and began to eat. *Hello, what's up with that?* Charlie said to himself, but was too busy to reflect on the strange antagonism that Jacob and Sam held toward each other.

An uneasy social stability persisted as the ship churned southeastward. Around midnight Sam, too tired to maintain his aggressive attitude, called the galley for a snack. When Charlie arrived on the bridge, Sam told him to stay on the bridge to relieve Jacob, then left for his bunk. Having given Charlie enough information to maintain the ship on its heading, Jacob went to the shared quarters ready to fall onto his bunk. But before he removed his shirt, something told him to look in on Sid. He descended into the engine room briefly, returned topside and told Frank to fill in for Sid, who desperately needed a break and some sleep. Then he returned to his bunk to flop down and pass out.

The next day was spent in similar fashion with Jacob and his three companions on the verge of exhaustion, both physical and emotional. That evening they rounded the Florida peninsula, leaving the keys behind to port. As they entered the Atlantic proper a massive hurricane centered off the Bahamas began to make itself felt. The *Rising Star* shifted her heading to the northeast, beginning a race against the storm and attempting to put a comfortable distance between the ship and the dangerous weather.

Chapter Seven

Jimmy pulled off I-10 into the town of Kerrville, their spirits high as they left the barren land behind to enter the hill country of Texas. He pulled into a service station, intending to fill up with diesel fuel. Millie and Joyce dashed out to the women's restroom as Earl headed for the men's. When Earl returned he found Jimmy staring at the pump with a perplexed expression on his face. He was reading a notice taped over the credit card slot:

CREDIT CARDS NO LONGER ACCEPTED HERE.

HAND READER IN OFFICE.

When they walked into the office, the clerk asked them if they had the newly-mandated hand symbol. He held up his own hand to illustrate what he was talking about. They both shook their heads, which elicited a negative reaction from the clerk. "You need to get with the system," he told them. "You should report to city hall." He started to pick up his phone.

"Hold on," Earl said. "We're going to do that right now, if you'll just steer us in the right direction." The clerk put down the phone and described how to get to the city administrative complex. Leaving the office, they climbed back into the RV, where Millie and Joyce were waiting for them. "Something's come up," Jimmy groused. "They aren't taking credit cards any more. Now we have to go to the city hall and get whatever needs to be done to our hands to let us get fuel."

"Nosir," Earl countered this statement. "What this amounts to is the mark of the beast as described in Revelation Chapters 13 and 14. "Accept that and you'll incur the wrath of God."

"Say what?" Jimmy said. "We're almost on empty," he challenged, pointing to the gauge. "All I want to do is get some fuel so we can continue on. You want to call that a sin, go ahead. I'm going to do whatever it takes to get some fuel. He started the rig, but Earl reached over and yanked out the key, stalling the RV.

"No, you're not," Earl said. "I won't stand by and see you self-destruct. Just listen to me for a moment. Revelation 13 describes the hand identification system known to Christians as the mark of the beast, a means of exchange that was designed and implemented by Satan himself. Anyone who accepts that mark gives the government *carte blanche* to track and control every movement of that individual. It's the ultimate prison. More importantly, Revelation 14 describes how the person who accepts that mark instantly and automatically forfeits any possibility of remaining in a relationship with God, but receives His full wrath instead. It's a very serious business. By accepting the mark, a person declares his allegiance to the antichrist."

He brushed off the hand that had clamped over his wrist and reached over to Earl's hand, attempting to grab the keys. Joyce came up and separated them. "He's right about that, Jimmy," she said. "We've suspected years ago that this eventually would happen. Well, now it has, plain as day. Please understand that Earl is only trying to save you from coming to a terrible end."

"Well then," he snarled to cover up his helplessness, "what do you propose that we do?"

"Let me see the map." After looking it over, Earl pointed down the main street. "That road seems to head out of town toward San Antonio. There's a little town about 25 miles away called Bandera. Let's see it they have the same policy."

Jimmy agreed to the short diversion, and they soon found themselves within the city limits of Bandera, driving beneath a banner that proclaimed the town to be the cowboy capital of the world. Jimmy pulled into the first service station he saw, and was greatly relieved to see the credit card slot open and ready for use. Either the town had not yet reached the sophistication of the larger cities, or its citizens were fighting the transition. Having filled up, they continued down the secondary highway toward San Antonio and stopped at an RV park before they reached the outskirts of the city. Joyce immediately went into the deserted clubhouse, where she scanned the extensive library until she found what she was looking for. Latching onto the Bible, she returned to the RV and opened up the Bible to Revelation Chapter 13. "Here," she said to Millie, handing her the open Bible, "read this, and then continue on through Revelation 14."

After reading the passages, Millie handed the Bible to Jimmy. "Read this," she said, "and then maybe I'll make dinner for us." Jimmy grumbled a bit, but he read the passages. "Sounds real serious," he conceded. "But what can we do about it if it's a universal thing?"

"I hate to say this, Jimmy," Earl told him, "but either we'll get help from outside the system, or we'll just have to die."

"You really mean that?" Jimmy said in wonder.

"I do. It's not always easy being a Christian. I have a feeling that the easy times are over for us."

"After what you and Joyce just came out of, that's saying a lot."

"We may escape the worst of the situation for a while if we play it smart. Starting tomorrow, we'll have to ferret out a black market system, if one exists around here."

They were fortunate. The next morning they saw a truck parked across the street from a popular chain grocery store. The driver sat idly behind the wheel, listening to country music. Jimmy parked his rig in the store lot, where they had a good view of the truck, and sat watching. As they watched, another car came up and parked behind the truck. A man got out and walked up to the idle driver, who removed his ear buds. They conversed briefly. Then the man extracted a wallet and handed over several bills. The driver accepted them, got out of the cab, lifted the tailgate, and jumped up onto the bed. He reached down and picked up a hose, which he handed to the other man. They obviously were making a fuel transfer from the truck to the car. When the transaction was completed and the car drove off, Earl left the RV and wandered over to the truck. "Hi," he said to the driver. "We're almost out of fuel. Know where to get some?"

The driver looked him over, then made a judgment. "Sure. I might have a little if you really need it. Gonna be expensive, though."

"That's okay. Just asking for now. Actually, I don't need fuel. But how about groceries? Same deal?"

"Yeah, sure. Just spendy."

"Thanks. I might be back soon." He walked back to the RV and gave the good news to the others. "There must be a lot of them out there. At least until the government starts cracking down in serious. Maybe we should try to pay up-front for a long-term stay at the RV park."

"I grew up a Catholic," Millie offered over dinner that night. "I stopped going when I left home and got married. I didn't get much out of it when I went. There was just too much ritual. God seemed—oh, just so distant and irrelevant to my life."

"I can't blame you there," Joyce responded. "It's difficult for a person to understand God or to have a relationship with Him with any kind of intimacy until he gets a decent background from Scripture of who our God is and the love He represents. The Churches—and I'm talking about both the Catholic and Protestant ones, have done a miserable job in priming the pump of their congregants' interest."

"And to my thinking," Earl added, "the Churches have made things even worse through their theologians' and leaders'lack of understanding of some very fundamental truths about God"

How so?" Jimmy chimed in, his interest picking up.

"Take the birth of Jesus. It's common understanding that Jesus fulfilled a prophecy way back in Genesis that the seed of the woman would bruise the head of satan, which Jesus certainly did by making Himself as God the sacrifice for the shortcomings of mankind. But the Catholic Church has an odd take on the seed from which Jesus came to earth as a man, while the Protestant Church is indifferent to the whole business. Here, let me go get a Bible." When he returned to his chair, he opened it. "The beginning account is in Genesis 3:14 and 15:

And the Lord God said unto the serpent, Because thou hast done this, thou art cursed above all cattle, and above every beast of the field; upon thy belly shalt thou go, and dust shall thou eat all the days of thy life. And I will put enmity between thee and the woman, and between thy seed and her seed; he shall bruise thy head, and thou shalt bruise his heel.

"I get that Jesus is that seed," Millie said, "but what's the problem with that?"

"The problem is with the nature of the process by which God implanted the seed of Christ in Mary. There is general agreement, at least by Catholics, that the seed is the male sperm rather than the female egg. I agree with that. I also agree that it was the Holy Spirit who did the implanting."

"As do I, from what little I know," said Millie.

"But then the Church made a straightforward association of the male seed with a male Holy Spirit," Earl continued.

"Of course! How else could you interpret the account in Luke?" Millie said.

"Okay, then, let's go to the passage," Earl said, thumbing through the Bible. "Here it is, in Luke 1:34 and 35:

Then said Mary unto the angel, How shall this be, seeing I know not a man? And the angel answered, and said unto her, The Holy Spirit shall come upon thee, and the power of the Highest shall overshadow thee; therefore also that holy thing which shall be born of thee shall be called the Son of God.

"The seed of the woman as given in this passage is universally identified as Jesus Christ, who indeed in the fullness of time was born of the woman Mary. And, of course, it seems to follow logically that this makes Mary the woman spoken of in the Genesis passage we just read."

"So?" Earl was just coming out with common knowledge. Millie was expecting new or at least important information, and his statement of the obvious was starting to irritate her.

"Don't you see the problem with that?" Earl countered. "The seed, which is perceived as a male seed, couldn't have come from Mary, because she is just a normal human woman. The seed is also perceived as coming from the Holy Spirit, which is logically far more consistent with Luke's account."

"But the seed had to come from Mary," Millie asserted with a militant attitude. "Remember, it was the seed of the *woman* that was spoken of in Genesis."

"Ah," Earl assented. "Now we get to the heart of the problem. The seed can't come from Mary, but it must come from her. You can't have it both ways. Let's put everything we've talked about up to this point on hold, and go back to Genesis—this time to the creation story, of which Genesis 1:1-5 offers us a very brief glimpse:

In the beginning God created the heaven and the earth. And the earth was without form, and void; and darkness was upon the face of the deep. And the Spirit of God moved upon the face of the waters. And God said, Let there be light; and there was light. And God saw the light, that it was good; and God divided the light from the darkness. And God called the light

Day, and the darkness he called Night. And the evening and the morning were the first day.

"Keeping that in mind, we'll turn now to the other end of the Bible, where in Revelation 3:14, Jesus commands John to write his commentaries to the seven representative Churches. For each Church He gave himself a unique name. As for the last of these Churches, Jesus gave Himself this name:

And unto the angel of the church of the Laodiceans write: These things saith the Amen, the faithful and true witness, the beginning of the creation of God.

"With Jesus' own claim in mind that He represented the first act of creation, the Light of Genesis 1:3, we can now go back to the creation overview given in Genesis 1:1-5 and put in a rational, self-consistent way the process of creation and the roles of the three Members of the Godhead in accomplishing it.

"The usual supposition," Earl continued, "both Catholic and Protestant, presents the Godhead as all male, wherein the absence of gender differentiation in the process of creative birth renders their masculinity pretty weak. This supposition leads to an awkward interpretation of the passage in Genesis 1:1-5 as we had read above, as thoughtful theologians of both Catholic and Protestant persuasions see in that passage an interaction among the Will and the Spirit such that the creative power of the Holy Spirit acts in response to the Divine Will to endow the Will with the reality of Creation. What is awkward about that relationship under the usual interpretation of the Godhead as all-male is that it puts the Holy Spirit in the role of responder, or, as Warfield put it, as Executor of the Will, which clearly gives the Holy Spirit a feminine attribute.

"If the Protestant theological community has chosen to address that conflict, their thoughts on that topic have not been made accessible to the general Christian public. Catholic theologians have indeed opted to pursue this difficulty, with the result that they have developed a school of thought, ably presented by Father John MacQuarrie, that all three Members of the Godhead possess attributes associated with both male and female genders.

"For multiple reasons that I won't go into right now, there are grave theological difficulties with assuming that bi-gender attribute, worse in fact than the creation issue that such an arrangement would resolve."

"Yes, please don't go any farther right now on that topic," Joyce laughed. "I've had my fill of your reasonings, not that I don't agree. And, Earl, you may want to start thinking about winding up. If you'll notice, their eyes are getting glassy."

"Okay, if I can just say this: if you can assign the female gender to the Holy Spirit, these logical discrepancies go away and you have a much more coherent picture of the roles that the three Members of the Godhead played in the epic of creation. In this alternative view, a functionally female Holy Spirit responds to a functionally male Will by implementing the Will's vision. The result: reality, as embodied by the Divine Word, Jesus Christ. Thus the creation epic becomes a gender-based act wherein the Will in union with the Implementer, or divine Means, gives birth to the Reality. I suspect the process to be a romantic one, and one that at the deepest level superbly represents the notion of family.

"I also view this alternative understanding, unlike that of the usual presupposition, to be fully compatible with the beginning of John's Prologue in Chapter 1 of John's Gospel:

> *In the beginning was the Word, and the Word was with God, and the Word was God. All things were made by Him, and without Him was nothing made that was made. In Him was life, and the life was the light of the world.*

"But what about the many instances in Scripture where male pronouns are used to reference the Holy Spirit?" Millie asked. "Even I know that much."

"I'll save my rebuttal on that point for another time, but just understand this: there are numerous ways in which the use of male pronouns in reference to the Holy Spirit can be made compatible with a functionally female Entity, one of which actually makes this usage a wonderful promise to mankind. Actually, what I just said may be a moot point, because there's some impressive evidence that suggests that references to a feminine Holy Spirit were in Scripture all along until they were deliberately switched to the masculine several hundred years after the beginning of the Church in an attempt to sterilize Christianity from all sexual connotations.

"I'll end this long-winded discussion with the comment that the Catholic Church, which clings to the notion that the apparently male Holy Spirit impregnated Mary, claiming as a result that Mary's spouse, or husband, in the process, being the Holy Spirit, endows Mary with the role of wife to the Holy Spirit. This, in turn, leads to the elevation of Mary in the economy of God beyond what Protestants consider to be proper. Indeed, the Catholic Church not only considers Mary to be mother of God, but also mother of the Church, residing at a higher level within the Church of all other humans. It is a major source of contention between Catholics and Protestants.

"But if one considers the alternative view of the Godhead, wherein a female Holy Spirit responds to the Divine Father in the process of creation, one appreciates that the original creation of Adam, including the formation of his male seed within him, was simply one instance among many of the creative acts of the Holy Spirit. In that context, the formation by the Holy Spirit of the perfect male seed within Mary was no different in nature than the uncountable multitude of other creative acts performed by the Holy Spirit, and therefore can be viewed as a birthing event that was entirely consistent with the office of the Holy Spirit. That makes the functionally female Holy Spirit the true source of the male seed, permitting a wonderfully natural attribution to the Holy Spirit of the "seed of the woman" of Genesis 3:15.

"While Mary certainly deserves the veneration of all Christians, whether Catholic or Protestant, for her participation in the cosmic drama of salvation," Earl concluded, "the "seed of the woman" properly refers to the Holy Spirit rather than Mary, as do so many of the companion attributes that the Catholic Church assigns to Mary."

"Whew," Millie said, theatrically wiping the back of her hand across her forehead, "I'll have to think about that. Maybe harder than I'm used to. But I kind of understand. One thing I'll say, the thought presents a more loving God than I'm used to. And more like a family."

"That's a big part of assuming a female Holy Spirit. In the face of the functional differentiation I've outlined, nobody can come back with an accusation that I'm pushing the heresy of tritheism. In a family context, and only in that context with the Members united in perfect love, the One God of a functionally-differentiated Godhead is the Divine Family."

"Now that really does make sense," Millie said. "But with that, I'm going to head to our bedroom. I've had enough thinking for one day."

Chapter Eight

"Don't you think it's time to radio an SOS?" Green water came over the bows every time the ship plunged into a trough. Some of it remained every time that happened, leaking aboard through the numerous cracks and holes in the ancient vessel. The troughs were getting deeper and the walls that surrounded them steeper. All of Jacob's strength was focused on remaining in a standing position as he grabbed various objects for support. Even the captain was on the bridge, peering outward toward the chaotic sea with a worried expression on his face.

Sam didn't respond immediately to Jacob's suggestion. With a grimace he finally turned to Jacob. "Can't," he said.

"Why not?" This time Jacob's question came out as a plea.

"Radio probably doesn't work," Sam replied. Jacob knew the radio worked; just yesterday he'd overheard voices in the radio shack as he passed by. The real problem with using the radio, Jacob surmised, was that if the ship didn't sink under them, its cargo would incriminate them. He wondered what made their anonymity more valuable than their lives. Just then the ship smacked into a trough and an ominous shudder ran through the vessel as it twisted into the beginning of a broach and tilted alarmingly. A mountain of green water cascaded over the bridge, ripping off some appurtenances. As the vessel struggled to right itself, the radio mast appeared in front of them, hanging down over the bridge. The next wave took it away. One of these was the radio antenna. Even if they had wanted to, now they wouldn't be able to communicate with the outside world.

An apparition appeared in the side port. It was Frank with a pot of coffee. He was struggling to open the door. Jacob moved toward him to help, but before he could reach the door the ship was engulfed by an enormous wave. Jacob waited anxiously for the water to subside, but when it did his terrifying fear was realized. The port was now empty. Jacob struggled to the door and opened it, but Frank was gone. Sam, who had watched the event, shrugged his shoulders. "Get down to the galley and bring up another pot of coffee," he said offhandedly. "And while you're down there, have Charlie spell the guy down in the engine room."

Jacob angrily complied with the order, choosing his timing carefully to avoid the same situation that had ended Frank's life. When he reached the galley he gave the bad news to Charlie, who went reluctantly, with an eerie sense of impending doom, down into the bowels of the struggling ship. Jacob waited for Sid to arrive in the galley. His bedraggled companion looked like he was about to drop from exhaustion. He staggered over the sink and puked until nothing more came up. Then he slid down to the deck and leaned back against the stove, hugging his belly. Saying nothing more, Jacob picked up a coffeepot and left, heading back to the bridge.

The captain had left to return to his bunk. As the interminable afternoon wore on, their situation became ever more desperate. Creaking noises became louder and the shuddering more pronounced, signaling the onset of serious, ship-threatening metal fatigue.

Late in the dark, sunless afternoon the vibration of the deck from the engine suddenly stopped. Shortly after that an apparition appeared once more in the side port. This time it was Sid, whose ghastly features registered extreme anxiety. Jacob opened the door and shut it tight against the screeching wind just as another wave crested level with the bridge. "What's wrong?" Jacob asked.

"We're shipping water. We're going to sink. I tried to get to the ladder down to the engine room, Jacob," he wailed, "but it was too late. The engine room's flooded. Water's rising up the ladder. Charlie's gone, Jacob."

Without a word Sam darted for the side port, scrambling outside and leaving the door open to the tempest that surrounded them. They attempted to wake up the captain, who sat up and belched, saturating the room with alcohol fumes. As he wobbled to a standing position, Jacob and Sid ran outside to follow Sam, who was struggling to free the single lifeboat from its davits. He slipped and with a scream that was overwhelmed by the bellowing wind he fell headfirst onto the deck. Before Jacob or Sid could reach him a wave washed him out to sea, where they quickly lost sight of him. The ship was dipping noticeably lower into the water, the waves higher to their perspective. Jacob and Sid struggled together with the davit release lines. As success approached, Jacob signaled to Sid to stop, tied the line off again, and headed back to the bridge. The captain flung himself outside before Jacob reached the door and, oddly, continued on a straight line directly into the next wave. Jacob rushed back and the two finished untying the lines and dropped the boat into the water. They rappelled down the lines and, once in the boat, pushed off from the now-derelict and rapidly-sinking ship. The little boat bobbed like a toy in the huge waves. It was all either man could do just to remain aboard. When the boat crested a wave they could see the ship. Each time it was visibly lower in the water until, eventually they crested a wave and saw nothing but water. The ship was gone, and along with it, they were certain, were the weapons intended for Israel's enemies. But they were alone, terrified, nauseous and without food or water.

After an eternity of misery they came to a semblance of cognition, where Jacob led them in a prayer that they might continue to be of service to their Lord Jesus Christ. Another seeming eternity ensued, after which the raging wind began to moderate. A long time after that the violence of the waves had noticeably lessened. Another day following that daylight appeared for the first time, and they were able to survey their craft. It had weathered the storm admirably, but the crew of the ship obviously hadn't taken thought that its use might sometime be necessary, for there was neither water nor food aboard. As the sea continued to calm their nausea vanished, to be replaced by a painful thirst that occupied their every thought.

That afternoon a large cargo carrier appeared on the horizon. It seemed to be headed for them, and as time went on it approached so closely that they were convinced that someone aboard the vessel had sighted them. It passed so near that its wake rocked the boat. But it never slowed down, much less stopped. It just kept on going, despite their arm—waving and shouting, completely ignoring them. Eventually it vanished into the distance.

"Might as well pass the time constructively," Jacob said to Sid. "Maybe God will be more inclined to help us out if we plan ahead on what we're going to do if we get to Israel."

"Well, I have a question. It's about something Earl said about Genesis being a Gospel of Jesus. I've been thinking about that. I never really thought of Genesis—especially the first part—being anything but a myth. I mean, nobody really thinks that the Flood was anything more than a local thing that got hyped up totally out of proportion. Do they? Anyone with brains?"

"You ever read Homer's *Iliad*?"

"Of course. But maybe now's not the time to go into that," Sid said, looking out at the vast ocean. "We're kind of vulnerable at the present time."

Jacob laughed. "What would you say if I told you that his epic actually happened? That what he wrote was an eye-witness account of an actual event?"

"But that's absurd," he replied. Jacob noticed that the thought had ramped his fear up to a new level.

"Not so. He was describing a battle between errant planets,

and his descriptions were too vivid and detailed to have been conjured up in his mind. And there's corroboration elsewhere in the Bible. Joshua's long day, for example, and the strange scene in the wilderness where the Israelites started worshiping a golden calf. Why would they, all of a sudden, worship a calf? And why do the people of India still worship a cow? And why is a dragon such a big deal in China? All these things were the shapes that the atmospheres of the clashing planets assumed as they interacted gravitationally and probably electromagnetically as well. Joshua's long day, as a matter of fact, was duplicated by a long night in the Americas halfway around the world.

"Say what?" Sid responded. "Next you're going to bring up that crackpot Velikovsky. Remember him? He said the same thing, until he got trounced by his scientific betters."

"I was going to bring up Velikovsky. He was attacked all right, but not by his betters. Carl Sagan was a fool. He embarrassed himself by spouting out quasi-scientific nonsense that was refuted by his real betters. Sagan and the others were nothing but schoolyard bullies. Their refutations were entirely void of substance. They simply out-shouted their opponent. If Velikovsky was such a crackpot, why did his very detailed predictions, which were scoffed at by the scientific community at the time, turn out to be real and to the profound surprise of his scientific adversaries? The Van Allen Radiation Belt was a big surprise. And, of course, the temperature of Venus, which Sagan attempted to dismiss after the fact and his own surprise about it, on the basis of the Greenhouse Effect, which was demonstrated to be false. And much more recently, the discovery that Mars had suffered a terrible collision, losing its water, most of its atmosphere, and half of its surface. All these things, while being radically inconsistent with the science of the day, are entirely consistent with Velikovsky's thesis. Sorry, but you lose that argument."

"Enough, Jacob. I'm really not in the mood to be talking about catastrophes. Not here and now. Maybe later." He stared moodily out to the surrounding water.

"Besides," Sid added much later, "Joshua's long day and the other catastrophes you were talking about were from a much later time than Noah's Flood. They didn't have anything to do with Noah."

"Wrong again," Jacob countered. The Great Flood catastrophe was the beginning shot of a series of planetary disasters that stretched all the way from that event to the shifting of the sun ten degrees as Isaiah had spoken to King Hezekiah. What first happened was the destruction by a comet of the canopy of ice that surrounded the earth. The mayhem that accompanied the gravitational interaction with the comet also broke up the fountains of the deep. The Flood wasn't just a rainy day, or even forty rainy days. It was an immense catastrophe that involved huge tsunamis, screeching superhurricanes and boiling earth. During that time the Grand Canyon was carved out of the surrounding mountains, perhaps over the span of a single week. The entire planet became a stinking cesspool of decaying bodies and vegetation.

"Then the comet continued on through the solar system, threatening other planets and, most importantly, periodically threatening the earth," Jacob went on. "Its erratic orbit may have taken it around the sun about once a year or so, but it continued to threaten our planet every time it approached us. Over a period of fifty or so of our own yearly revolutions, it would approach ever closer until it almost touched us, and then retreat until the next fifty-year cycle. On one of these cycles its closest approach coincided with the Exodus event, contributing, Velikovsky was convinced, to the parting of the Red Sea. Joshua's long day took place on the next cycle. After that the earth seemed to have a temporary respite from this comet, but then it got entangled with mars in the eighth century B.C., opening a new period of planetary disturbances that were observed by Isaiah and Homer. And then. . ."

"Just stop, will you? Do you have to go on and on about it? Leave me alone." Sid turned his back on Jacob and continued to stare out to sea. Eventually he turned back to face his companion. "I have to be honest with you, Jacob."

"What now?" Jacob responded harshly.

"Just that in case we don't get rescued, I don't want you to have the false impression throughout eternity that I like you." He turned away from Jacob. They both sat bleakly staring out to sea, each set of eyes occupying opposite hemispheres.

The next day they began to lose hope. The ocean was just too vast, their chances of being seen so small as to be nonexistent. Around noon Sid sighted another ship on the horizon, but after the previous episode with a passing vessel the sighting evoked a sense of mockery, of an insubstantial mirage. It was smaller than the other and had the color and appearance of a war ship. He looked at it indifferently and began to close his eyes again, but the memory of his outburst against Jacob intruded sharply into his mind. "Jacob," he said, shaking his companion. "Jacob, please."

"What?" Jacob responded shortly, his eyes still shut.

"I'm sorry about what I said yesterday. I spoke in anger. I do like you. You're my best friend. Forgive me, please."

"Okay. I knew that. I forgave you yesterday. Not that it makes much difference." He went back to sleep.

Sid mulled over this latest conversation, but within less than a minute he drifted back into sleep also.

When he opened them again, his entire vision was taken up with a wall of grey. Raising his head, he saw a number of faces peering down at him. They were dressed as sailors. He was assaulted by a range of emotions in rapid succession: joy at being rescued, quickly replaced by fear that the authorities had recaptured them. But then his eyes saw the proudly-waving flag. It was white with a blue Star of David. Hope returned, and with it a great joy. *God has provided!* he thought, giving thanks to the Lord. He nudged Jacob awake, laughing and crying at the same time.

They were brought aboard, given doses of water, examined and then set at a table, where they were given plates of food.

"What's this?" Jacob asked, looking dubiously at the tiny morsel in the center of the plate. It looked like a dot. "Don't get me wrong," he said to the sailor who served him. "I'm grateful for anything, but are you guys on starvation rations or did we mysteriously end up in an upscale restaurant that just looks like a ship?"

The sailor laughed. "No, but we do need to conserve. Captain's worried that if we give you too much at first you'll just upchuck it. Don't worry—keep that little bit down, and I'll give you more right away."

The two wolfed down their bites of food and in unison handed back their plates. "Next course, please," Jacob said with a smile.

The next course took longer to serve, but it also was much larger. When they finished their meal a steward came to their table and, in perfect English, asked them to follow him. They were shown into the officers' mess, where the captain introduced himself and bade them sit.

"Who are you?" he asked without preamble. "Your pockets were empty. No identification. Where are you from?"

Jacob spoke for the two refugees. "We're from America, sir. And we're Jews, which got us into trouble with the regime. We were hauled off from our homes and tossed into a prison camp. They were about to put us to death. We. . ."

"That bad, huh?" the captain broke in. "We knew it was bad over there, we've been hearing from our relatives about mistreatment. I have cousins in New York, or at least I did at one time. They couldn't get exit visas. But up to now we haven't heard of actual death camps, but I shouldn't be surprised. The old hatred has come back and it's not just in America. It's a worldwide thing now. By the way, my name's John. Go on."

"Maybe so, but there's a higher Power at work too. Would you believe me if I told you that we're here because we were trying to get to Israel? As a matter of fact, sir, what brought you out of the Med?"

The captain chuckled. "Don't we know about that higher Power! Half of us aboard have become Christians, including me!"

"As are we!" Sid exclaimed.

John returned their smiles. "There was a ship inbound to Israel from Brazil, loaded with Jewish refugees escaping a vicious persecution there. They were endangered by Hurricane Emma to the south of us. After their distress call, we were dispatched to give them assistance. Turned out that they were able to make it out of the danger zone without our help. They're just behind us now. The hurricane, on the other hand, is now heading directly for Galveston. Odd, that," John reflected. "America's been getting hammered by weather for several years now."

"And nobody seems to make the obvious connection," Sid added. "I remember one popular televangelist talking about it years ago. There was such a huge public uproar that he backed off. I'll bet he wishes that he was bolder before he was permanently shut up. But ever since that fiasco, Christians everywhere have been silent about what to me is an obvious link."

"As a matter of fact," Jacob said, "way back when Bush Senior was president, he was the first to try to peddle America's answer to the Israeli-Palestinian conflict, which was called "The Roadmap to Peace". He was at the peace conference in Madrid offering it to the world when the perfect storm hit the northeastern United States. You know, the one they made a movie of, where George Clooney meets his end trying to climb a huge vertical wave."

"I saw that too," John said. "You're saying that there's a connection. Maybe so, but. . ."

"Oh, the best part's yet to come. The storm generated huge waves that trashed Bush's Kennebunkport home."

"Ah." John laughed, adding "that connection is pretty direct."

"And when Israel was evacuating Gaza in preparation for the Palestinian takeover there, the one that was forced on Israel by America, New Orleans also was being evacuated in preparation for Hurricane Katrina. After that the American Midwest began to get hammered with drought, tornadoes and generally bad weather, a process that's continuing even as we speak."

"Well," John said, "there's no doubt in my mind about God's

involvement in today's affairs. It's a pretty comforting thought. As I read the Bible, I find that when things look really grim here on earth for God's people, that's when our Lord makes His presence felt the most. Anyway, glad to have you aboard. We should be docking at Haifa day after tomorrow, after which I'll hand you over to immigration. Don't worry about that," he added when he saw their anxiety. Just tell them what you told me. They'll treat you like natives. In the meantime, you have free run of the ship, providing that you don't interfere with its workings." He shook their hands and called for the steward, who recited the ship's mess schedule and showed them to their bunks. Other sailors gave them friendly smiles as they passed through the ship.

CHAPTER NINE

During that night Hurricane Emma made herself felt to the two couples in Jimmy and Millie's motor home. They were now in an RV park on the northwestern outskirts of San Antonio, where the buffeting became so pronounced that they awoke in fear. The screeching of the wind terrified Millie, who hurriedly dressed and commanded Jimmy to do the same and exit the park forthwith. "I knew we should have left the area," she wailed. "Now we're going to have to run for it."

"Calm down, Millie," Jimmy countered, inwardly as fearful as his wife. "The authorities told everyone to stay put. The only thing we can do now is pray." He looked at Earl with a pleading expression. "But I don't know how." Earl got on his knees in front of the couch that he and Joyce had just vacated, and Joyce joined him. Millie shook off her claustrophobic sense of entrapment and got on her knees too. Jimmy soon followed.

"Dear God," Earl began, "We know that everything, even this storm, is in your hands. We simply ask that whatever happens, we remain in your will and that You use this storm for Your glory. Amen."

Jimmy looked over to Earl, expecting to hear more. Finally he asked, "Are you through? Don't you want to say more?"

"Not right now," Earl responded. "I don't seem to have the call right now to do that, maybe because God is dealing with a whole bunch of long-winded pleas for help. Anyway, God knows our situation better than we do." The simplicity of his plea to God impressed Jimmy. *Maybe Christianity is more real than I thought,* he reflected, having been subjected once to a pastor who delivered in fruity-voiced eloquence a sermon that went on interminably without saying anything of real substance.

The storm rocked their rig and threatened to overturn it, but as the winds abated with the movement of the front to the northeast their home remained upright. The dawn broke to a dark, cloudy and wet sky, but the winds were no longer a threat to their lives. Jimmy opened the door cautiously, peering out at their surroundings. He ducked back in with a frown. "I don't know how we managed to stay intact," he told his companions, "but the entire park except for us seems to have suffered major damage."

"I do know how we came through it," Earl said. "Our Lord indeed answers prayer—if it's spoken with the right attitude." He immediately went down to his knees and offered his thanksgiving to the Lord.

"Hey, wait for us!" Joyce said as she went down beside him. He repeated his thanksgiving as all four held their hands together and joined in with a fervent "Amen".

Power was out in the park, but the motor home was equipped with a generator and, with that and their propane they enjoyed the comforts of heat, light, and an operable stove. Joyce was thrilled with the availability of all the essentials of home in such a compact vehicle that could move at will. *Not at will,* she reminded herself as the depressing reality of governmental repression intruded into her mind. She shook off the impending anger and offered to help Millie with breakfast.

After breakfast they went outside to look around. There was a break in the rain and they waded dry otherwise through ankle-deep water to their neighbor's rig which lay on its side. "Help!" a feeble voice called in despair. After that plea there was nothing but silence. Earl reached down and grabbed a rock, which he used to smash the windshield. He squeezed himself in, bloodying his arm on the sharp glass, and searched inside for the source of the voice. He found it underneath a pile of cartons that had cascaded out of the cupboards when the vehicle had turned over. He quickly removed the mess on top and discovered two people beneath. "Ow!" the man said when Earl attempted to tug him upright. He looked at the arm he was holding and saw by its distorted shape that it was broken. "Sorry," he replied, and after several more gentle attempts he succeeded in getting the man to stand. He handed him over to Jimmy, who had come into the rig after him, and Jimmy managed to extract him through the broken windshield. Earl focused next on the woman who had lain beside him. She was dazed, but despite her grogginess she also stood with Earl's assistance, and extricated herself from the vehicle with Joyce's helping hand on the outside. Without being asked, Millie helped them over to her vehicle and went in with them to get them into dry clothing.

The next victim of the storm that they came upon was an actual doctor. "My name is James, and I'm grateful for your kind assistance," he offered as they helped him to emerge from the wreckage of his motor home. "I'll try to pass it forward." Fortunately, his bones had remained intact during the night of terror. Earl directed him to the first victim he had encountered, the one with the broken arm. The doctor immediately improvised a splint and went back to his own demolished rig to acquire some pain medication, which he offered to the man.

CHAPTER TEN

The war ship crossed from the Atlantic into the Mediterranean under a crystal blue sky that complemented the warm breeze and the scent of African desert. Jacob and Sid leaned against the rails gazing out over the benign sea, Jacob thinking *free at last.* Looking toward the stern, he saw the other ship trailing behind at some distance. He turned back and looked at the water below, visualizing how its warmth would feel against his skin, now that survival was no longer an issue. The thought tempted him to strip down to his shorts and dive right then into the water. But before his imagination could take him any farther, their day was quickly ruined by Sid's finger, which was outstretched and pointing toward a dot in the sky. A sailor came up and ordered them down below.

The crew was polite enough to them as they sat in the mess, offering them coffee and even some pie left over from last night's meal. But though they could sense the tension in the ship, they couldn't see what was going on topside. Their ears registered plenty that seemed to be happening. Commands were shouted and turrets moving. Muffled *booms* echoed in the hull. A startling *whoosh* told them that a rocket had just been fired. After a long time a couple of sailors came in chatting excitedly, poured themselves coffee and sat down at their table. Jacob and Sid looked at them, obvious questions on their faces. The nearest seaman smiled in response and moved down the table to sit next to them. "Plenty of action today," he started, ramping up Jacob's impatience. "Helicopter. U.N. We sent you down in case they came closer. We should never have let you go up topside. Didn't think about satellites."

"Is it still around?" Jacob asked him.

"No, no, it's gone." He pointed downward. "Chopper went after the civvy boat instead. Started firing on them. Even dropped some depth charges. They won't be doing any more euthanizing. But there'll be others now. We'd be hightailing it to port, but now we're really on nursemaid duty to that other ship. We'll be going alongside with the ship's surgeon to patch up any wounded aboard."

The two seamen left. Soon they could feel the ship slow and eventually come to a stop. Still later, amid clanking and banging, the hatch opened and in poured a group of civilians trailing behind a corpsman. They were obviously wounded, most sporting white bandages wrapped around various parts of their bodies. A makeshift sick bay was set up at one corner of the mess. As the last of the wounded were accommodated there, the change in vibration signaled that the ship was again underway. The two refugees went over to them and offered their help to the corpsman. He happily took them up on their offer and picked two of the most severely wounded, explaining what they could do to mitigate their suffering. Jacob and Sid were both relieved to be occupied with something that would take their minds off the situation developing outside.

"Nuts to them all, those U.N. cretins," a wounded man with a bandaged arm muttered nearby.

"What happened?" Sid asked. "We couldn't see."

"Shot right into our boat. Didn't even hail the captain. Like rats in a barrel. It's Hitler's Germany all over again—ridding the world of Jews was on their minds."

"Good thing this ship was in the area," another wounded man

spoke up. "We'd have been goners for sure."

"Where are you from?" Jacob asked him.

"Germany, where else," he replied caustically. "Home of the Jew-killers. It's happening all over again."

"But this time you have a homeland," the corpsman spoke up.

"Yeh, and thanks. We do appreciate that, but how long is your homeland going to last?"

"At least as long as I'm alive," the corpsman said.

"Amen, brother," the wounded man replied. There was a murmur of assent from the others.

A meal was served in the mess. Some time after that the ship slowed again, the sounds informing them that they were in the process of docking. A lieutenant came into the mess and signaled them over while the noises outside indicated that the work of completing their voyage was still in progress. "See those refugees over there?" he said, pointing to the small group of wounded they had just left. "Might be a good idea if you two just joined them. Not that you won't eventually be welcomed into Israel, but it just might take longer if you stay separated. A lot longer. Get what I'm saying?"

"Yes, sir, and thanks," Jacob replied.

The lieutenant tipped his cap in acknowledgment of their understanding. "Compliments of the Captain," he said, and turned back toward the hatch.

Jacob told the corpsman what had just transpired. "Good idea," he said. "But we need to make it better."

"How so?" Sid asked.

"I'll show you if you'll sit down." When they complied, he bandaged Jacob's arm and Sid's leg.

As the ship approached the port of Haifa those refugees capable of walking were allowed topside for a view of their destination. The scene was magnificent, with Mount Carmel and surrounding hills rising up from the Mediterranean and white buildings shining in the sun. Trees were abundant, lending the large city a homey, settled look. "It looks beautiful," Sid said to Jacob. "Like what home should look like."

"There's much history here, too," spoke another refugee. "This is where the *Exodus 1947* came to rest briefly after being boarded and commandeered by the British. The boat was carrying over forty-five hundred Jewish Holocaust survivors, whom the British refused to allow onshore. Instead, they were taken back to refugee camps in Germany. But the Jews in losing the battle won the war. A huge stink was raised over the heavy-handed manner in which the British treated the Jewish refugees, and all the more so as by that time their suffering under the Nazi regime had become common knowledge. Then there was the popularity of Leon Uris' *Exodus*, a fictionalized account that did much to advertise the plight of the Jews. I'd be willing to wager, in fact, that the incident of the *Exodus 1947* helped the Jews enormously in their quest for statehood and international recognition."

"Is the boat still here?" Sid asked him. "Can we visit it?"

"Yes and no. It's here, but it was allowed to fall into neglect and eventually burned to the waterline and sank. At the present time it's buried beneath the port facility. And that's probably where it will stay for a long time to come."

As the man pointed to the facility, Jacob marveled at its busy industrial modernity. This city wasn't some backwater town, but a major economic powerhouse. As he saw the modern high-rises in the background, he thought to himself that Haifa could just as well be an American city.

Closer in as they approached the breakwater, the industrial section of the port came into the fore, confirming the impression that Jacob had acquired before. A major cruise ship was docked at a quay. At other locations, huge cranes offloaded containers from freighters.

They went through customs as part of the European group. The trauma of injury evoked compassion from the officials and sped up the process. They all were issued identity cards apparently based on nothing more than their solemn oath that they were truthful in giving their names. Behind the scenes, of course, they accessed the Interpol face-recognition database, but nobody in their group was apprehended. Samples of their DNA were also taken for confirmation of their Jewish identities and their right to make aliyah under the Right of Return, law 5710. They then would be full Israeli citizens. When they refused further treatment for their wounds, they were endowed with a starter stipend, enough to get them something to eat and a place to stay for a week, and were directed to the Ministry of the Interior for temporary visas. There they would be directed further to help with employment.

When they emerged from the customs building, the colorful bustle outside forced Jacob to amend his impression of Haifa as being reminiscent of an American city. *Maybe once it had been that*, he reflected, *but now Haifa's incomparably better.* Under the present regime, America had lost its color and optimism. Now the streets of its cities, under the watchful eyes of millions of cameras, were drab, its people grim, fearful and colorless. This city, in stark contrast, was healthy, happy and alive, despite the ever-present threat of incoming rockets, improvised explosive devices, and the huge mass of people outside its borders who wished its destruction and death.

As they walked away from the dock at Haifa, they saw a small knot of people waving enthusiastically at them. "Messianic Jews!" Jacob exclaimed, heading over to their apparent leader, a busty blonde woman in khaki shorts waving a sign. Jacob smiled as he approached her. He waved off her hand as she attempted to hand him literature. "That's okay," he said. "We're already Messianic Jews. But we have a whole lot to share with you about our Jesus. Information that should make your mission a whole lot easier. Care for a cup of coffee? I'll buy."

As they sat at an outdoor table sipping lattes, Jacob couldn't help but notice her blue-grey eyes and her attractive mouth with its charming smile. His priority shifted momentarily from his need to share about Jesus to an urge to kiss her. He caught Sid's annoying wink and reshuffled his agenda back to the task at hand.

"Moira, is it?" he asked, and with her confirming nod he began telling her about his own entry into Messianic Judaism and what he'd learned about Jesus from Earl at the concentration camp and afterward, during their escape from the authorities. He began with the Passover connection. She listened politely as he spoke.

"Most of us are well aware of the link between Jesus and Passover," Moira told Jacob when he finished with that issue. "But it's always grand to hear the story again." She smiled to soften her words.

"Okay, then," Jacob responded. "I'll just cut to the chase and give you some information you don't have. Or if you do, I'll eat this napkin."

"Go ahead, then," she laughed.

Borrowing a pen from her, with the help of diagrams on his napkin he gave her the details behind Jesus' feedings of the multitudes and the patterns by which five thousand were fed with five loaves and produced a remainder of 12 baskets while four thousand were fed with seven loaves and leaving a remainder of seven baskets. "Given the simple miracle of a loaf becoming whole after its breaking, the rest is all in the pattern," he concluded.

"Amazing," she answered, clapping her hands in enthusiasm. "How beautiful is Scripture!" She covered Jacob's hand in hers. "You blindsided me," she laughed. "I was expecting to rib you again about telling me something I already knew, so I didn't see this coming. I'm very grateful for the knowledge, and, believe me, I'll do everything I can to share it with as many people as I can."

"But Wait! There's more!" he exclaimed, mocking a huckster's pitch. He added Elisha's feeding of the hundred prior to those of Jesus, and of Peter's subsequent feeding of the three thousand.

"Now that's extremely interesting," she said. "I had no idea that there were more than the two feeding events given in the Gospels. But there you have it, in black and white in the Old Testament. And

I immediately caught the connection between Jesus' commandment to Peter in John 21 to feed his lambs and the symbolic feeding of the people with the Word of God. The feeding details fit right in with Scripture and amplify it. How about this Earl? He must be quite a Messianic Jew himself."

"He's not. He's a Gentile, and not even an educated theologian. He said it took him ten years to figure it out about the feeding."

"Well, thank God for him. But I'm not really surprised about his lack of credentials. Look at all that the theologians—ours and the Gentiles'—have done throughout history to garble the message. The man must have had a close relationship with the Holy Spirit."

"He did indeed," Jacob continued. "But I haven't even finished with the story."

"There's more?" she asked, surprise in her eyes.

"Oh, yes. The best part's to come. Remember in Mark 8 how Jesus responded when they asked for a sign? He told them that their generation wouldn't get a sign. But in His feedings Jesus actually was developing a sign. It wasn't for that generation, but ours."

"The implications of that last statement are pretty big, Jacob," Moira said. "There are some eschatologists out there who claim that prophecy must be interpreted according to the knowledge and customs common to the people during the time that the prophet spoke. What you're saying is that that convention isn't correct."

"I can see by your smile," Jacob said, "that you don't believe that convention anyway. We both know that the Book of Revelation as well as those of Daniel and Ezekiel are given for us, not for the people of the prophets' time."

"Of course. Just keeping you on your toes. So go on—I'm still waiting to get the sign."

Jacob picked up Moira's pen again. "As I'd told you, the companies of fifty and a hundred can be combined into a larger rectangle to encompass five thousand. But in a perfect rectangle there's fifty-one hundred, not five thousand. Restoring the number to five thousand leaves a gap of a hundred in that rectangle." He drew a rectangle with a little indentation to describe the missing one hundred. "But if I add Elisha's one hundred into the five thousand, I get a perfect rectangle again, and that suggests something. It suggests that maybe all the feeding events can be combined together to form a sign." He turned the napkin over and drew the rectangle of the five thousand and the one hundred. On top of that he drew the rotated rectangle of the four thousand, and on top of that he drew the rectangle of Peter's three thousand. Moira's eyes widened in astonishment as he finished.

"Oh!" she exclaimed. "Oh, that's huge. It's a cross! I can't believe it!" But as she looked at it further a frown darkened her features. "Yes, but what about the hundred fifty left over from the feeding of the four thousand? You said that a perfect rectangle for that case involved thirty-eight fifty and put the rest into a much smaller rectangle."

Jacob grinned. "I was just waiting for you to come up with that. So here's the deal: there are three companies of fifty left over, right?" Before she could respond he continued. "Remember that the saying 'THIS IS THE KING OF THE JEWS' was placed on the cross. It was called a Titulus. Now here's the amazing part: the inscription was given in three languages, Greek, Latin and Hebrew, one language for each of the representative companies left over in the feeding of the four thousand."

Moira was speechless. Finally she softly but deliberately placed her hand over his. "I'll remember this day the rest of my life," she said. "Thank you so much."

"Thank you for listening. And maybe we can work together to spread the word about it."

"Deal. Got any more gems like that?"

"Sure. Probably not as big, but there are some more. What do you know of Migdal Edar?" When she shook her head, he told her about how the manger where Jesus was born was a special place for the birthing of sacrificial lambs, who themselves were wrapped in swaddling clothes to prevent injury. He continued on from there, with Sid helping out from time to time, to share with her all that they had learned from Earl and Joyce. By the time they wound down it was late afternoon.

"Do you have a place to stay?" Moira asked them.

"Not yet. We were going to look for an inexpensive hotel, but got carried away here."

"I can help you there. We live in a kibbutz about twenty miles away, but we're staying at a boarding house while we're here in Haifa. I'm sure there's room for more. Why don't you join us?"

Jacob and Sid didn't need any further urging to comply. As the three departed the café, Moira gave them something to look forward to. "You've given me—us—something to share with the yet-unsaved. I want to do something for you in return. Tomorrow, how about me taking you on a tour of the city?"

"I'm not going to complain," Sid said.

"Thanks," Jacob added, touching her hand.

When they entered the boarding house, Jacob instantly could tell by his surly expression the fellow who had had a claim on Moira. Oblivious to his attitude, she walked over to him and introduced the two. "Hi, Jer," she said. Meet a new refugee from the States, who also happens to have a Messianic bent. Jacob, this is Jerry." Jerry reluctantly offered a hand, which Jacob clasped with misgiving. When he released it, the hand moved to Moira's shoulder in an obvious demonstration of his prior claim on her. Feeling somewhat left out but grasping the reason, Sid also understood the antipathy of the two men and moved into the circle, introducing himself and offering a hand. Confronted with the outstretched hand, Jerry was forced to release his hold on Moira, who quickly departed to engage another group. An awkward silence ensued, put to an end with the abrupt departure of Jerry. Sid rolled his eyes at Jacob, and they wandered over to another knot of people, who were considerably warmer with their welcomes. Paul, an elderly man with Santa Claus features and a white beard to match, showed them the ropes, including a trip upstairs to the dormitory where he pointed to two available bunks. They returned downstairs to a simple but hearty meal. After the dishes were cleared, a chore that Paul had told them would be their turn in a few days, Moira told them to stay and listen to a story she had to tell. In repeating the information that Jacob had given her earlier, she both simplified and embellished upon it, proving her rare ability at storytelling. Even Jacob and Sid were mesmerized by her account. She stood talking for two hours before finishing. Before sitting back down, she pointed to Jacob, inviting him to address their questions regarding these new revelations about Jesus. Both he and Sid responded for another half hour to their eager thirst for understanding. By that time everyone was ready to turn in for the night.

Moira approached Jacob after breakfast the next morning. "Are you and Sid ready for a hike? Jacob assented with a smile, looking around for Jerry. He couldn't be seen. *As a matter of fact,* he thought, *I didn't see him at all this morning.* "Let me go fetch Sid." But when he told Sid that Moira was ready, his friend begged off, pointing to a small knot of people. "Moira's talk last night was a real hit with them," he explained. "Now they want more, and I'd like to accommodate them. Have a good time." Sid watched Jacob's retreating back. *Good luck, old friend,* he thought.

Moira brightened when Jacob returned without Sid. *What about Jerry?* He asked himself for the hundredth time since they had arrived at the boarding house. She pointed the way and he followed her outside. "Our first stop will be a treat for you," she said. "Being an illegal refugee yourself, having pretended to come from Europe instead of the States, I thought you might appreciate how our little country has enshrined our first illegal refugees as heroes." They walked together under the warm blue sky, her carefree attitude filling Jacob with the simple joy of being in this new and wonderful place with this beautiful woman at his side. They crossed the broad Haganah Avenue and took a number of winding streets until they reached a museum. "It's called the Clandestine Immigration and Naval Museum," she offered, "honoring the holocaust survivors who attempted to come to their homeland in opposition to the

British post-war policy of forbidding mass Jewish immigration into Palestine. All that ended, thank God, when Israel became a nation in 1948."

"Speaking of which, I have another story to tell you. I'm sure that you know of Daniel's amazingly accurate prediction of when Jesus would make His entry into Jerusalem as King of the Jews."

"Oh, yes," she said, pausing under the shade of a palm. "Waving these very branches," she said, pointing upward, "and to the very day, exactly a hundred seventy three thousand and eight hundred eighty three days after Artaxerxes' decree. I know it well—it's one of our most important messages to the Jewish community."

"Well, there's another precision forecast in the Old Testament, one that was just very recently discovered by the late Grant Jeffrey, a well-known Bible scholar. It's very important too. It predicts the return of Israel as a nation in 1948, again to the very day, but this time almost a million days in advance."

"Oh, you have to be kidding!" she exclaimed.

"No, it's right there in your Bible, in Ezekiel 4 and Leviticus 26." He gave her the details, including the companion passages in Hosea about Israel's eventual return to her homeland in modern times. She took his hand in hers and they entered the building, where she gave him a personal narration of what they were viewing. After an hour they emerged back into the sun. "Are you ready for some serious climbing?" she asked him.

"Sure," he replied, his heart giving another jump as she again took his hand. They headed south away from the seacoast and toward the wooded hills.

"We're on Allenby Street, as you can see," she said. "Do you know anything about the British General Allenby and why he is so honored by us?"

"I do know something. But I'd like to hear it from you." He loved the sound of her voice.

"This land had been under the control of the Ottoman Turkish

Empire for a four-hundred year stretch beginning in 1517. During the First World War in 1917 General Allenby marched into Jerusalem, ending the Muslim hold on our sacred city. This Allenby, Jacob, was a committed Christian who knew his Bible. In particular, he was aware of Isaiah 31:5, which says *'As birds flying, so will the Lord of hosts defend Jerusalem; defending also he will deliver it; and passing over he will preserve it.'* Under his command was the 14th Bomber Squadron, which he deployed over Jerusalem, routing the entrenched Turks, who fled the city without waiting for orders to do so. There's no controversy whatsoever about this event having fulfilled Isaiah's prophecy, but there is some regarding its timing. That seven-fold extension of time from Leviticus 26 that you described regarding Israel's return as a modern nation in 1948 has also been applied to Allenby's victory in 1917. In this case, the twenty-five hundred twenty-year period was applied from the beginning of Israel's first captivity rather than its end. Actually, I think it's more logical, given the conditional nature of the time period, to think that it's more relevant to your application to 1948, but who knows? Maybe both events are relevant to prophecy. At any rate, I'll spread the word around about 1948, and thanks ever so much for that information."

They crossed over from Allenby onto the picturesque Stella Maris and began to climb in earnest. When they reached the Stella Maris Square Jacob was panting. "Are you okay?" Moira asked with concern.

"Yeh, sure," he replied between breaths. The starvation rations at the death camp haven't helped me any. I'm hoping to recover in these new surroundings. So far things seem to be working out real well."

"I hope that I can help," she said, looking deeply with her striking grey-blue eyes into his.

"Yes, well, there's something I need to say to you about that. By this time—short as it's been—you must know that I find you attractive. I have the impression that you may feel the same way. Am I out of line?"

"No," she smiled shyly. "You're quite right."

"But then, what about Jerry? He seems to think that you belong to him."

"Jerry thought I belonged to him the first time we shook hands. He never bothered to check with me. That's been a big problem for weeks, and it came to a head last night when he demanded that I break off all communications with you. I told him where to go and he left our group early this morning. So you see, not only were you not out of line, you solved a very big problem for me."

Jacob tried unsuccessfully to hide his elation. She grinned at him. "I just hope that I'll be more than a problem solver to you," he said. "At least I won't get all possessive."

"Are you sure that that's what I want?" She linked an arm in his. "Let's go eat." They strolled down the street and stopped at a charming outdoor café, where they had lunch. It was evening by the time they arrived back at the boarding house. They sat together for dinner, after which Moira once again took center stage to pass on to the others Jacob's prophecy about the return of Israel as a nation in 1948. After her talk, briefer this time, they drifted off to the sitting room to read. Jacob noticed Sid at the other end, continuing his tactful separation from them. He smiled, and Jacob noticed that he, too, was sitting near a girl, a dark-haired beauty who seemed to be enjoying his company. Jacob picked up a magazine but the contents didn't reach his mind, which was occupied elsewhere with thoughts of grateful thanksgiving to God for the vast gulf between Haifa and his bleak memory of America.

The next morning Moira met him as he emerged from his room and they went down together to breakfast. "How about catching some sun today at the beach?" she asked.

"That sounds wonderful, Moira. But what about your work?"

"I'm in very good standing right now, with all the information you've given us. They want me to stay close to you, maybe interrogate you for more. I'm happy to give them what they want. You might ask Sid along. And Mary. They seem to enjoy each others' company.

The four took a bus to Kiryat Haim Beach, Mary's favorite. A picnic table complete with sunshade was available, but they bypassed it and spread out their towels on the somewhat rocky sand. Moira took off her smock, displaying a spectacularly healthy body, and lay down on her back for a quick dose of sun. Mary sat with her arms around her knees, looking out at the water. Jacob and Sid immediately ran splashing into the water. "What do you think, Sid?" Jacob called. "Think it might be an acceptable life?"

"I don't know," Sid called back, flopping his arms joyfully in the warm water, "I'd hate to think of us never again seeing the chow line at the camp. And there's a scorpion over there that I'm really beginning to miss. And, of course, a really cute female guard."

"Speaking of cute," Jacob replied, "You're not hurting." In her own way, Mary was just as pretty as Moira.

"Neither are you," Sid said, laughing.

Jacob lay on his back, basking in both water and sun and letting the small waves rock his body. *He's right about that. No wonder Jerry was so possessive of her.* He looked toward the beach, where Moira was sitting up now, applying tanning lotion to her legs. His interest suddenly shifted from water to Moira. He waded back to his towel next to hers and sat. "Need some help with that?" he asked.

"Sure. You can do my back, if you don't mind."

"Oh, I don't mind." *Back off, pal,* he thought. *Eager isn't becoming.* But he complied with plenty of inner joy. Transient thoughts of his dead wife threatened to encroach on his happiness, but he pushed them away. He lay down beside her when he finished, and they engaged in talk of the beauty of the day and other pleasant trivia. He loved to hear her voice. Another topic intruded in his thoughts. "How did you come to be a Messianic Jew?" he asked.

"I'm an orphan," she replied. "An older one to be sure, and capable of handling my own life. But I'm still an orphan. My parents died before their time."

"What happened?"

"They were at a party in Tel Aviv, celebrating their friends' twenty-fifth wedding anniversary. It was at a popular night club. A suicide bomber thought that would be a perfect place to acquire his seventy-two virgins. I used to hope that they'd be very beautiful, and he'd be very castrated."

Jacob held in his urge to laugh. "When?" he asked.

"It happened a little over two years ago. I'd always thought of myself as a good Jew, but I harbored this rage inside of me. Their passing left me with enough money to finish out my last year in college. I did okay, I guess, but just. I couldn't shake my anger toward the bomber and his family, and all Muslims, to be honest. It occupied so much of my mind that I couldn't focus on my studies as well as I should have. I'm certainly capable of more than I accomplished that year. I knew it at the time, but, well, you know, I was preoccupied. Then a group, the one that I'm with now, came onto campus to talk of Yeshua, and how He's the One foretold in our own Tanakh, the Christian Old Testament. I was sitting on the grass eating a sandwich and I couldn't help but hear what Peter—you've met him, the one with the beard—was saying. I was particularly struck by his recitation of Isaiah 53. Then he went on to speak of the real meaning behind the Passover, and he linked that with the twenty-second Psalm. I went over to him after his talk. I wanted to thank him. But before I could speak, he looked into my eyes and saw the mixture of sadness and hatred there. He invited me to join him at coffee. Then he dragged the story of my parents out of me and spoke of Jesus' love towards those who wanted to kill him. He talked for hours, going over the way that Joseph pointed to that kind of love, and of how Jesus turned the Apostle Paul from a Pharisaic Christ-hater into the most devoted Christian who ever lived. I was completely won over and accepted Jesus that night as my personal Lord and Savior. My hatred fell away immediately, and I've been living a joyful life ever since."

"Thanks for sharing that beautiful story, Moira," Jacob said. "Aren't you a bit—*cautious*—about meeting up with another suicide bomber? Isn't everyone living here a little edgy about the hatred of so many people beyond the borders of Israel?"

"I'm not the least bit cautious any more. Having an intimate relationship with Jesus makes all the difference. What will be will be."

"A wonderful attitude. I share it with you. One thing, though, about your turning into a Christian. As a Jew, didn't you kind of think of the Holy Spirit in feminine terms?"

Yeah, Jacob. I know that the New Testament refers to the Holy Spirit in terms of a masculine Entity, and yes, it does bother me. I've just personally worked around it by sticking to my Jewish belief in a female Holy Spirit and not talking about it to anyone. But I expect that a lot of our fellow Messianic Christians feel the same way about the issue that I do." She looked into Jacob's eyes. "How about you?" she asked.

"I'll answer that by saying that I've got great news for you. Remember me telling you about the guy—the *goy, the gentile*—who brought me a saving knowledge of Jesus Christ in the death camp?"

"Sure."

"Well, this fellow Earl, without any kind of Jewish background, had come to the same conclusion regarding the female functional gender of the Holy Spirit. More than that, he and his wife were able to back up their claim with a lot of Scripture, both in the Old and the New Testaments. They said that in the very early days of the Church, a substantial percentage of the new Christians thought of the Holy Spirit as being female.

"For the first several centuries of the Christian religion it was customary for those non-Christians in the surrounding Roman society to worship a pantheon of gods and goddesses along with their devotions to the Roman emperor. The ceremonies devoted to the goddesses, in particular, were openly sexual and even degenerate, but always lurid and base. A number of early Church fathers, including Justin Martyr, Polycarp and Irenaeus, even up to Augustine in the fourth century, were influential in denouncing what they considered to be the perverted and disgusting rituals associated with paganism. On top of the pagan religions, heresies like Gnosticism also were attempting to sidetrack the Gospel message, and they, like paganism, were abusing the association of sexuality with God by bringing the notion down to the materialistic level, the domain of humanity at its basest."

"During this prolonged period of intense debate over issues of heresies, particularly Gnosticism, the Church Fathers were motivated to clean up their religion, to purify it. To them, that meant the purging of all hints of sexuality within the Godhead. According to Earl, it was a terrible mistake, one that Christians have had to live with for almost two millennia."

"So are you saying that you believe in the Holy Spirit the same way that I do?"

"You bet I do, and better yet, thanks to Earl I know plenty of Scripturally-based reasons to hold to that understanding. UH!" he exclaimed, and fell back on the towel. The towel wicked out a copious quantity of red blood from beneath his body.

"Jacob!" Moira screamed, jumping up. "What happened?" Sid shouted, jumping up himself. Moira grabbed her smock and wadded it up beneath his unconscious body to stanch the flow of blood. She put her head against his chest to reassure herself that his heart was still beating, and then grabbed her cell phone for emergency assistance.

Jacob awoke to see three troubled faces hovering above him. "What happened?" he asked.

"Stay still," Moira told him, tears streaming down her cheeks. "You've been shot." She had his undershirt wadded up in her hands and was holding it against his chest. "An ambulance is on its way now." She looked up toward the road. "Oh, please hurry," she wailed. There was no pain. In fact, there wasn't any feeling at all. The numbness crept up to his brain and darkness prevailed.

He woke again to white surroundings. Looking around, he immediately saw Moira, whose expression changed from concerned to joyful. "Welcome back!" she cried. Sid and Mary were next to her, and he nodded to them.

"What happened?" he asked them.

"You were shot, Jacob," Moira answered. "Through the chest, where your heart would have been if it had been on the other side. Bad enough, though, for you to need some lengthy recuperation. You lost a lot of blood, and some lung tissue as well."

"Is my lung gone?"

"No, the doctors don't think so. But right now it isn't working too well. The doctors are hoping for a full recovery, but they told us not to get our hopes up."

"What about—"

"Yeah," she interrupted. They got the guy all right. It was a drive-by shooting, some fanatic who wasn't quite fanatic enough to meet his virgins. He'll be away a long time. I hope."

"There's lots more where that came from," Mary offered. "It's just something we have to live with. If we let these things get to us, we'll have let them win. That just won't happen. I hope you feel the same way."

"No, I want an immediate repatriation to America, where I can return to the chow line and re-establish a relationship with my pet rattler." Jacob grinned at his sarcasm. "Of course I feel the same way. With or without a choice, I fell in love with this country even before I left the boat, and that hasn't changed a bit." He looked again at Moira's eyes. *I think I have another love too. No, not think. I know.* But then the thought returned of the wife that he'd left behind at the death camp and a sharp misery returned. He tried to shake it off, but couldn't. *Please, Lord,* he pleaded. *Never let me forget, but allow me to step into this new life without carrying the baggage of my past.*

Sid saw his sudden distress and recognized it for what it was. He spoke up, attempting to break the dark spell. "Good news, Jacob," he said. "They're saying that the information you gave them has picked up the response. Several people came to a saving acceptance of Jesus Christ as their Lord and Savior, and another person has joined the group."

"It's not me. It's us," he said, embracing all of them in his stare. "As a matter of fact, it's not even us. It's all about God."

"Amen to that," Moira breathed. "Is there anything we can get you?"

"A Bible for starters."

"Already done. It's in your drawer."

A nurse came in. "I'll have to ask you to leave now," she said. "He needs his rest, and Doctor Frank is making his rounds now. Come back in the morning, please."

Jacob remained in the hospital for another three weeks. One afternoon while he was alone reading his Bible that same nurse came in to check his vitals. She lingered afterward. "You're Jewish," she declared. "I can see it in your face. What gives with the Bible?"

"Yes, I'm Jewish. I'm also a follower of another Jew, Yeshua, Jesus. He was our God all along, but we were so wrapped up in our traditions that we failed to see that He's as much a part of our own Torah as of the Christian Bible. Here," he said patting the edge of his cot. "Sit and let me show you something." He turned the pages to Isaiah Chapter 53 and handed the open Bible to her. "You know and respect the prophet Isaiah, as do all observant Jews. Read that."

After reading the passage from Isaiah, she returned the Bible to him. He proceeded to explain the Gospel to her. At the end of his talk she got down on her knees and gratefully accepted Yeshua as her own Savior and Lord. Almost immediately thereafter another nurse came into the room looking for her, and they left together. But as she reached the doorway, she turned her face back to him with a smile.

The smile was on her face the next time the nurse came into his room.

"Thanks for the message," she said. "I'm getting more into the Bible now. Any more gems like the last one?"

"Sure," he said. "Read Psalm 22, written by King David. It speaks of Jesus' crucifixion a thousand years before the event. Then read Exodus 12 about the initiation of the Passover. That's really about Jesus. We'll talk about it when you've read it."

"There's something I want to tell you now," she said, the smile broadening into a grin. "Your friend, the girl. She's in love with you."

"Well, I sure hope so, but how can you tell?"

"Trust me. It's a girl thing. But I'll tell you this: among other things she's been here alone for hours while you've slept. I'd say that's a real commitment."

His three friends had come to visit periodically during daytime visiting hours, but when the time came for him to leave, only Moira showed up. "Where's the others?" Jacob asked her, looking up from his wheelchair.

"I wanted to pick you up myself. I hope you don't mind."

"If you can lean down so I can whisper in your ear, I'll give you an answer to that." When she complied, he turned her face and kissed her on the mouth. Startled, she began to withdraw, but returned to kiss him back. "I wanted to do that at the beach and ever since," he murmured. Are you okay with it?"

"What did my kiss say?"

"Enough said." They left the hospital in her car and in a happy state.

"Things are really starting to happen, Jacob," she told him as she drove back to the boarding house. "In fact, our movement is taking on a life of its own, with other leaders emerging, and ones who are more capable than us. Some are theologians and others are well-known in the entertainment industry. We're thinking of moving on, maybe to Tiberias on the Sea of Galilee."

"That's wonderful," Jacob exclaimed. "Like we planted, and now Apollos is watering, is that it?"

"Right. People are already starting to pack for the move. I wonder, though, if you're up to it yet."

"Of course I am. I'd be honored if you'd let me tag along with you. Wither thou goest and all that. Please."

She didn't speak. Instead, she reached over and kissed his ear.

Chapter Eleven

"Get offa me!" the injured man yelled. He hauled back his left arm and brought it forward, slapping Joyce in the face. "Can't you see I'm hurting?"

Joyce ignored her smarting cheek and attempted once more to free the man from the debris surrounding him. This time she was more successful and examined his extremities for breaks. From the angular appearance of his right leg she knew that it was broken. "I'm so sorry for hurting you," she told the elderly victim. "Your leg is broken below the knee. Someone will be by soon to set it. Would you like some water?"

"Yes, please," he said in a subdued voice. She put a glass to his lips and he helped her hoist it while he gulped it down. "I gotta pee," he said when he finished. "Real bad." She brought out the red plastic pail she'd been carrying around just for that purpose and helped him get onto his left knee. She left him then to take it from there, and when he'd finished she took it outside the heavily damaged trailer and dumped it in an inconspicuous place. Now wasn't the time to be trying to obey the sanitation laws. Not with a defunct and already overflowing park septic system and the probability that no attempt would be made to empty it for at least another month. *That has to be up there among the worst effects of a natural disaster,* she reflected as she searched for Earl. *The filth of it all—the mountains of trashed human contrivances and the human waste on top of that. We're an ugly lot when our civilizing systems break down.*

She found her husband helping Doctor James set a broken ankle. It had to be the fifth one they'd come upon since they'd started their rescue effort. *And in this park alone,* she thought, wondering what the situation was outside. "Earl, when you're through with this fellow, there's another broken leg two rigs down," she said, pointing to the trailer from which she'd just emerged. She left them and went past the trailer to the next semi-demolished vehicle, another likely candidate for a suffering inhabitant.

They repeated this process throughout the morning and early afternoon, filling up their motor home as they did with frightened, injured and dispossessed people. After having completed a circuit of the RV park with their first-aid assistance, they returned to their own rig, where Millie with Joyce's assistance prepared a meal of sufficient size to serve the entire assembly of refugees. Before they ate, however, Earl led them in saying grace. His prayer, directed by the Holy Spirit, turned out to be significantly longer than his earlier thanksgiving. It turned out, in fact, to be a Gospel message.

This new "band of brothers" helped each other under Earl's guidance to restore some semblance of livability to their damaged homes. With the aid of a tow truck from a nearby auto repair shop, they restored many of the vehicles to upright positions. The refugees were spread over those RVs that were minimally damaged, and they continued, through frequent visits to an RV shop located a few miles away, to make those repairs within their ability to achieve. Personnel from the RV shop made some of the more demanding repairs. Throughout the process, Earl's unstinting help and leadership, coupled with his open, bold Christianity gained him the respect of many of his new companions, a number of whom began to express an interest in learning about this Jesus whom the government had denounced as a dangerous rabble-rouser with a dedicated terrorist following. Joyce, as she openly expressed her Christianity among the women as they worked to comfort and assist the ever-dwindling group of refugees, earned the same respect as her husband, and was establishing a growing cadre of women who wished to commit themselves to the Lordship of Jesus Christ despite the ever-present threats of the government against those who did so.

One of the larger rigs was the home of a ham radio operator, another dwindling breed of short-wave enthusiasts whose equipment survived the destruction about them with minimal damage. Within a week Seth had the system up and running again and was operating it at very short intervals to conserve the fuel in his generator. One evening two weeks after the destructive storm had hit, he ran over to Jimmy's rig and pounded on the door. When Jimmy opened it he came inside without preamble. "Something terrible's happened over in Arizona," he told them between gasps for breath. "There was a huge earthquake in the Grand Canyon, totally unexpected. They think it was a magnitude nine, or maybe even bigger. It happened last week. There wasn't much ado about it until the Colorado River went dry. Some of the canyon collapsed and a big lake is forming behind it. It's way too big a deal to move the dirt, and now they're rationing the water from Lake Mead. They're real worried about L.A. and Phoenix."

"Yes, but both of those cities have other sources besides the Colorado," Jimmy said. "I studied the water situation once when Millie and I were thinking of moving. Phoenix and Tucson both get some water from the Colorado by way of the CAP canal from Lake Mead via Lake Havasu, but they also get water from other river systems and groundwater as well. Los Angeles and the California southland gets Colorado water from Lake Mead, but the canal running from the Sacramento River Delta is another major source, as well as groundwater. I'd think that with a some careful rationing there wouldn't be a real problem. Maybe there'll be some dry lawns and a few defunct golf courses, but by and large it shouldn't be a huge disaster." Jimmy's reassurances took the air out of Seth's sails. Millie asked him to stay for dinner, and he agreed with alacrity.

Three days later Seth again pounded on Jimmy's door, and again he entered their domain out of breath. "There's been another earthquake!" he announced. It hit Central California this time. A new volcano's popped up west of Yosemite. It's growing by the hour and, guess what, the quake's trashed the canal bringing water south from Sacramento. Folks are really worried now about the developing water shortage in Southern California. And there's another new factor. The authorities had kind of tolerated us hams in the past, but now they're getting heavy-handed. One of my airwave pals told us that he'd been watching a truck with a directional antenna coming down the street and I haven't heard from him since. Everybody's tightening up their act and shortening their air time."

Over the next several days Seth kept them posted on the deteriorating situation in the major southwestern cities. But as their condition continued to decline the information about them became sketchier. From what they were able to glean from the spotty news, riots of unprecedented magnitude erupted from Los Angeles to San Diego. These were met by an even harsher governmental response that was leading to massive slaughter. Apparently the entire Southland had been cordoned off and the authorities were simply allowing it to die. At first they heard of selected elites being airlifted out of the ensuing chaos, but one-by-one the major airports were being overrun and rendered inoperable by desperate mobs.

A vicious earthquake struck the Mississippi River Basin forty miles north of Memphis, Tennessee, reprising the famous New Madrid earthquake of 1811. Immense as the earlier temblor had been, this was stronger and the destruction it wrought more extensive. It completely blocked the mighty Mississippi River, creating a huge flood that extended all the way up to St. Louis. To the southward of the epicenter, the event threatened to deplete the water supply of New Orleans.

The government responded to these varied events with a siege mentality, commandeering food and water supplies and sequestering shelf goods within enclaves reserved for the elite, into which much of the government and its loyal army retreated. As an immediate consequence, there was a general lifting of the closely-maintained supervision and micromanagement of local authorities outside the areas most directly impacted. The locals began to perceive that support from their superiors was declining. This new attitude opened up a new and very welcome opportunity for Earl and his group to evangelize their area. Earl started a Church within the RV park and held open services. Borrowing from his knowledge of the Bible and his experience as a lay pastor during the Seattle riots, he was an effective preacher, particularly in driving home to his expanding congregation the relevance of Scripture to current events. The Church quickly outgrew its home and expanded into the outside community, first in an abandoned shop and then in a community hall, its membership fueled by backlash from the recent state oppression and a general public surprise that the heavy-handed attempt to enforce political correctness at swordpoint hadn't succeeded in stamping out all vestiges of Christianity.

"What I want to do," he told his growing congregation one Sunday, "is first to get you to know some of the early Bible characters who fleshed out the Jesus to come. In the process, I'm hoping to lead you to an appreciation of the Bible as truthful. Along the way I'll also address some of the issues that have led people to think of the Bible as being a mythical book and one that was written by man alone. But it wasn't. It contains too much information that goes way beyond the capability of the human mind to put together to be a product of man.

Let's start with the Great Flood of Noah's day. So many would-be theologians with PhDs behind their names have asserted that Noah's flood was local that a distressing number of pastors have come to accept the account in Genesis as mythical. And, having come to the impression that the Genesis account made a big deal out of an event that merely was local in nature, they proceeded to pass on that belief to their congregations, thereby infecting much of the Christian community with a notion that is completely unjustified. In actuality, there is far more scientific evidence that the Great Flood was of planetary scope rather than a local event. Those who insisted upon a local flood may have been cowards at heart for whom a catastrophe of worldwide proportions was way out of their comfort zones. Either that or they simply were too myopic to be able to picture something so far out of their range of experience. They couldn't comprehend a mechanism that huge as to be so destructive. Nor did they want to.

What clinches the Flood as being of a universal nature is that it entirely changed the weather regime of earth. There are a number of hints of that in the first chapters of Genesis. Why, for example, did it not rain at the beginning? Or why was there no rainbow? The answer was right there in plain sight with the statement that the waters were divided from the waters. The obvious answer from that information is that the earth was surrounded by a globular canopy under which the temperature of the atmosphere was more uniformly distributed." He paused to let that sink in, noting a few gasps of surprise from the congregation. "And, by the way," he continued, "it was an atmosphere more suitable for some ancient animals than at present, so much so that many of them died out. But the experts were too busy scoffing at the Bible to think for themselves, insisting instead that the Genesis account was written by someone so naïve and unsophisticated of mind that he wrote of physical impossibilities. They were so blinded by the myopic popular view of natural history that they couldn't perceive a cause for the destruction of the canopy until our modern technology created a stir with the glimpses it gave us of the destructive havoc that has been wrought upon our neighboring planets. Finally someone looked skyward and said to himself, 'Oh! It came from there.' Soon after that the 'string of pearls' that in 1994 smashed into Jupiter, creating planet-sized holes in its atmosphere, shoved an actual mechanism of destruction into everyone's face. You can't argue with reality. But before that happened, mainstream science insisted, always with vehemence and sometimes quite viciously, that no such mechanism existed. In the mid-twentieth century, Dr. Immanuel Velikovsky put together a logical and self-consistent account of a world-wide disaster during the time of the Exodus. For piecing together that remarkable story, he was verbally torn to shreds by a cadre of scientists who set upon him like a pack of rabid dogs. While his logic prevailed over theirs, the violence of their assault upon him convinced the generally shallow and intellectually apathetic public that it was they who were right. Well did Peter speak of their mindset in 2 Peter." He opened his Bible and began reading from the beginning of Chapter 3.

> *This second epistle, beloved, I now write unto you, in both of which I stir up your pure minds by way of remembrance, that ye may be mindful of the words which were spoken before by the holy prophets, and of the commandment of us, the apostles of the Lord and Savior; knowing this first, that there shall come in the last days scoffers, walking after their own lusts, and saying, Where is the promise of his coming? For since the fathers fell asleep, all things continue as they were from the beginning of the creation. For this they willingly are ignorant of, that by the word of God the heavens were of old, and the earth standing out of the water and in the water, by which the world that then was, being overflowed with water, perished. But the heavens and the earth which are now, by the same word are kept in store, reserved unto fire against the day of judgment and perdition of ungodly men. But, beloved, be not ignorant of this one thing, that one day is with the Lord as a thousand years, and a thousand years as one day. The Lord is not slack concerning his promise, as some men count slackness, but is long-suffering toward us, not willing that any should perish, but that all should come to repentance.*

Earl closed his Bible and looked out at his audience, noting Joyce's smiling face. "Peter goes on with an exhortation to the reader," he continued, "telling them that despite the scoffers, there will be an end to God's forbearance. At that point, which, as he refers to Jesus' commentary of the end of the age in Matthew 24, will come as a thief in the night, the heavens shall pass away with a great noise, the elements will melt with a fervent heat, and all of man's works will be burned up. So much for the scoffers. "

When Earl came up to Joyce after the sermon, she continued to wear a smile. "What's up?" he asked her. "I didn't say anything that you haven't heard before."

"Oh," she replied, "but, judging from the whispered comments from those around me, it's something new to them. It's good to know your sermon was having an affect. So how's it feel to be back in the saddle?"

"Real good, honey. Even though I know it's not going to last very long. The world is so closely following the script that the Bible laid out that we can't be very far from closing time."

"Well said. But let's enjoy it while it lasts."

In his next sermon, Earl brought up the topic of evolution, building upon the foundation he laid the previous week of countering the common mistrust of Biblical truth. "Darwin's theory of evolution," he told his audience, "has, perhaps, done more to cause an alienation of people from their God than any other notion of man. In the first place, it mocks the creation story in Genesis, supporting the attitude that the Bible represents something less than absolute truth. Secondly, it turns God from an intimacy of love that knows every hair on our heads into a remote and alien Diety who is indifferent to the daily affairs of mankind. That, too, mocks the Biblical message of God's passion toward us. The figures of the Bible have little purpose in that context. Instead of portraying Jesus as was intended, they represent nothing more than a collection of stories. Evolution is a huge can of worms," he said with feeling. "Secular science has so muddled the issue that it'll take me at least two or three sermons— perhaps they should be called lectures on real science instead—to get the point across that evolution is totally false, itself actually no more than a myth." He paused.

"No! Wait!" he gestured theatrically. "Evolution isn't false at all! It actually works! To explain what I mean by that, I need to qualify the notion of evolution, separating it into two distinct branches. There's micro-evolution, and then there's macro-evolution. Micro refers to tiny changes, while macro refers to large changes, of the kind that can create new species, or even life from non-life. At the level of tiny, one can even say trivial, modifications, evolution actually works. Such microevolutionary changes are of the kind that permitted moths in England to change to a darker color during the smoke-filled years of the coal-fueled industrial revolution, and back to a lighter color when the air became cleaner again. Such also has been shown to work, for example, in the constant battle between the malaria parasite and the human body's response to it. Some Africans have the ability to resist malaria, but they gained that resistance at enormous cost, which is the propensity for acquiring the debilitating and deadly sickle-cell anemia. The modification of the blood cell into a sickle shape was tiny, involving just one, or at most two, chance changes at the molecular level. But while it worked against malaria, it generally degraded the body into something inferior than it was. Research has demonstrated time and again that micro-evolutionary modifications always result in a net loss of information regarding the body, and always end up deteriorating the systems of which the body is composed." He paused again. So far, his audience remained interested.

"At the macro level, evolution doesn't work. Nor can it. To understand why it can't you're going to need some background in molecular biology. Don't get too worried about that. I'll try to keep it as simple and painless as possible. And I promise not to give you a test at the end. But you will have to pay close attention. From now on, what I say about evolution refers to macro-evolution.

"As you yourselves know, most of us were thoroughly exposed in school to Darwinism as a valid theory, even a fact. And we have attempted to embrace it in parallel with our Christian beliefs. Despite its basic nature as antithetical to Christianity, our Christian leaders have remained apathetically on the sidelines as our children have been indoctrinated into the system of beliefs associated with evolution, offering little in the way of guidance toward an understanding of its moral pitfalls and essential Godlessness.

"Perhaps the source of this failure of our leaders to act in behalf of our youth is their own lack of understanding of evolution and how thoroughly modern science has undercut its presumptions. I intend to help correct that deficit right now. What you need to grasp immediately about evolution is its moral bankruptcy, which thoughtful and committed Christians have understood for years, and its intellectual bankruptcy, which modern science is now in the process of exposing. It turns out that evolution, as most of us understand it, is false. If this fact didn't have moral implications as well, evolution still would be bad, because it's basically nothing but an ill-conceived myth. As such, it represents a monumental waste of time and energy that could have been spent in far more useful pursuits. Some quasi-official publications, including articles in National Geographic Magazine, school textbooks, governmental placards located in National Parks and other popular tourist attractions, do indeed present evolution as fact. They do so in violation of that scientific standard. The Theory of Evolution, my friends, is precisely what this title suggests: evolution is a theory. It is not a natural law like gravity, but merely a proposition. It is merely a proposition because it is unproven and unverified in accordance with the standard that science itself has erected for differentiating a law from a mere theory. Every so-called 'proof' of evolution to date, including the numerous 'missing links', subsequently has been exposed either as an intentional fraud or a misapplication of scientific tools or knowledge.

"In 2 Thessalonians 2, Paul talks about the mystery of iniquity. In verses 8 through 12, he describes a grave indifference in the time just prior to Christ's second coming to the truth represented by the Word of God. Paul then indicates that because of this indifference, God will allow those who are infected with this attitude to be deluded even more:

> *And then shall that wicked one be revealed, whom the Lord shall consume with the spirit of his mouth, and shall destroy with the brightness of his coming. Even him whose coming is after the working of Satan with all power and signs and lying wonders, and with all deceivableness of unrighteousness in them that perish, because they received not the love of the truth, that they may be saved. And for this cause God shall send them strong delusion, that they should believe a lie, that they all might be damned who believed not the truth, but had pleasure in unrighteousness.*

We have been describing the theory of evolution as a falsehood that is generally accepted as truth in today's sophisticated, technology-embracing world, one that is glaringly overt in nature. As I get out of Scripture, God has something to say about it too. God tells us in First Timothy Chapter 6:20 and 21 that such a condition will prevail in the last days. Moreover, the falsehood will be distinctly scientific in character, and it will even be accepted among some ill-informed Christians:

> *O Timothy, keep that which is committed to thy trust, avoiding profane and vain babblings, and oppositions of science falsely so called. Which some, professing, have erred concerning the faith. Grace be with thee. Amen.*

"Next week I'll go into the theory of uniformity, a companion notion to evolution that's just as false as its brother. Then I'll offer some details of evolution's intellectual barrenness that I'm hoping you'll find interesting."

"Well, that didn't go over too well," Earl said to Joyce as they walked back to Jimmy's motor home. Did you see the people who walked out as I was speaking?"

"There weren't all that many who did," Joyce replied. "Most everybody stayed put, and from the looks on their faces, they were very interested in what you had to say. You're always going to have people who'll disagree with you. I don't have to tell you that. Look at Judas. God Himself spoke to him, and he still didn't get it."

"Then you don't think I should change the subject?"

"Don't you dare! They need to hear the truth about evolution to bolster their faith. That theory did as much to weaken faith in God than anything else Satan has come up with."

"Okay. I hear you." In fact, Earl didn't have to wait a week to speak about it. That Sunday afternoon a contingent out of the congregation knocked on Jimmy's door and asked him to turn his sermons into lectures, more like a Bible study, so they wouldn't have to wait a week for each lecture. Earl compromised with them, agreeing to speak on Wednesdays as well as Sundays. "But," he told them, "we still need Church on Sunday. It's important that we not only hear the Word of God, but worship Him in prayer and song as well."

As he had promised, Earl held Bible study that Wednesday evening. He had expected to see a portion of the Church attendees there, but was surprised that what looked to be the entire congregation had showed up, with the exception of those who had walked out on last Sunday's service.

"Tonight we'll go into the theory of uniformity, as I'd mentioned last Sunday. Evolution demands the theory of uniformity, because even its supporters know that evolution is an inherently weak process. The probabilities involved are so tiny that the operation of chance needs a big boost in the form of huge amounts of time - time of such enormous quantities as to obscure the gigantic odds against its workability to make it believable at all. So here's the deal: science came up with the notion that every geological feature we observe today came about exclusively through processes that can be observed today, such as the action of water, wind, ice and rain working like tiny chisels to scrape away entire mountains and to build up others. Oh, there might be the occasional earthquake or volcano to speed up the process of change in certain places, but, to paraphrase Carl Sagan, that's all there was or is or ever will be. So, without the slightest justification, science enshrined this notion as a rigid principle and applied it to evolution to answer the numerous initial critics of that theory. Demanding its validity is equivalent to demanding that the earth be flat, or that something is true merely because we wish it to be so. It wasn't until science finally accepted a catastrophic collision of an asteroid with the earth as the probable cause of the extinction of the dinosaurs that such infrequent but huge events were even possible. And even then they insisted upon a uniformity-based dating of that event. Worst of all, they were very reluctant to enlighten the public about it. They made no effort to convey this radical change in position to the schools or to the public at large, nor did they consider the implications of this change on evolutionary theory.

"Peter sheds further light on the nature of this falsehood. According to Second Peter 3:3 and 4, the lie will involve a deep sense of unpunctuated continuity of the earth and the life within it, such as is embodied in the principle of uniformity, the notion of the great age of the earth, wherein all geological changes are of extremely modest proportions that produce measurable results only over vast intervals of time:

Knowing this first, that there shall come in the last days scoffers, walking after their own lusts, and saying, Where is the promise of his coming? For since the fathers fell asleep, all things continue as they were from the beginning of the creation.

"As I have said before but want to emphasize again, the principle of uniformity as attributed here by Peter to scoffers represents such a necessity to the viability of Darwin's theory of evolution that uniformity and evolution may be considered to be two halves of a common philosophy.

"Scientists compounded their error by applying evolution and uniformity together to come up with what they call the 'Standard Geologic Column', which is an interpretation of the many different layers of soil, or strata, that make up the surface of the earth. In comparing the characteristics of different strata exposed in ravines and canyons throughout our planet, they assembled what they consider to be a theoretical template of all the layers accumulated from the beginning of the earth to now. They apply dates to the various layers based on the complexity of the fossils that they find within them. This amounts to guesswork and a basic presupposition that both evolution and uniformity are proven fact, which, of course, they aren't. Then they apply the result of this effort to the assignment of dates to arbitrary fossil specimens. A neophyte of logic can see the circular reasoning in this process, but so-called scientific 'experts' are too myopic to do the same.

"Now, let's for a moment suppose that these various layers were established by huge tsunamis, driven by some catastrophic collision upon earth of some wayward heavenly body, such as might have happened to cause Noah's Great Flood.   The raging water and enormous winds, along with super-volcanic action, would have ripped up soil, vegetation and animal life and re-deposited it, maybe time after time, in a variety of patterns. In the midst of that turmoil, the first lifeforms to be re-deposited would have been the most streamlined, thereby sinking the most rapidly. They wouldn't necessarily be the oldest at all, or the least advanced.   Such a scenario actually is far more likely than the uniformitarian one. And do you see how it throws a monkey-wrench into the application of evolutionary theory?

"With this little digression into uniformity, we'll return next Sunday to the topic of evolution. See you then, and thanks for your interest."

CHAPTER TWELVE

Coffee in hand, Jacob glanced around the small cafe seeking an empty table. His eyes caught a woman seated alone. Her beauty took his breath away and his attraction startled him. The attraction wasn't sensual. Moira had already imprinted herself on his heart and mere beauty, gorgeous as this woman was, made no inroads into his romantic commitment to his companion. It was more like kinship, that he not only knew her but felt in some indefinable way as if she was intimately connected to him. A hazy memory of a woman and a dream caught his attention, but before the image clarified the seated lady motioned with a finger, pointing to two empty chairs at her table. Before committing, Jacob turned around to Moira, who was following close behind, his eyes asking her for approval. Surprisingly, she stepped past him and reached over to the woman, introducing herself with a fervent hug. Surprised at the easy association between the spectacular woman and Moira, Jacob settled for a handshake, but as the woman held his hand she smiled broadly, saying, "We've met before, Jacob. You don't remember much about it, but I know that a yellow school bus with an angry driver already has started ringing some bells. And you, Moira.

We've talked several times before. You do remember me and I'm happy to see you progressing so well. I'm particularly happy to see you two together.

"You're Wisdom, aren't you?" Moira declared. "I'm so very glad to see you again, but You don't usually show up outside of my dreams. Is there a special occasion?"

"I do like to get out and about, and the coffee's very good here," Wisdom responded. But yes, there are two items. The first is personal. I enjoy seeing you two together. The second is important. You plan to head over to Tiberias. I don't want you to do that. Bypass it and go northeastward instead, to the other side of Galilee in the area called the Golan Heights. It's closer to Syria, and you'll be able to accomplish your main objective with more results, which is to bring more of your fellow countrymen into the Christian fold. You'll be heading toward Mount Hermon at the northern boundary, and you'll be passing through a number of agricultural settlements along the way. When you get close to Hermon, you'll be in a position to witness the fulfillment of prophecy taking place before your very eyes. It'll be dangerous, but I know that you're both beyond the fear of injury."

"I feel very privileged," Jacob said. "This is the first time that the Holy Spirit has actually commanded or forbidden something."

Moira looked at him strangely, appalled at what he had said. Wisdom laughed. "Tell him, Moira," She said.

"Jacob, you need to catch up on your New Testament Scripture. This is by no means the first time. Paul was forbidden by the Holy Spirit to preach in Asia. It's in Acts—" She looked at Wisdom for the answer.

"—Acts sixteen, verse 6," Wisdom supplied. "The reason that I'm directing you to Golan is that even as I'm communicating with you satan is assembling his forces for the massed assault on Israel as foretold by the prophet Ezekiel. It's generally common knowledge among Christians, being called the Ezekiel 38 War. In the process, Golan's going to be trashed, and so will Israel's enemies. You'll be in the thick of the action there, but even before the flag goes up you have much to do. With the ramping-up of persecution against Christians in the surrounding Islamic nations, the only remaining haven for them is little Israel. They're coming here in droves and, with little education or sophistication but with a godly work ethic, they're heading for the most part to the many agricultural communes east of Galilee in the heart of the Golan Heights. Once they hear of your own contributions to the understanding of God, they'll be on fire in support of evangelizing the nation. Christianity—the real thing—is going to hit that area in a big way, bigger than you can imagine, and spread outward from there and Hebron to all Israel. Enjoy your coffee, but when you're finished, go and tell your friends about your change of plans." She arose and, giving them a long loving look, departed.

"Here, let me take one of those bundles," Jacob said to Moira as the climb became steeper. "Looks like Wisdom healed up my lung rather well."

"Whew," she replied, handing it to him and wiping her brow. "I won't argue with that. But look at the view we're getting."

"I'm amazed at how beautiful it is here. Things are growing everywhere. I heard that it was pretty barren before 1948."

"So it was. The prophets had foretold of how the land would lay waste until God's people came back to re-occupy it, and of how it would blossom when they did. Did you know that during the entire period of the Diaspora, from 70 A.D. to 1948, the land was in the grip of an unrelenting drought? But the rains came back when we did."

"Pretty impressive. It's the kind of thing that the godless would be blind to. But it sure gives me a boost—WHOA!"

The jolt tossed them off their feet and they slid backwards several more. All the way up the hill they could see others who had fallen like they did. Moira reached out to Jacob as the earth continued to shake. "Help me," she cried. "I'm terrified. I have a phobia about this."

Jacob scrambled up to her and embraced her tightly. She clung to him with a desperate strength. *If this is what it takes,* he thought happily, *bring it on!* Within a little over a minute the shaking had stopped, but Moira continued to cling to him. He decided to press his good fortune by stroking her hair and kissing her on the mouth. It got him nowhere. She was too frightened. "Something must have happened to you before," he murmured in her ear.

"It did," she said in a small voice. She twisted in his arms and looked around. In the valley below, a small cloud of dust rising out of an overcrowded settlement marked a location where some destruction had occurred, but most of the civilization below them appeared to be intact. Quakes weren't that common in this region. Fortunately, it was a small one. "I was in a very bad earthquake when I was a child," she told him. Color was returning to her cheeks, and her beautiful eyes began to register another emotion. "How about another one?" she asked. He complied and they remained in their embrace for several minutes. Reluctantly they stood up, picked up their bundles and set out once more up the hill.

"Something happened to me, too, Moira," Jacob said presently. "Maybe you've noticed that I haven't been as . . . aggressive toward you as you might have thought. I love you, Moira. But something's been holding me back."

"Yeah, what's the deal?" she replied.

"I was married once before. We had a baby together. Our marriage ended for all practical purposes when we got tossed into a death camp and our baby was murdered before my wife's eyes."

Moira tugged at his sleeve, halting him and turning him to face her. "How awful!" she exclaimed. Like the holocaust. I didn't know America had turned so evil."

"Yeah. Anyway, I want you to know that you've helped put that behind me. I love you with all my heart."

"Prove it."

They embraced for several minutes before they continued their upward trek.

"She must have made you very happy," she said after a while. "I'll try to do the same." They left unspoken the obvious fact that a baby was not a tenable prospect in today's world.

CHAPTER THIRTEEN

"Today I'll venture into a brief history lesson," Earl told the congregation the next Sunday. "I want to give you a little background regarding the time and environment in which the theory of evolution came into being.

"The world that Darwin was born into in 1809 saw the rapid ascendancy of science, beginning to nudge against the Word of God but not yet in open conflict with it. The spectacular achievements of Isaac Newton in the fields of mathematics and physics a century earlier had laid the firm groundwork for the rapid advance in understanding the natural world and the exploitation of it for the supposed betterment of mankind. The industrial revolution took off, and soon men no longer had to rely on the wind for ocean travel, nor on animals for transport over land or working the farm. Despite Newton's own grateful understanding that God had given him a gift of comprehending facets of His creation, others saw his insights as products of man himself, particularly of that superlative organ, the human mind. It was a heady time, full of promise.

"The latter part of the eighteenth century was marked by a growing conflict between two very different views of both the earth's history and the origin of life. Not long before Darwin's entrance onto the scene of naturalistic speculation, the present condition of the earth, with its hills and valleys, meadows and barren outcroppings that revealed layers upon layers of different soils, was commonly viewed by the scientists of the day as having been formed by sudden, catastrophic events. This more traditional view articulated by the eminent French spokesman Georges Cuvier maintained that the earth had suffered periodic catastrophes, most likely great floods, causing widespread extinctions and subsequent creations. He was a harsh critic of the emerging notion of evolution, forming well before Darwin's birth, and championed during his time by fellow Frenchman Jean-Baptiste Lamarck.

"The prevailing paradigm that the earth's features had largely been formed through the agency of catastrophic events was aggressively challenged by two investigators of the natural world about them who held very different viewpoints from those of the catastrophists. Scottish naturalist James Hutton, born in 1726, proposed in his 1788 paper *Theory of the Earth* the uniformitarian notion that the earth was influenced more by small changes occurring over large intervals of time than by sudden and large-scale events. Charles Lyell, born in 1797, the year that Hutton died, picked up his uniformitarian torch and expanded on it. A copy of his 1830 work *Principles of Geology* came aboard the Beagle with Charles Darwin, and greatly influenced his thinking. Among other concepts, the large time frames proposed by Lyell furnished the huge durations required to make his theory of evolution a workable proposition. Darwin also was influenced by the other individual, Jean-Baptiste Lamarck, who was born fifty-five years earlier, and whose speculations had the effect of questioning God's ongoing involvement with mankind. Lamarck preceded Darwin in proposing a naturalistic mechanism for the development of man. Although his concept was similar to Darwin's later evolutionary theory, Lamarck differed from Darwin in his proposal that the inheritance of acquired characteristics was the primary force behind the ongoing progress of living beings. This mechanism has since been discarded as not viable through direct observation. Lamarck's own speculations regarding evolution weren't completely novel, as they were preceded by those of ancient Greek thinkers including Anaximander, who proposed that life evolved from non-life through purely naturalistic processes.

"Darwin developed the heart of his theory regarding evolution early on aboard the Beagle, where he spent the five years from 1831 to 1836. He first published in 1859 the work for which he is most famous, *The Origin of Species*. In this work Darwin proposed that life is in a state of flux, continually undergoing change. In this context, the life that we observe today represents an advancement over its predecessors, in that it descended, with modification, from simpler forms. All life forms, according to Darwin, are related by common ancestry back to the first instance of life. This general assertion, that life developed by naturalistic processes independent of intentional design, is accepted not as mere theory but as established fact by today's scientific community at large, who cite direct observation of changes due to breeding as well as similarities across species boundaries in support of that assertion. I'll comment as an aside that the appearance that breeding results in positive change is a falsehood. Different characteristics are always produced at the expense of the loss of genetic information. Then, too, the existence of "missing links" once was used as a powerful argument in that regard, but since has come into disfavor due to the exposure as fraudulent of virtually all such exhibits.

"Darwin went further than his predecessors in that he furnished a potential mechanism for the process: natural selection operating on genetic mutations. Natural selection, proposed almost simultaneously by his contemporary Alfred Wallace, asserts that if a life form acquires a genetic change through chance that is beneficial to his survival, the quality intrinsic to that change will be preserved by the fact that its increased chance for survival will afford it an increased chance to reproduce.

"According to scholar of logic Phillip Johnson, Darwin's theory involves three related propositions: first, the mutability of species, which is their intrinsic capability of change beyond species boundaries through the process of "descent with modification"; second, the ability of this process to account for virtually all of the life forms extant in the earth today from a very small number of very simple original ancestors; and third, that this transformation was guided by the undirected naturalistic mechanism of "natural selection", often described as "survival of the fittest".

"Darwin's mechanism, as opposed to his general theory, isn't faring too well at the present time. In fact, there is general agreement even within the community embracing evolution that the process proposed by Darwin as well as all subsequently proposed naturalistic mechanisms are deeply flawed. This disenchantment on the part of evolutionists with regard to specific mechanisms is largely due to insights into the phenomenon of life acquired over the past few decades. Nevertheless, they vehemently continue to insist, although the specific explanatory mechanism is yet to be found, that it is out there awaiting discovery. Their insistence that evolution is factual is based primarily on the companion insistence that all processes associated with life must be naturalistic, a notion that itself resulted from the definition of science as excluding all non-naturalistic processes (i.e. God).

"Like the theory of uniformity, which has been thoroughly discredited as a geologic necessity by recent observations and events in our solar system that we have witnessed first-hand, the declaration that God must be excluded from science has no relevance to the real world. It merely represents wishful thinking on the part of the more vocal members of the scientific community.

"Stephen J. Gould was a recent representative of the attitude that attempts to place the stamp of 'fact' on evolution to distance the concept itself from the prevailing 'theories' of evolutionary mechanisms. Gould is well-known for his concept of 'punctuated equilibrium', which his followers have shortened to the cutesy 'punk-eek'. This notion asserts that life forms remain virtually unchanged over long periods of time, then suddenly in a uniformitarian sense, spanning a duration of perhaps a hundred thousand years, undergo large-scale modifications. This concept suffers from the truncation of time, which all naturalistic mechanisms of modification, due to the weakness of undirected chance, require huge quantities of for viability. Another highly-vocal modern supporter of evolution was Richard Dawkins. Dawkins, however, was not unbiased. One could rather easily interpret his commentaries as displaying a hatred of God that borders on insanity.

"I was going to say more, but I've already put a lot of information on your plates. We'll continue on Wednesday. Once again, I'd like to thank you for your interest—and your patience. By the way, bring some writing materials with you to the Wednesday Bible study. There'll be some memory work involved. See you then."

That Wednesday evening Earl delved into the meat of the subject of evolution. "There are several obvious weaknesses in Darwin's presentation," Earl began. "All of them have been and continue to be ignored by the more uncritical of his adherents.

"First, his basic theory and its lengthy string of implications are all based on speculation. Darwin had little choice in resorting to so much speculation for two reasons: the scientific insights available to him regarding life at the submicroscopic level were quite primitive, leading to a very simplistic understanding of life, including a view of the cell basically equivalent to a simple jelly-filled rind; and his presupposition of enormous time periods precluded him from direct observation of the process he espoused. Instead of observations of change in the wild, he was forced for confirmation to look to the results of artificial breeding processes. The problem with that, of course, is that artificial breeding involves intelligence rather than pure chance. His reliance on mechanisms and observations associated with artificial breeding processes guided his speculations into the domain of intelligent design, confusing not only himself but generations of his followers regarding the true boundaries of the operation of true chance.

"Second, he extrapolated his suppositions without any justification whatsoever from the primary microevolutionary domain of his speculations into the macroevolutionary domain. The microevolutionary domain with which he was familiar included such developments as the length and curvature of a bird's beak or of a creature's coloration, whereas macroevolutionary changes, if even possible, would include such changes on a wholesale scale as the development of life from non-life or the gift of wings and sustained flight from a four-legged land animal.

"Third, he proposed his theory on the basis of a very limited and extremely simplistic knowledge of the essence of life. Our intellectual advances in the domain of living systems since his time, from the level of major organs, their functions and operations, through that of cellular operations down to the level of molecular biology, are as distant from his knowledge as an atomic weapon is to a hand-held club. You have to thoroughly understand the workings of the cell to comprehend the complexity of the processes that take place within it. To those who have that familiarity, the cell seems as sophisticated a machine as a computer or even modern airliner.

"Fourth and possibly most important, his theory doesn't square with the archaeological record. This is extremely important, as it puts the lie to the Academy of Science's attempt to include evolution into its definition of science as being concerned with matters that are observable and testable, as opposed to religion, which, it claims, is not. Darwin, having expected that fossils would be found in much greater profusion than reality gave him, and that transitional species would predominate, was forced to consider the fossil record to be very incomplete, particularly in its glaring absence of transitional forms. Knowing, however, that the exploration of fossils was in its infancy, he was hopeful that further exploration would uncover the evidence that he sought. Now, well over a century and a half since the publication of *The Origin of Species*, the earth, having been subjected to a much more thorough search, still contradicts his theory. Virtually all of the supposed transition forms of man that were regarded as intermediary steps up from apehood have been exposed as frauds. Worse, the sudden profusion of life known as the Cambrian explosion suggests an abrupt introduction of life followed by rapid extinction. Modern neo-Darwinist Stephen J. Gould attempted to capitalize on this problem with his notion of "Punctuated Equilibrium", which suggests that evolution was more abrupt than Darwin envisioned. His theory suffers even more from the lack of a convincing mechanism than Darwin's.

"In his book *Darwin on Trial,* Professor Phillip Johnson addressed the first issue, the attempt to liken artificial breeding with the operation of chance. He said that it missed the point of his theory by attempting to substitute the operation of intelligent design for the working of chance. He further suggested that the fact that so many fellow scientists failed to pick up on that flaw only proved that his audience was uncommonly uncritical. He also made the observation that there are limits to the amount of change that breeding can accomplish, noting that dogs don't change into elephants because they don't have the genetic capacity for that degree of change.

"Darwin himself was quite concerned over the absence of transitional forms in the geologic record, and exerted much effort toward the development of a plausible argument to explain away this situation. It is to his credit that he made the attempt. Nevertheless, his answers are not satisfactory. In Chapter VI of his work entitled "Difficulties of the Theory" he identifies four problems, which he declared were so serious that he could hardly reflect upon them himself without being staggered by them. The first of these was the lack of transitional forms—in our lingo, the lack of missing links. He was hopeful that with time these missing links would be found. In truth, the passage of time hasn't helped. Secondly, he was concerned himself that if evolution worked for small changes, it also would work for the larger ones. As we've found out, he was entirely justified in having this doubt, because while science has indeed found evolution to work for tiny changes, it has also found that this finding does not justify the application of the theory to larger ones. Darwin's third point of self-doubt was that changes in form would require changes at the same time to instincts as well, and the knowledge that some instincts were of profound complexity. His final doubt involved his awareness that the attempt to cross species boundaries through breeding, even among very similar forms, always resulted in sterile offspring.

"Nevertheless, Darwin was comforted by a multitude of

supporters.   Actually, his only real detractors were from the Christian community.   One of his most ardent supporters was the German biologist Ernst Haeckel, who not only helped to popularize Darwin's theory in Germany, but added something of his own to the theory, which was the well-known notion that 'ontogeny recapitulates phylogeny'. This maxim, which is forced upon every student of biology to this very day, means, in effect, that various stages of ontogeny, or embryonic development, revisit phylogeny, or the history of evolutionary change. The problem with this is that Haeckel essentially cooked the books with his drawings of embryos, employing such a high degree of artistic license in creating these pictures that they have since been recognized by experts in the field as being fraudulent. For example, what were once thought of as gill slits in embryos are nothing of the sort, being nothing but folds. Amazingly, Haeckel's notion is still being peddled to biology students despite this recognition.

"Now we'll delve into the working essence of evolution, but very briefly. The purely naturalistic mechanism for what Darwin regarded as the continually-increasing organization of life is what he termed 'descent with modification'. According to him, the process of 'natural selection' automatically preserves those changes that give an organism a competitive edge in the never-ending struggle for survival. The thought here is that if a modification renders an organism more suitable for survival than its unmodified siblings, its increased likelihood of survival also increases its likelihood of procreation, thereby enhancing the odds that the modification will be passed on to its descendents.

"In this scenario all life undergoes a constant struggle for existence within a fiercely competitive environment. If by chance a change occurs in an organism, and if that change offers the organism a competitive advantage in that struggle, the advantage, through the undirected, mindless mechanism of natural selection, will tend to be preserved through inheritance. On the other hand, if no change occurs, or if a change represents a competitive disadvantage, that situation will be less likely to be preserved, eventually threatening complete extinction of that change.

"At the individual level, the changes that Darwin proposed were tiny, becoming significant only over their accumulation over large periods of time. He refused to countenance the possibility of benevolent large-scale mutations, called saltations, realizing that such changes, being of a miraculous nature, could be considered to be instances of special creation. He wrote to Charles Lyell regarding this point, telling him that if he were convinced that his theory required the involvement of changes more than the tiny ones he envisioned, he would reject as rubbish the entire theory. As a side point, modern biologist Michael Behe demonstrated the necessity of that very thing in his observation of biological systems that he called 'irreducibly complex', ones for which multiple steps would be required to make a component functional.

"Darwin's primary genius was a rich imagination coupled with a capacity for developing his ideas in meticulous detail. By the application of intricate detail to his speculations he was able to develop plausible scenarios for what naturalists were able to see with their own eyes, the causes of which had eluded them prior to Darwin's proposed sequence of events. The very profusion of Darwin's speculative corollaries almost leads one to miss altogether the fact that the qualitative nature of his use of vague words like 'multitude', 'extremely few', 'almost as well', and 'so few' increase the confusion regarding the true boundaries of his notions and the consequent difficulty in rebutting them.

"But Darwin was not alone by any means. He was also a product of his time, being greatly supported by peers who were more than willing to elevate his thoughts to positions of common acceptance. He was, in fact, hurried along in his effort to publish by his contemporary Alfred Wallace, who was coming up with ideas on his own that were remarkably similar to Darwin's, including the notion of natural selection. The scientific and intellectual world was not only ready to accept Darwin's ideas, but it was eager, almost impatient, to receive them. Darwin's theory, right or wrong, offered them the perfect opportunity to do so. A naturalistic process by definition presupposes the absence of a Designer. It demands that no guiding hand is at play in either the creation or the maintenance of life. Given specificity with Darwin's descent with modification, it also implies that life, on its own, is continually improving itself in an ever-upward process of complexity and organization."

CHAPTER FOURTEEN

Topping a rise, Jacob reached down to grasp Moira's hand, helping her up. They stood together looking out over the valley and the beautiful Sea of Galilee to the south. The boat-dotted lake was quiet beneath a cloudless sky, the pastoral scene calm but filled with life. Nearby they saw a group of local farm hands working a field. Women moved alongside the men, the farmers working in what looked to be cheerful harmony. The sound of singing reached their ears. "Hallo!" Jacob called out. The field hands stopped their labors and stood silently, awaiting their approach. As Moira drew near, she assessed the laborers. *They're healthy, that's for sure*, she thought. *Happy, too. I'm going to like this.* She reached out an arm toward the nearest woman, a young blonde, who noticed the glance at her hair. "Hi! the woman responded. I'm Edith, and yeah, I'm so dumb they have me working outside to minimize the damage. Where're you from?" she asked after the laughter stopped.

"Haifa," Jacob responded, grasping her hand. My name's Jacob, and she's Moira. Moira's been here a while, but I haven't. I came here from the United States."

"Oh?" The question had an intense interest behind it. "We've been hearing some pretty bad things about it. But then, we haven't exactly been having a picnic. Most of us here are refugees from Egypt," she said, looking at her companions with compassion. "We still have family there. Or maybe not."

"Then you must be Christians," Moira said.

"Yes, we are that," Edith said with conviction. "Fresh out of the furnace. I gather you are too."

"Yes, we are indeed. Both of us," Moira said, pointing to Jacob, "have had flames licking at our heels. And there are some more of us, too," she added, pointing to heads emerging onto the trail from the depression below. If your community wouldn't mind parting with a little food and a place for us to spend the night, we have some things to tell you that you'll find to be real faith-builders."

"Not a problem," Edith replied. "We've had so many travelers come through in the past several months that we always keep something extra on the stove. And blankets too, if you don't mind sleeping on the floor. I, for one, can't wait to hear what you have to say. So much new information has come our way from travelers like you that we're about ready to set up a revival tent. And it sure beats what we used to get from satellite television. And I guess that we can fill you in as well on what's been happening here."

That night Jacob shared with them his understanding of Jesus' feeding of the multitudes and the sign that came out of those events, which brought some murmurs of appreciation. Moira told them about events in Haifa, as well as Wisdom's forecast of violence heading their way.

"We've been expecting something to happen for some time now," a man named Josh told them. "You can see plain evidence of troops massing up around the border with Syria. It's out in the open for everyone to see, like they're certain that this time they'll be able to toss us into the sea."

"Same 'ol," Edith replied. "They pretty much thought that way before every war they started with us. I think they're unteachable."

"Yeah," Josh said. "And if they'd bother reading our Scripture, they'd know that God isn't especially happy about what they keep trying to do. We've been talking the situation over for a while now, and we're not really afraid. We're convinced that the story of Gideon is a prophetic warning from God that He's going to handle the situation pretty much by Himself."

"Not only that," Edith added, "but we know from Ezekiel 38 and 39 that war with them is inevitable, and that it's not going to end well for them."

The evening lightened up with a song fest, which the travelers were told was a nightly event. They stayed for another two days of mutual companionship.

As they prepared to leave the commune and their new friends, one of their number, Ralph, came over to Jacob. "I'm sorry, Jacob," he said after hesitating for a few embarrassed moments, "but I won't be going with you."

Jacob laughed. "I didn't expect that you would," he told the other man. "I saw how you were looking at Dyan."

"Was it that obvious?"

"It wasn't only you. She was looking right back, like you were her favorite dessert. Did you manage to get the approval of the kibbutz, or are you sticking your neck out a mile and a half?"

"I asked the leaders this morning. They assented. Actually, they were smiling. They must have expected it just like you. I know this is quick, but I've really fallen for her."

"Hey, don't apologize. It's natural and healthy. It speaks of the continuation of life, even in the midst of a brewing disaster. You might as well get as much out of life as you can, because none of us may have much time left. So stay. With our blessings."

This dropping-out of Ralph established a pattern that would be repeated throughout the group's journey. It was welcomed by all as a sign of the resilience of life.

CHAPTER FIFTEEN

That Sunday at the Church service, Earl was heartened to see so many of the people equipped with writing tools. Evidently they still were on board for his prolonged discussion of evolution's numerous problems. "Well," he told them, "if you're looking for information about evolution with some real meat on it, I don't think I'll disappoint you today.

"Our body—all life, in fact, is a collection of molecular machinery, all coordinated with each component interacting with a host of others within a system of such complexity and sophistication that even a little bug makes a 747 airliner look like a cheap little toy. Much of the direction and coordination comes from the deoxoribonucleic acid molecule, commonly known as DNA, of which every one of the trillions of cells in our body has a copy, which is not insignificant, considering that each one of those DNA molecules consists of about ten billion components. DNA is a very long molecular chain with a double backbone, each of which consists of alternating sugar and phosphate molecules. Embedded within this backbone is the software that runs the show. Yes, I said software, because the pattern of the embedded chemicals represents pure information. There are four specific chemical coding elements whose arrangement within the DNA chain makes up this pattern, exactly the way that electronic software directs the operation of computers. Only DNA does more, because it includes instructions for building the machinery first that it later directs. The coding chemicals always appear in pairs of two, but since reversed positions of them also are unique codes, these pairs represent an alphabet of four code elements. This is more efficient than the electronic '0' and '1', with its alphabet of only two code elements. To add to the degree of sophistication of the DNA molecule, it exhibits a property called chirality that forcefully hurls a monkey-wrench into the notion that life came about purely by chance. Chirality essentially means that while there are two equally-probable directions in which the sugar and phosphate molecules can bond together, in living systems they may only be of a single form, which is right-handed. This requirement alone virtually eliminates the possibility that the first DNA string was formed by chance—can you imagine how tiny the probability is that a million tossed coins will come up heads, let alone billions?

"I hate to say it, but I'm leaving out a whole bunch of interesting facts about DNA and its cousin RNA, and about the fascinating molecular machinery that's involved in pattern replication and protein formation, as well as the many other machines and power plants within a cell. But for this kind of broad-brush overview there simply isn't time. I'll just say this: embedded within the DNA code are segments called genes. Genes operate exactly like software subroutines, containing instructions devoted to the specific tasks of assembling proteins out of amino acids. Each protein requires a precise sequence selected out of an alphabet of twenty life-supporting amino acids. There are long stretches of DNA code in between the genes. Researchers are still learning about them, and so far they've found items like punctuation marks and other edit characters, as well as shipping labels for the transferal of molecular components inside and outside the cell. Years ago in the early days of DNA investigation, some of the scientists involved were rather arrogant about the role of those portions of DNA that weren't specifically associated with the manufacture of proteins. Being of the evolutionary persuasion for the most part, they considered the portions of DNA for which they could find no specific use to be 'junk DNA', DNA that represented earlier stages of evolution and was no longer useful to and was ignored by the living system. Those who possessed this attitude were pruned back a bit by later discoveries of uses that included error-correcting codes like checksum values, and sequence-control commands, of which punctuation marks are a very simple example. I'll add—WHAT WAS THAT?"

The community hall in which Earl was speaking was over sixty years old and, like many of the public facilities of that era, was constructed of cinder blocks, one of which flew into Earl's hip, knocking him breathless. As he struggled to regain his breath the floor upon which he now lay jumped up in rhythmic bursts, knocking his head and driving him senseless. A rumble broke the initial ominous silence of the congregants, but was soon drowned out by shouts and screams as the ground beneath them swayed and the building continued to collapse. One man gave voice to the obvious: 'Earthquake!' he shouted, and began to run for the door. Others behaved more nobly. An individual started to herd the crowd toward a stable corner of the building, and others, seeing his intent, chipped in to help. Joyce had eyes only for Earl, who was lying helpless on the floor. Attempting to run toward him, she was hindered by the violent shaking of the ground beneath her. She fell once, but determined to reach her husband, she got up and continued to move. Once by his side, she held his head up and was relieved to feel a pulse. A man came up, and together they dragged Earl to the corner where the congregants were huddled. Eventually the shaking ceased, and at virtually the same time, Earl regained consciousness. "Stay put," Joyce ordered him, cradling his head in her arms. She prayed that his head was merely bruised and not bleeding.

"Who ever heard of an earthquake in Texas?" he asked in wonder. "This is really strange." He struggled to get to his feet. Noting that he was lucid, Joyce let him go. The congregation headed toward their homes in knots of friends, noting structural collapse and devastation around them and dreading what they might find back in the RV park. The damage there looked more serious than it actually was.

One modular home had slid partly off its cinder-block foundation and a fifth-wheel trailer had been partially overturned, having been prevented by a tree from going on its side. The insides of the RVs were, of course, jumbled messes. But with people helping their more seriously affected neighbors, it didn't take long to restore order and livability to the community. Electricity was not available, but they made do with their generators, those without their own hooking up to neighbors who had them. Gasoline wasn't really an issue. Provided that they didn't try to leave the area, there were enough vehicles scattered about inside and outside of the park that they could tap for gas that it would be some time before they would run out. Food was an issue that eventually would force them to leave, but for now they had everything they needed for their near-term survival.

The community hall was unfit for use. Earl and two friends searched for an alternate site and found an old VFR building several blocks away. It had remained intact and was large enough for their use. They had been too busy restoring livability to their homes to conduct a Wednesday evening service, but by the next Sunday they were able to hold a Church service. Earl decided not to revisit the events of the past week. Everybody was fully and painfully aware of what had taken place.

"Having given you just a taste of the complexity of life in what was a very short overview of evolution and biology," Earl began after they had sung two hymns, "I want to jump to some of the major, you might say insurmountable, problems with evolution that our new understanding of life has uncovered.

"The first of these is the issue of anticipation. Naturalistic processes are, by intrinsic definition, non-intelligent. A fundamental feature of non-intelligent processes is that they are unable to anticipate. They can't form *a priori* an objective or goal for a system. If a system function or feature doesn't yet exist, a non-intelligent process cannot anticipate it. This is the essential thought behind Michael Behe's concept of 'irreducible complexity', first noted in his book *Darwin's Black Box* and further refined in his book *The Edge of Evolution*. In actuality, Behe found, chance is capable only of performing changes requiring at most one or two sequentially meaningful steps, with even those insignificant changes involving information loss. That's the limit—and it's like a rock wall, preventing any truly useful changes. And, by the way, that problem is entirely oonsistent with the information-based version of the Second Law of Thermodynamics, under which information can only be lost without the input of information.

"An irreducibly complex system, to paraphrase Dr. Behe, requires so many mutually-supportive subsystems that while the operation of naturalistic evolution is limited to small, incremental and undirected advances, the very existence of the top-level system without the input of anticipation is out of the question; yet the existence of such systems is so ubiquitous in living entities that such input must be acknowledged as having been present.

"A few years back, a few books were written by pro-evolution authors that claimed to rebut Dr. Behe's notion. Their argument, in addition to being superficial, was irrelevant to the thrust of Behe's finding. It was nothing but a red herring.

"The next issue is modularity," Earl said, but as he spoke he was interrupted by one of the congregants. "Yes?" he asked a man who was waving an arm for attention.

"I know that this is good information you're giving us," the man said. "But what's the use? We seem to be reaching the end of the road, so it's not like we'll be trying to convince others. Sure, I know we have kids—I hate to say it, but they might not have much of a future, so what good is this lecture going to do?"

"Good question, but think about it," Earl replied. "We've all been brainwashed about evolution to some extent, and, whether you care to admit it or not, it has to have affected your faith to some extent, and more so to our kids. Faith is what will keep us going, and particularly keep us in favor with God. The fat lady hasn't sung yet, and we're going to need all the faith we can get for the days ahead. At least that's what I'm thinking."

Hearing a murmur of assent from the congregants and seeing

the man who had questioned Earl return to his seat, Earl continued. "Thanks for the question," he said. "It was a good one. Now, back to the modularity issue. Evolutionists of the modularist persuasion have claimed that the similarities between a number of biological subsystems in entirely different functional settings shows how evolution has taken advantage of opportunities for natural selection to considerably shorten the evolutionary path by borrowing large modules from other subsystems and, with minor modifications, utilize them for their own purposes. This concept of modularity supports and attempts to revive the earlier notion of 'punctuated evolution' proposed by the late Stephen J. Gould with the more advanced knowledge base of modern molecular biology. What the modularists have actually accomplished instead is to undercut the central feature of the Darwinian mechanism, which is modification through a huge number of tiny, incremental steps. With the arrival of the concept of modularity, many evolutionists have come out of the closet to acknowledge that Darwin's original mechanism was unworkable. They were more than happy to do so, because in finding this new mechanism they were able to admit the obvious problems with the 'old' evolution while keeping God at bay with another purely naturalistic process. But there are at least three reasons why the concept of modularity fails to provide the breakthrough that evolutionists were hoping for. Number one, it fails to explain how the modular components came into existence in the first place. Number two, these so-called modular components aren't perfectly modular, but require considerable modification to be useful in a new context. And then, there's the huge problem that the new situation would demand a corresponding control system on top of the modular component. Think of it this way: getting a bird to fly doesn't just require wings, but a birdlike nerve structure to operate them. Dr. Behe notes that in his study of the evolutionary histories of viruses, bacteria and humans he encountered no evidence whatsoever of modular evolution. There is a big reason why this is so: rather than supporting evolution, both modularity and control circuitry work against it.

"This subject of modularity brings up the general issue of

coordination. The added complexity of developing and integrating the control structure for an improvement, along with the improvement itself, into a higher-level structure is but one element of a very broad category of evolutionary difficulties, that of coordination. Evolution works on single-point changes with absolutely no consideration of the systems-integration aspect of such modifications. That's a huge problem that evolutionists are blind to, because life exhibits coordination everywhere. Symbiosis among self-contained but mutually-supporting systems stretches the improbability of the combined systems far beyond what it would be if the systems were independent of each other.

Take DNA, for example, which as a software code is useless without the supporting hardware. Specifically, the DNA code for protein synthesis is meaningless without the supporting systems of messenger RNA, transfer RNA and ribosomes that utilize the DNA code in assembling proteins out of amino acids. But the constituents of ribosomes are proteins, which means that proteins cannot exist without the prior existence of proteins—DNA and certain proteins had to exist together in a coordinated manner. This poses a huge problem for evolution. An example of this that I find to be particularly amusing is the notion of some poor four-legged creature possessing one or two features of a bird, perhaps wings and a beak, without having yet acquired all the features necessary to actually fly. We can imagine this unfortunate beast wasting energy uselessly flapping its wings when if it just ran without the added encumbrances it might escape being eaten.

"Another serious issue with evolution is chirality. I've already talked about this property, but I want to quickly revisit it to emphasize its importance. Chirality is a property of some chemical structures that describes their ability to come in different orientations. This property applies particularly to some molecules essential to life like DNA, RNA and amino acids, all of which come in 'right-handed' and 'left-handed' versions with equal probability in nature. The problem is that molecules like DNA must consist entirely of one version or another. Even the inclusion of one component of the wrong chirality is enough to gum up the works.

"Chirality in living systems isn't a problem, because the machinery in the body automatically takes care of it. It's getting from non-life to life that's the real problem, and it's a very big one. Even the most dedicated of evolutionists would realize, if he allowed himself to do so, the vast improbability of flipping a coin millions of times and coming up with nothing but heads. That's exactly what chirality demands.

"The bottom line in all this is that evolution is basically unworkable because life is based on information. The essence of life is information that resides in the cell, and especially within the pattern of base pairs in the DNA molecule. This molecular-level information is of the most sophisticated and complex nature, which is something that neither Darwin nor his supporters have understood. Only recently has science begun to scratch the surface of this new understanding.

"Much as I myself have only begun to scratch the surface of our present understanding of this extremely fascinating field of molecular biology, I've probably devoted way too much time to that one subject when there are so many other issues that must be addressed to prepare us for a difficult future. But at least you should know by now that evolution is the real myth, rather than Scripture. Keep the faith. And now that your children are no longer participating in the public school system, it's the responsibility of you parents to undo the harm that their teachers have perpetrated by attempting to cram this false notion into their heads."

CHAPTER SIXTEEN

Signs of hostility became increasingly evident as the group continued their journey toward Mount Hermon and the border with Lebanon and Syria. At every stop, though, they imparted their Messianic message to generally enthusiastic listeners. Attrition among them also continued, as individuals and sometimes couples remained behind in the towns and kibbutzim they visited.

When the party reached the kibbutz of Dafna the stay-behind bug bit Moira hard. Two days after they had arrived, their mission with respect to the inhabitants was complete, but Moira balked at leaving. The next day after asking permission to stay in the community for another day or so, Moira was again struck by their cheerful generosity. They were advised by Jerry to visit Shulman's sweets before leaving. Without saying a word, Jerry called the chocolate museum and booked their tour for that afternoon. Excited, Moira headed into the little village with Jacob in tow. There they rented bicycles and toured the area, returning to a charming little café at midday. They found themselves afterward on a small bridge overlooking the tree-lined Dan River. "Oh Jacob, this place is so beautiful!" she exclaimed as they gazed down at the picturesque scene. "I feel like I'm home."

They spent the afternoon at the little museum of chocolate, ending their tour by purchasing way too many of the famous sweets, eating them right on the spot. That evening, still exuberant over what Moira thought of as the prettiest spot in the world, they strolled back toward the town park under a full moon. I want this to be home. Our home. Can we?"

She asked me, Jacob thought with a glow in his stomach. *Does that mean a commitment?* They walked over to a nearby park bench, where they sat. Jacob took a hand in his.

"It is pretty," he responded. "Let's ask God about it." Jacob did just that. "I need to ask you something, too, Moira," he said after they had prayed for guidance. "I know that we haven't known each other that long. There's still lots that we don't know about each other. But I do know from what I've seen so far," he quickly added, "that you're everything I ever wanted in a companion., and more than I have a right to expect. I'd also like to pray for God's guidance in this relationship the two of us seem to be getting into. Is that okay with you, or am I just assuming—"

"Stop," she said, putting a finger to his lips. "Father," she began without preamble, "in the name of our blessed Savior Lord Jesus Christ, we ask you to bless and honor our commitment to each other, for which we are grateful. Thank you. Amen."

"Gee," Jacob said, "that didn't sound like much of a question. So do you—"

"Sometimes you talk too much, my darling Jacob," she said, placing her finger back on his lips. "There wasn't any need for it. In the first place, the Holy Spirit obviously set this up. And then, we know what's on each others' minds whether it's too soon or not. And more, have you noticed the commune—that everyone there's married and very obviously happy? They're living every day in joy like it might be their last on earth. Look around. You've seen the war drums beating. Who knows what's going to happen tomorrow? If we're serving the Lord, we can certainly continue to do so as a couple."

"Well, then—"

"Just be quiet. I haven't finished talking. When you ducked into the bathroom before we came into town, I had another talk with Jerry. I asked him if we could possibly stay on at the kibbutz. I told him that we're both hard workers, but before I could say anything more, he welcomed us into their commune and gave me a big hug. The rest of them began to get excited, but I asked them not to let on to you about it before I had a chance to tell you about the ceremony."

"Ceremony? There's a—"

"No. Not for that," she broke in. "I also asked Jerry if he could arrange for a wedding. Ours, dear. I knew you were getting ready to ask, so I just anticipated a little. So now let me ask you a question. Am I being too forward?"

Jacob's teeth glowed whitely in the moonlight. He didn't have to say a word. Instead, he reached over and gave her a deep kiss, which morphed into a serious embrace that grew more heated with passion. "Whoa," she finally gasped. Let's save the rest for after our marriage." They both laughed and very reluctantly got to their feet.

"But what about our prayers?" Jacob asked as they strolled hand-in-hand back toward the community. "We didn't exactly wait for a response from God."

Moira laughed again. "You may recall that my prayer didn't ask for anything. It was all thanksgiving. Wisdom visited me last night, Jacob. I asked Her then, and Her big smile said it all. She was very enthusiastic about our marriage, as a matter of fact. And She blessed our stay here as well."

CHAPTER SEVENTEEN

For several weeks the small community in the RV park had not been molested by government authorities. But now a new situation intruded upon them: an enraged population was rising up to fight back against the dictatorial, self-serving and corrupt government bureaucracy. Having begun in small, independent hot-spot enclaves scattered throughout the country, the rage fed upon itself like a wildfire as it expanded and began to merge together into a cohesive network. Now, taking open advantage of the retreat of government forces in the face of the numerous natural disasters afflicting the American countryside, it was baring its teeth.

Texas was already primed for civil war. Now in the historically conservative hill country near San Antonio, it manifested itself in the presence of an armed band of patriots, who came into the RV park one Saturday afternoon looking for the local leader. They were directed to Earl, and were invited in by Jimmy into his motor home, where Ron Bowling sat down in a face-to-face discussion with Earl and Jimmy about who they were and what their short-term objective was all about.

"We're heading over to Austin," Ron told the two men. "First thing we're gonna do is take over the capital as a symbolic gesture. We'll see what happens after that, probably combine forces with other groups. We know they're out there."

"An admirable plan," Earl began. "But it doesn't even begin to solve the real problem behind every bad thing that's happened to this country."

"What's that?" Ron asked, surprised.

"The real problem with America didn't start with a corrupt government. It started when our population in general lost interest in following God or even in understanding who He is. Everything else came down automatically."

"Yeh, but don't you feel a duty, as an American, to help clean up the mess?"

"I have a greater duty to my God, Ron. He tells us to love our enemies, not to kill them. A man called Peter once said to a different group that we ought to obey God rather than men. We're committed to that call. But I'll tell you what we can do for you. While our first duty to God is to tell the story of Jesus to those with whom we come into contact, we also can support you as Christian advisors, kind of like chaplains, if you wish. That way we'd be working together instead of against each other."

Ron thought it over. "Maybe you're afraid," he said with narrowed eyes.

Earl grinned. "Those are fighting words to a Marine," he shot back. "You and me—bring it on." In jest he assumed an offensive stance.

"Whoa, back off," Ron replied. "We have real enemies to fight. We don't need to waste our energy on each other."

"Glad you said that," Earl replied. He remained at the physical ready.

"Yeah," Joyce broke in from the background. "You might have

bitten off more than you could chew." Ron turned his head to look at her and was taken aback by her hands, cupped into claws. His glance moved up to her eyes, which appeared ready to ignite. There wasn't a trace of jest in her demeanor.

"Okay, okay," he said. "I get the picture. Only you have to know that we've come up against some cowardly people this past month. They'd rather live like mice than stand up like men."

"You think being a Christian is easy?" Joyce continued. "Let me set you straight. The mistreatment of Christians separated the men from the boys a long time ago. Earl and I have had enough crap heaped our way—because of our Christianity—to last several lifetimes. Including a death camp, which we survived only by the grace of God. And we've seen so many other brave Christians persecuted and tortured and killed that we know that the only reason we're still alive is that God has more for us to do. When we've finished our jobs here, we'll be more than happy to meet our Lord. So you tell me if we're afraid to fight."

"I hear you," Ron said apologetically. "We'd be honored to bring you with us. If you'd care to come along," he added. He frowned. "But what would that accomplish?" he asked, more to himself than to the others.

"Only the most important thing of all," Earl replied. "To have God with you. Secondarily, to buck up the troops. What do you know about the father of our country, George Washington?"

"Well, I know about Valley Forge, and how Washington beat the odds of cold and starvation to win the war."

"Yes, but did you know how strong a Christian Washington was? Or of how many times that God intervened in his life and during the Revolutionary War to bring him—and his country—to victory? Even the misery of Valley Forge was initiated by God to harden the troops for the battles ahead. Yes, I know what you're planning to say, that Washington was both a Christian and a fighter. To that I'll say that we all have our calling, and what God has put into our hearts to do we must be obedient. If God wants me to fight, well, then I'd take up a weapon and fight. For the present, at least, that's not what God would have me do. In fact, He's been telling us here at the park to love even our enemies, as He'd said during His earthly ministry. I have the feeling that the nature of this war is different. In Washington's day, God wanted America to be a unique country, independent of Europe and especially England. Like in ancient Israel, America would have to fight to be free of secular forces. But now, as I see it, the situation seems to be different. America may have come to the end of that road. At this point America has been thoroughly secularized and is ready to be integrated into a world government, just as was foretold by Daniel and also by John in Revelation. Now the battle is far more spiritual, and, like Paul has told us, we need to fight it with spiritual tools, not man-made weapons. That's not to say that there isn't a physical component. In some way, I'm sure that you have a useful purpose in what you're trying to do. But our job"—he looked at Joyce—"is to bring the Light of Christ to a dark and evil world."

Ron nodded his head, but then a frown came upon his features. "You sound like everything that happens in this country comes from God. If that's the case, then why isn't America mentioned in the Bible? I do know that much."

"Oh, but it is," Earl said, laughing. "You're digressing, but I don't mind. I never turn down an opportunity to preach. You'd have to go back and read Daniel Chapter Seven to understand. He notes several beasts in that prophecy, each of which had a short-term representation that history confirms already has been fulfilled. The first was a lion, which stood for Babylon. Next came a bear, which was Medo-Persia. After that was a leopard, which stood for Greece, and then a savage iron beast that represented Rome. But in line with Revelation Chapter thirteen, those beasts also had a long-term future representation as components of a final world government. In this other representation, each of the beasts is identified by the icon of its associated government. In this context, the icon for England always has been a lion, and just as obviously the bear represents Russia. The leopard is associated with Germany and, like the four-headed leopard of Daniel 7, Germany has held center stage three times and is now in the midst of her fourth manifestation—the fourth Reich, if you will."

"Great," Ron interrupted. "But where is America in all that?"

"Wait for it—" Earl told him, half in jest. "Returning to Daniel seven, the lion had an eagle's wings, which were plucked off of its back and made to stand up like a man. I don't have to tell you that the icon of America is an eagle. Nor do I have to say that the Revolutionary War was primarily against England, considered by mostly everybody to be our mother country, so America is indeed mentioned in the Bible. The ominous thing about that, though, is that there's no mention of our country in Revelation thirteen, which leads me to believe that America won't be occupying center stage at the end of the age."

As Earl wound down, Joyce softened toward the visitors. "It's not an easy thing to argue religion with my husband," she said with a smile. "Would you like to stay for a bite to eat?"

The men willingly complied, sitting on the floor as Joyce and Millie prepared soup. During the meal Earl reinforced the reality of God's presence in their lives, while Ron laid out his plans for taking Austin by force.

CHAPTER EIGHTEEN

Jacob and Moira were married the next week. After a brief celebration, their companions left to continue their northward journey.

They were given a room of their own, which they immediately put to use, and were integrated into the kibbutz with specific tasks. "First order of business," Jerry began as they sat before him awaiting their assignments, "is our common defense. Nobody's exempt from standing watch, which is required for everybody over the age of twelve, men and women alike. And everyone must be capable of defending their comrades. That means that you must be able to shoot at least one weapon and preferably two, and be reasonably accurate at it, even when being fired upon. You'll be attending a firearms course together beginning this afternoon. It's up to you when you'll be ready to stand guard, but we expect you to be reasonably quick about completing your training. Now for the good news," he said, looking at Moira with a smile. Word's out that you like chocolate. I'm assigning you to kitchen duties. Right now, we're short of a good dessert chef, which I have a hunch you might just be very good at. As for you," he continued, directing his eyes toward Jacob," the news isn't quite that good. I'm sorry, but we really need help with the farm work. Go see James after I'm finished with you, and he'll give you more detailed directions as to what you'll be doing. I expect you'll have a lot of different chores to do, depending on the season and the weather.

"I'm rather happy for the assignment," Jacob responded. "I could use some exercise, and, besides, I think my new wife would appreciate a buff body." Moira grinned her assent.

"One more thing before I let you go," Jerry said. "You've given us some valuable information about Jesus and the Godhead. You need to keep doing that. We'll set up some meetings with our neighbors, both here and there. I'd like to see you put some of that information in writing, too. Perhaps you two can collaborate on that in your free time. If you aren't too busy on other matters," he added with a smile.

That afternoon they each were handed weapons by their instructor Jesse. "I understand that you came from America," he told Jacob. "So did I, before the flag went up over there. As a matter of fact, I was in the Marine Corps for a tour, a fact that you'll find somewhat uncomfortable, but very helpful to you and our kibbutz." Jacob was given an old Weatherby bolt-action .30-.06 rifle, with a scope. Jesse gave Moira a much more sophisticated-looking Ruger mini-14 gas-operated semiautomatic rifle chambered for the .223 round and equipped with a banana clip that held thirty of the deadly rounds. "We want the little lady to be well-equipped," Jerry said. "Most important, the mini-14 has a much lighter kick to it than the Weatherby, which should keep her from flinching. You look like you can handle a heftier weapon," he said, eyeing Jacob. "After a month in the field with a hoe, this will seem like a toy. I'm hoping that we might make a sniper out of you. Well, we'll see."

Jesse took them over to the range and went over the operation of the weapons. He next had them disassemble the rifles, clean them thoroughly, and apply light coatings of oil at the necessary places. Moira took to the instruction with enthusiasm and was surprisingly adept at putting the many pieces together. Jacob was a little less enthusiastic, having a clearer idea of what Jesse had in store for them.

"Okay, people," Jesse began for their next phase. "Now we'll get into a snapping-in exercise. For starters, hold your rifles at port-arms like me," he said, dropping down into a squat, holding his own weapon horizontal. "See that target over there?" he asked, pointing to a distant square of white after they had assumed his position. "We're going to duck-walk over there. Quack-quack. Get moving."

That evening after supper they hobbled to their bedroom. "We might as well start on that book," Moira said. "I'm sure not good for anything else. I think our honeymoon just ended."

Jacob gave her a sympathetic laugh. "Nor I. But at least you get to go to the kitchen tomorrow. They gave me a hoe and they expect me to wield it in the morning. I'm afraid that the book will have to wait too." He undressed and fell into bed. Moira followed soon afterward. They both fell into sleep almost instantly.

The next two weeks were a living hell for both of them, but as their bodies gradually adjusted to the physical demands laid upon them, they started to pick up in strength and attitude. During that time Jesse added various positions from which to shoot effectively, and had them snap-in to those as well as the squat. Using their slings as braces, their positions of fire began to be comfortable and natural, as the U. S. Marine Corps had successfully taught generations of recruits. Despite the added burden of work with the crops, Jacob began to feel more alive that he had ever experienced. Both he and Moira glowed with health, and they began to participate in the communal activities as well.

With their collaboration on a book, interspersed with lectures on the topics with which they were familiar, their lives were full beyond their imagining. Their happiness was complete.

Until a night-time raid on their kibbutz changed everything. Up to that time the ever-present threat of violence was a background fact that the community had successfully managed to work around. Now it became a central feature of their existence.

Moira was on guard duty the night their enemies' hatred exploded into another bout of violence. She had heard noises nearby and was alert to the danger, but the suddenness of the attack surprised her. Fortunately, she was in a hidden, well-protected position and, having undergone extensive training, she kept her head and reacted automatically. When the lead intruder set off a tripwire that illuminated the area, she placed a well-aimed round into his neck, dropping him instantly. Shifting her aim, she dropped two more in quick succession, but one of their bullets hit its mark and she cried out in shock. Refusing to give up, she quickly sighted on the offender and dropped him as well. By that time reinforcements arrived and routed the band of intruders. Jacob was among them and, seeing that Moira had been hit, he ran up to her and cradled her in his arms. He surreptitiously looked for the wound and saw that it had penetrated her left leg near the thigh. With vast relief he noted from the blood that the bullet hadn't severed a major blood vessel. Lifting her up, he went back down to the infirmary, where he placed her tenderly on a cot. He watched anxiously for a doctor but the one nearby was working frantically with an assistant to save the life of another injured person. There was nobody else available, so he did what he could. First praying for Moira and the wounded man nearby, he ripped off his shirt. He wondered briefly if his sweat would infect her wound, but remembered a classic secular proverb. *When you're up to your ass in alligators, you don't think about draining the swamp,* he repeated under his breath, and pressed the bunched shirt against the wound to stop the flow of blood. Only when the doctor finally came over to Moira's bedside did he let up on his compress. He stepped back to let the doctor do his work and bent over the cot. "I'm going to have a very hard time sleeping without you tonight, honey," he murmured in her ear. "Just get well soon, okay?"

CHAPTER NINETEEN

That Sunday morning as Earl faced the people assembled in front of him, he was mildly surprised to see Ron and a few of his fellow fighters among them. *Good*, he thought, picking up his notes. But then he frowned, thinking of the impact of their presence on what he should be saying, and returned the papers in his hand to the upended box on his right that served as a makeshift podium.

"Hi, everybody," he began. "I already had a talk on my mind for this morning, but I suddenly realized that there's a more important topic that needs to be addressed. So if you'll bear with me, I'm going to speak out of my heart, calling upon support from the Holy Spirit rather than my usual notes. If I were going to give the subject a title, I guess that 'What's Really Wrong with America' would be as good a one as any. I don't need to tell anyone here that there's something wrong." His statement of the obvious brought a few half-hearted laughs, but the mouths of most turned grim.

"What really happened to America started before most of us were born," Earl continued. "Like a serious disease such as cancer, it started slowly, with hardly any symptoms at all. Only when it got to the terminal stage did we all become aware of what had happened, but by then it was too late.

"What was this dreadful disease? I'll tell you what it wasn't. It wasn't a failure of leadership. Nor was it a takeover by unprincipled, self-absorbed rulers who cared nothing for our God-given American constitution. The sickness is a disease of the heart, of our indifference toward the Judeo-Christian God who played such a vital part in the founding of the American dream. This disease didn't turn our leaders into evil, vicious persons. It infected us instead, creating the environment in which evil people could thrive and prosper.

"The sickness began within four of the institutional systems upon which we base our understanding of the world around us. The first of these is the secular media, which provide us with news and entertainment; the second is the scientific community; the third is our schools, wherein our children are supplied with a formalized version of knowledge; and the fourth is our seminaries, which supposedly offer us a specialized knowledge of God. These institutions were the first to get sick, and then the disease metastasized from there, branching out to infect the general public.

"The secular media was infiltrated long ago by selfish, godless people, to whom the physical world in which we reside is the only world there is because that's the way they want it to be. They were repulsed by the thought of some higher being looking over their shoulders, or knowing their thoughts, which probably did run into some colorful fantasies and mean-spirited notions. But in their torrid love affair with their own minds, they embraced the ever-expanding world of science as much as they were put off by religion. In their wholesale rush to glorify mankind's scientific achievements, they bought into some very bad and very false ideas, being so incredibly shallow of mind as to unthinkingly accept these ideas simply because they were generated by so-called experts in the field.

"The sources of these very bad and very false ideas were people of the same kind of godless self-absorption as the media representatives. Encouraged by the adoring media, they assumed the intellectual authority of the God they had in mind to replace.

The only difference between these self-styled scientists and their media counterparts is that the scientists possessed some knowledge of the subject upon which they made such weighty pronouncements. But their education in some cases actually was as sparse or nearly so, as that of the public at large, because the scientific disciplines were in their infancy, with very little knowledge to be obtained through formal training. Such was the case in the fields of natural history, geology, and biology. I could go into a very detailed expose of the reasons why, for example, the theory of evolution is a misleading, dead-end path, but time doesn't permit that. The reasons involve some very important and revealing scientific discoveries in the field of biology by Darwin's far more knowledgeable modern counterparts. If any of you are truly interested, see me after this meeting and we'll set up a workshop on the subject.

"But just as the media controllers bought into false scientific notions that confirmed and increased their distance from God, so did the educators, who also infiltrated the school system all the way from kindergarten to the great universities. John Dewey was among the worst of that lot. After assuming dictatorial power over the machinery of public education, this godless Marxist developed curricula that opposed Christianity at every turn. His ideas also began to sway students away from nationalism into a world citizenry, and fostered quasi-scientific notions that supported our alienation from God. His most devastating weapon was his appreciation that he wouldn't accomplish his objectives in a day, or even in a decade or a generation. His gradual insertion of bad ideas into the classroom began in the classrooms of the teaching colleges, infecting the teachers first with false notions, and letting them be his unwitting tools in disseminating his notions to the public at large.

"The same thing happened in our seminaries, the schools that supposedly train men and women for Christian service as pastors, chaplains and religious instructors. Just as John Dewey infiltrated the secular teaching system, so did self-centered and basically godless men invade the seminaries, attempting to turn theology into a strictly intellectual endeavor. They elbowed God aside with their false theories that the Bible was nothing more than a work of man, and attempted to strengthen that assertion on the basis of literary reviews that claimed various books to be written by several authors and at widely different dates, all of which were established on the false presupposition that prophesies could not have involved a God-given knowledge of the future. Not all, but way too many of the pastors that came out of these wicked seminaries were just as self-centered as the secular educators. After having avidly internalized the false teachings to which they were exposed, they lost their focus on God, which was tenuous to begin with, and concentrated instead on the task of creating successful income-producing congregations based on the false pictures of God which they had uncritically embraced.

"So what? What is the bottom line in all this? It is that the public at large perceives that the Bible was a work of man and riddled with errors and fuzzy, unsophisticated and basically meaningless passages. In line with that understanding, the God of that Bible is seen as either imaginary or a very distant and essentially alien being. Considering the Bible to be less than profound, the general public long ago released itself from the odious task of attempting to read it. Refusing to understand the Bible as the only reliable Word of God, these same people lost most of their knowledge and understanding of God. In the end, God became to them at best a stern taskmaster and at worst a distant, alien being who was entirely indifferent to the daily affairs of mankind. Perceiving God in that way, they themselves distanced and alienated themselves from Him.

"But as history has demonstrated time and again, mankind needs God. We certainly need God for the salvation that offers us a ticket into the next world, for which there's reason to believe that it's much more colorful and real than this one. But we also need God's Word and the Holy Spirit to impart to us the selfless nobility that is so necessary for us to get along with each other in this lesser world. Without the lofty standards established by God for human interaction, the world quickly descends into mean-spirited, selfish, hate-driven acts of people showing unkindness toward each other for their own profit. It becomes an insane hell of our own making. Does anyone doubt that this is exactly what has happened outside these doors?

"I'll wind up today's talk on that sour note. But think about the implications. The solution of our present distress isn't about patriotism or patriotic acts. We lost our patriotism to America when we lost our patriotism toward God. Our forefathers knew their God in an intimate way that is almost completely lost to us. They had their eyes on a greater world than our material realm. They knew, for example, what Paul had to say about that other, better world." Earl picked up his Bible from the upended box beside him and turned to First Corinthians Chapter 2.

But as it is written, Eye hath not seen, nor ear heard, neither have entered into the heart of man, the things which God hath prepared for them that love him. But God hath revealed them unto us by his Spirit; for the Spirit searcheth all things, yea, the deep things of God. For what man knoweth the things of a man, except the spirit of man which is in him? Even so the things of God knoweth no man, but the Spirit of God. Now we have received, not the spirit of the world, but the Spirit who is of God; that we might know the things that are freely given to us of God. Which things also we speak, not in the words which man's wisdom teacheth, but which the Holy Spirit teacheth, comparing spiritual things with spiritual. But the natural man receiveth not the things of the Spirit of God; for they are foolishness unto him, neither can he know them, because they are spiritually discerned.

"That, my friends," Earl said as he looked out to the audience, "is what we have lost in maintaining our focus on the material world to the exclusion of the spiritual realm. But it is in the spiritual world that the biggest battle is being waged. Paul was very clear about that." He turned to Ephesians Chapter 6 and continued reading from it.

For we wrestle not against flesh and blood, but against principalities, against powers, against the rulers of the darkness of this world, against spiritual wickedness in high places. Wherefore, take unto you the whole armor of God, that ye may be able to withstand in the evil day, and having done all, to stand. Stand, therefore, having your loins girded about with truth, and having on the breastplate of righteousness, and your feet shod with the preparation of the gospel of peace; above all, taking the shield of faith, with which ye shall be able to quench all the fiery darts of the wicked. And take the helmet of salvation, and the sword of the Spirit, which is the word of God; praying always with all prayer and supplication in the Spirit, and watching thereunto with all perseverance and supplication for all saints; and for me, that utterance may be given unto me, that I may open my mouth boldly to make known the mystery of the gospel, for which I am an ambassador in bonds; that in this I may speak boldly, as I ought to speak.

"Now, after hearing that, let me ask you: is it better to contribute our own violence to the mess we are surrounded with, or rather should we turn back to God and, as Jesus said in His Sermon on the Mount, show our love of God to the world by loving our enemies, no matter what that might cost us? While you're thinking about that, you might offer a prayer for me and all your fellow Christians that, like Paul, we may receive from the Holy Spirit the courage to continue speaking out about our convictions."

Ron and his group decided to stay among the RV dwellers for a time. He resolved, instead of the immediate action he had planned, to send a couple of scouts ahead to make a reconnaissance of the Austin area.

The deterioration of the modern infrastructure was nearly complete by this time. A major consequence of the cascade of natural disasters coupled with the self-serving retreat of government into shelters designed only for the privileged was a stampede of people from the major cities. They were driven by the self-fulfilling notion that the urban areas were doomed to destruction. The common notion was that food would be more plentiful at the source, which, of course was the rural backbone of America. And they were right, but only for a very short time. The city people, having been used to the luxuries of a wealthy and sophisticated society, were spoiled to the point of perpetual childishness. They were incapable of discipline, godless, as self-serving as their now hidden government officials, and utterly lacking in the concept of hard work. They had no idea that it required patience and backbreaking labor to grow food, prepare it for consumption, and renew the growing process.

Coming across farms, the first wave met the armed resistance of the occupants, who had been expecting this mass exodus from the urban centers and had prepared for this situation the best they could. Many within the mobs were wounded or killed in the one-sided battles, and the typical mob quickly retreated to safer ground, leaving their wounded behind to scream ineffectively for help. Eventually, however, their hunger overcame their cowardice and, shouting curses, they massed again for assault. The dead and wounded among them piled up outside enclaves, but eventually the defenders' ammunition ran out, interrupting the gunfire with a very brief silence, which ended as the hordes correctly interpreted the lack of gunfire. The battles then became one-sided in the other direction, overwhelming the defenders with their greater numbers, killing them without thought and looting their supplies.

The mobs that followed them were out of luck. Slowly starving, filthy and unruly, they turned in upon themselves in a long, slow, painful and inexorable process of self-destruction. Large areas of the countryside stank of decomposing bodies. With the abandonment of social order among those responsible for the maintenance of the utilities and systems necessary for urban living, the systems ceased to work. Electrical power would never revisit this area; it would remain forever absent from much of the country.

Workers in the nuclear power industry made half-hearted attempts to shut down their systems gracefully, but they, too, succumbed to the need to get out of the increasingly untenable cities in which they lived. As a result, radioactivity breached reactors throughout the nation, spewing deadly radiation into the atmosphere and making a heavy contribution to the death of the country along a corridor that spanned the Midwest and Eastern part of the United States.

Ironically, those who stayed inside the cities were comparatively well off, having ready access to the mountains of canned goods that were stocked by the chains and big-box grocery outlets.

For sleeping purposes, Ron's group occupied an abandoned apartment building close to the RV park. Without electricity they had the choice of eating food cold out of cans or of joining the RV dwellers for meals. They chose the former for three days, coming to Earl on the fourth day with a plea for at least some hot supplements. Laughing, Earl welcomed them for meals under two conditions: first, that they would search out the stores in the area, bringing back provisions for themselves and, hopefully, adding to the stores available to the original occupants as well; and second, that they would attend Church services on Sunday. On behalf of his people, Ron quickly assented.

The next Sunday Earl, noting that more of the newcomers were attending, but probably only because they perceived their attendance to be a condition to their feeding arrangements, kept his sermon simple but interesting and, most importantly, lighter-spirited than his last one.

"I'm going to direct my thoughts today toward those who have just joined us," he began. "But I think all of you will find most of what I have to say to be interesting. I'm pretty much of a Protestant, I guess, but what I have to say relates to an insight that I received from a book written by a Catholic. It's a good one, and it follows Scripture quite closely, although today in describing this insight I'm going to set aside my usual practice of reading from Scripture, again for the benefit of our newcomers.

"I believe that there are only two of you here who have heard of Migdal Edar, the Watchtower of the flock," he continued, looking directly at Jimmy and Millie with a question in his eyes.

"That's okay, Earl," Jimmy spoke out. "We don't mind hearing it again."

"Thanks, you two. Okay. For starters, we have to go all the way back to the Old Testament and near the beginning of the Bible. In Exodus 12, a great drama is about to begin. The Jews had been in Egypt for four hundred thirty years. For Four hundred of those years they were occupied as slaves to their Egyptian masters. God is about to bring them out of Egypt over the spiteful opposition of Pharaoh. The event is so important that God makes that month the first month of the year. On the tenth day of that month, every family is to take an innocent yearling lamb, perfectly healthy and without blemish of any kind, and bring it into their home. Four days later, after having learned to love this little lamb, they are to kill it and sprinkle its blood on their lintel and doorposts. Every family that does this is to be passed over by God on His way to kill the firstborn of every family in Egypt. That night they are to eat the lamb in haste, for the next morning they are to begin their momentous journey out of Egypt. This event is called the Passover, and God commanded the Jews to observe it forever as a memorial to the innocent lamb who died to save them from destruction. In fact, the Passover is observed by Jews to this very day.

The Passover is all about Jesus. Jesus died on the cross on that same fourteenth day of that same month, and for the same reason. In the Gospel of John, Jesus is described by John the Baptist as 'the Lamb of God who takes away the sins of the world'.

"Now, to Migdal Edar. The first mention of it is in Genesis thirty-five. It's a very brief account of a landmark tower near Bethlehem where Rachel was buried. The next reference to it is in Micah 4:8, and that passage links the same watchtower to the coming of Jesus Christ, just as the more well-known passage in Micah 5:2 pinpoints the town of Bethlehem as the place from where Jesus will come. They're actually the same place. There's more information about that particular place in Jewish history, which I'll get into in just a moment. I believe that most of you are familiar with the Christmas story, that Mary and Joseph went to Bethlehem for the taxation and, since there was no room for them at the local inn, they were forced to go to a stable for lodging, and that's where Mary gave birth to Jesus. According to Luke's gospel, angels told the shepherds in the fields to look for their Savior there, who would be wrapped in swaddling clothes.

"We usually form a mental picture of that scene that goes something like this: Mary is in a stable surrounded by horses or cattle, she and her Holy Child being forced to endure conditions of the most abject poverty by an uncaring world. We also see the bit about the swaddling clothes as unimportant and actually irrelevant information.

"While some small part of that picture might have some truth to it, most of it is quite false. Migdal Edar, you see, was quite special in the eyes of God. It was the watchtower of a very special flock, and the shepherds were more than the ordinary lot. The place where Mary gave birth to Jesus was no more than about five miles from the temple in Jerusalem. The stable where He lay was actually the birthing place for the sacrificial lambs reserved for the Passover ceremony. If there were any cattle there other than sheep, it's probable that the only one was the donkey on which Mary rode to Bethlehem. Now an interesting and very relevant fact in all this is that sometimes the sheep would injure themselves after their birth, which would result in a blemish that would render them unfit for the Passover sacrifice. In order to prevent this, the sheep would be wrapped in swaddling clothes after their birth.

"So you see, every aspect of where and how Mary gave birth to Jesus was pre-planned, including the lack of room at the inn. It was simply never an option for Mary to stay there. Instead, Jesus' birth precisely followed all the ancient pointers to that event."

After the meeting had closed with song, Earl walked back toward the RV park with Joyce on an arm. Ron caught up with him. "I want to thank you for that," he told Earl. "I'm not used to going to Church. I've had some pre-conceptions of what it was all about, and I want to tell you that if I'd known it was like this, I may have gone before."

"Thanks for that, Ron. But you have to know that I really don't have much to do with it, being just a messenger. The Holy Spirit tells me what to say, and how to say it. But I do enjoy having the privilege of speaking on behalf of God. I'm glad you're sticking around for a while. Maybe you'll want to come next week too."

"Count on it," he said.

The next week at the Church service, Earl continued along the lines that he'd established the week before. "Today I'll give you another tidbit of interesting information about Jesus that I'm pretty sure none of you have heard of. Including you, Jimmy and Millie," he added, looking at the couple.

"This one's about the Ark of the Covenant. This ark was a wooden box, overlaid with gold and topped with two cherubs. Inside the box were relics of past interactions between God and man, including the staff that Aaron used, the one that turned into a snake in front of pharaoh, and a sample of the life-sustaining bread that fell from heaven during the great exodus from Egypt and, most important, the tablets upon which God had written the Ten Commandments and which he gave to Moses on the mountain. These tablets of the Law represented the first Word of God covenant between God and man, or the Old Testament. The Ark of the Covenant was placed within the Holy of Holies of the Tabernacle in the wilderness, and later in Solomon's temple. At the dedication of both of these temples the glory of God, called the Shekinah, descended in a cloud and dwelt within the temples. There is a great significance to this indwelling of the Shekinah glory, and I'll probably go into it in another sermon. But for now I want to focus on the Ark, which has had a very colorful history. There's a question as to whether Menelek, the queen of Sheba's son with Solomon, went back to Ethiopia with a copy of it or actually had stolen the real thing. To this day, that version is jealously guarded by Ethiopians. Nevertheless, it was eventually lost. Apparently, the prophet Jeremiah buried it in a cave toward the end of the sixth century B.C. when Jerusalem was in danger of being overrun by enemy forces. There's another story in that too, but to forge ahead, the Ark of the Covenant is finally mentioned again toward the end of the Bible, in the Book of Revelation, where John sees it in heaven. But this may be a different Ark altogether.

"Let me tell you why. In Revelation 12, immediately after John's sighting of the Ark in heaven, he goes on to describe another heavenly wonder: a woman clothed with the sun, who gives birth to a man-child who is to rule the world, obviously Jesus. This woman has variously been identified as several different personages by people of differing faiths, each one being the favorite of one faith or another. Many have thought of this woman as representing Israel. Catholics have picked up on this passage, claiming her to be Mary. For reasons that I won't go into now, I don't think that's quite accurate. But it's very close. Whether this woman actually is Mary or not, it does evoke an image that makes me want to say, 'Of course! It can be no other way.' That image, which I cherish now with all my heart, I know to be true, and I want to share it with you now. Mary herself, in containing the Word of God in her womb, was herself the flesh-and-blood Ark of the New Covenant in Jesus Christ. That may well have been the Ark that John saw in heaven."

Over the next several weeks Earl gradually led into a direct exposition of the Gospel story of Jesus Christ, referring ever more frequently to Scripture itself. He finally had the opportunity to tell the complete story of Jesus' feeding of the multitudes, with a logical development of how five thousand could be fed with five loaves and leave a remainder of twelve baskets, while four thousand could be fed with seven loaves and leave a remainder of seven baskets, and the ultimate symbolism of the events, which was a cross. As the weeks went by, more and more of Ron's people, beginning with Ron himself, accepted Jesus as their Lord and Savior and were baptized in His name.

The two scouts returned six weeks after they left. They fell into the RV park starving and emaciated. Joyce and Millie stopped what they were doing and prepared a thick broth for their immediate consumption. "Don't eat that so fast, Joyce cautioned the men. "Take it slow, or you're going to upchuck it and waste our precious food." The men complied for a short time, but they were too greedy for nourishment to care about the long-term effects of their eating habits, long-term being measured in seconds rather than hours.

They had interesting news, which they related after allowing the quick meal settle for a while. "Nobody's home in Austin," Jack told the assembled crowd after completing a lengthy round of belching.

"All the government workers have wimped out and gone into hiding or something. There is no force to do battle with, which I guess is good news."

"Yeh, but it's a real jungle out there," Matt added. "People are going crazy and I sure don't want to mess with them."

"Me neither," Jack said. "Mobs, everywhere you look. Man, I hope they don't get an idea to come back here. From what I see, this is the only place worth defending."

"Well, okay then," Ron said. "So be it. Maybe here's where we'll stay and, if need be, here's where we'll take our stand."

CHAPTER TWENTY

Master Sergeant Ellery MacAfee, USMC, sat rigidly at his desk looking out the window at the rural Maryland countryside. Cows grazed contentedly in a nearby pasture, their tails swinging to ward off the ever-present flies. The sky was a deep blue with just a hint of a gathering thundercloud off to the west. His tense posture had nothing to do with military bearing or the discipline ingrained in him over a sixteen-year enlistment.

The ringing of one of his three desk phones diverted his attention. "Seattle Central," he intoned into the phone. "How may I help you?"

"This is Waylon Deeds for POTUS," the phone responded. "We want a conference with POTEUR, to be arranged for thirteen hundred hours in the Colorado room. Have the usual refreshments available, and, El—make sure of the additional security. This is a special get-together."

"Will do," MacAfee said, and rang off. His gaze returned to the window and his posture stiffened further. His problem was personal. He'd succeeded so far in hiding it from those with whom he interacted, from the White House staff down to his buddies, but with every year that went by the problem seemed to get worse. He was claustrophobic; he had thought of this affliction as mild, but it was beginning to intrude more forcefully into his everyday life. *And here I am in probably the most phobia-producing situation in the world*, he thought. *I might was well be sitting in a tank, or living in an elevator.*

Gazing out at the rural scene, he couldn't see the green fields or the blue sky or the cows with swishing tails. All he could see was the reality of five feet—maybe even ten, for all he knew - of rebar-reinforced concrete behind the images on the high-definition screen. And the mountain of earth and concrete that lay between him and the Washington countryside above, which, his monitors told him, was awash in the usual cold rain. *What was that?* he asked himself in sudden shock, one that had been recurring more frequently lately. Two weeks ago a substantial earthquake had frightened everyone living in FEMA Post 415, particularly after someone had gone screaming down a hallway after seeing a "window" fall to the floor and a large crack appear in the concrete behind it. He waited, finally acknowledging to himself that he was just getting jumpy.

To say that the government was in hiding would be to grossly overstate the situation. True, following the numerous natural disasters that had crippled much of the infrastructure of topside America, most of those employed by the government, including the military, were ensconced in underground accommodations. But that situation had been planned for months beforehand and actually had little to do with natural events. The government was well-aware of what a serious infrastructure breakdown would do to the indolent American populace. Unruly, unthinking mobs would form and ravage the countryside. This would lead to wholesale starvation, which is precisely the situation that the government wished to produce. Having been softened up by the disorder, those topside losers would fall all over themselves to accept the bio-ID system already implemented within large portions of the government workforce. With a draconian ban on the use of cash for transactions, each sorry member of the topside population would be controllable down to the time he would be permitted to take a leak. Then the government controllers could come back topside too. If they wanted to.

MacAfee thought about the mindset that had prompted him to join the Marines after high school, and how his motivation had been so seriously betrayed by the government. He knew that he wasn't cut out for an academic career. His grades in high school weren't too bad, maybe a notch or two above mediocre. His real yearning was to be active. He didn't want to get tied down to a desk, but he wanted his life to count for something, maybe even something noble. He thought he'd found it in the Marines, and for much of his career he was confident that his service career was everything he'd hoped for. It was only after the most recent presidency got underway and had made its plans apparent to the American public that he began to question whether there was any America left in America and started to regret that he was serving this out-of-control abomination by continuing on active duty. The only mitigating factor in his present life was his Christianity. His wife, who lived with him in their underground quarters, finally had succeeded three years ago in getting him to accept Jesus Christ as his Savior and Lord. Since then he'd taken up the reading of the Bible, and every added bit of information he'd acquired from this Word of God had increased his enthusiasm for more. He'd read the entire Bible through at least once. Lately the Book of Daniel had recaptured his interest.

Something Waylon had said intruded on his thoughts. *POTUS?* MacAfee reflected. *His aides had best shape up, and be quick about it.* The title no longer suited the American leader. The United States no longer existed as an independent nation. POTNAR was the correct term—President of the North American Region. Much had happened since POTNAR went underground. After his two terms had expired, the ex-president had allowed a political hack to assume the office of president, but only for a very brief time. Having undercut the leaders of both Canada and Mexico with the aid of the European leadership, he had employed Machiavellian tactics to integrate the three former nations into a single entity—one of ten regions that constituted a government approaching worldwide status.

MacAfee often had wondered what Daniel had meant in Chapter 7 regarding the "little horn" who had plucked up three of the first horns by the roots. Why a little horn? Were there bigger horns? He had remained confused about it until last night, when he suddenly realized with a shock that there actually were little horns and big horns. With the advent of world government divided into ten regional jurisdictions, the regions themselves were automatically bigger than the old system of nations that they had just superseded. *And that means that our trusty POTNAR, who used to be a national leader—a little horn—in the process of first betraying and then killing the leaders of the three nations that now comprise the North American Region, just now made himself a big horn.* This potential insight greatly alarmed MacAfee, who woke up his wife Marge to tell her about it. "He probably didn't have the slightest clue as to what his move meant in cosmic terms, or that in doing so he fulfilled the ancient prophecy of Daniel Chapter Seven", he had told Marge.

"Oh, I wouldn't be too sure about that," she had replied. "If he's really the antichrist—and I think you're on to something there—he's probably had a number of conference calls with his boss, the devil himself.

"What are we going to do now, Marge?" he said.

"Not a whole lot we can do. They know that we're Christians. There's no way they'd let us outside."

MacAfee had begun to suffer the onset of a serious bout of claustrophobia. Sensing his growing discomfort, Marge had reached in the bedstand drawer and grabbed her prescription anxiety-relief pills. "Here, take these," she had said, thrusting three into his hand, "and don't argue about it. As for what we can do, well, we can stand fast as Christians. God will do the rest."

The United Nations remained a useful tool for the ten-region government. With the godlike authority vested in him, POTNAR now enjoyed the virtually unlimited use of United Nations troops, which he intended to deploy shortly in rounding up the topside survivors and herding them back into the cities. But the infrastructure basics first had to be restored, a task for which he planned to deploy the North American Army for supervision purposes.

The meeting with POTEUR went well. Every one of the apparent slipups, miscalculations and scandals during his administration of the United States while it was still an independent country was actually a well-planned event that had served to consolidate his power. Now, because of the well-hidden efficiency of his administration, the North American Region was among the strongest of the ten that comprised the new government. This meant that while ultimate control still remained within the unthinkably wealthy world leadership, he may well be slated to join that inner circle. Perhaps, if the fawning, obsequious behavior of his European counterpart in the face-to-face holographic meeting was any indication, he would assume overt headship of the entire governmental apparatus.

He began planning for the next step: restore the American infrastructure. He called another meeting, this time with his shakers and movers, who had maintained a fear-driven loyalty to him throughout his tenure. Among his greatest achievements, through them, of course, but actually through the cleverness of his own brilliantly imaginative mind, was the transformation of the army from the characteristically noble and independent nature of its members to a shallow, brutal and self-indulgent band of cutthroat pirates. This radical change had been facilitated largely through the removal of the Judeo-Christian influence within the ranks of military personnel, inspired by his spiritual mentor Adolph Hitler, who had been faced with the same problem. An avid student of military and political history, POTNAR recalled Hitler's lament that the German people had the misfortune to have the wrong religion. Why, he had questioned, didn't Germany have the religion of the Japanese, who regarded sacrifice for the Fatherland as the highest good? Or of the Mohammedan religion, which would have been much more compatible to his objectives than Christianity, with is meekness and flabbiness. *Well, sir, that's just what I think,* POTNAR observed. *Only I have one-upped you. We now have the Mohammedan religion as our mainstay.* He didn't formalize the additional thought that this religion, too, was just a temporary stopgap. Ultimately, of course, he himself would be the focus of their final religion. The notion of being the worldwide majestic overlord of a subdued and manipulated populace remained somewhat nebulous in his mind, but, nevertheless, it was there in sufficient clarity as to evoke a gratifying anticipation.

CHAPTER TWENTY ONE

The sudden brilliance outside startled Millie, causing her to drop a dish onto the floor. "We have electricity!" she cried, looking out at the streetlamp to be sure she wasn't dreaming. Jimmy turned off the generator and rushed outside to re-connect the large electrical umbilical cable to city electricity. Sure enough, the inside of the RV began to light up like a Christmas tree as Millie rushed around turning on various lamps. They enjoyed this newly-found comfort as if it actually was Christmas, but after they started to become used to it, a troubling notion came into Earl's head.

"I wonder what this means," he voiced aloud. "Is the government going to come back?"

"In force, you mean," supplied Ron, who was sitting on a hard-backed folding chair.

"Yeh."

"Well, maybe I'm thinking that we need to break out the ammo and saddle up."

"Probably not a good idea, Ron. I've already told you how I feel about that. I've been hoping that you'd get the message too that this particular battle's much more spiritual than physical. Besides, if they do come back, most likely it will be with overwhelming force. I've been bothered by the possibility for some time now. The government seemed to be capitulating to nature way too easily. That doesn't fit in with our leader's personality, coward though he might be. Now if the government is manning up for a huge assault, and you really do want to fight on their terms, it would take the Hand of God to make your effort meaningful. I know that God has been in the thick of the battle in the past for Moses, and Joshua, and Gideon, and, more recently, with the modern Israelis in their several battles against their Arab neighbors. But, I'm sorry to say, I don't have any indication from God that such is the case with this one. In fact, I do have indications that the opposite is true, that the battle this time is spiritual. If we pursue a physical battle our world will also be lost like when the Jews rebelled against Rome and were defeated by Titus, who destroyed their world in 70 A.D."

"If not that, what do you suggest?"

"I've already told you. Bring yourself and your troops closer to God, and fight the battle in the spiritual realm. That will require just as much courage to execute, and will probably leave you just as dead in the end. But if you die serving God, a whole new world awaits you. God help me if I'm wrong," he said in a small voice. "I'm going to have to pray that I've been giving you the right advice."

Wisdom returned that night, answer ready. "You have it right, you know," She began. "The government is coming back, and on a scale that you're no match for. Violence isn't your gig, anyway. Remember what Paul said in Ephesians six—the battle ahead's not physical, but spiritual. This is exactly what you've been preparing your people for. Now take your words to heart and buck up, because very soon now you'll be surrounded by events that will test your faith like never before. The good news is that you'll have some time to prepare, both mentally and spiritually. You've—well, We've—chosen your place well. It's such an insignificant backwater that nobody's going to come looking for you for the next month or two.

Eventually, though, they'll come for you, too. Remember what we told Polycarp when he was arrested and threatened with execution?"

"I—I think so," Earl responded. "Didn't You tell him to play the man?"

"Essentially, yes. You escaped from your death camp, but only because your work here wasn't finished. But, I'm happy to tell you, your prison mate Jacob has succeeded in reaching Israel, and he's doing Our work just as you'd hoped he would. You and Joyce have played your parts in the way We'd hoped you would. As a bonus, you've also brought a number of people to Us from here. Already a terrible slaughter has just taken place here in America. You missed the agony of that particular event, but you knew that time would come when you, too, would have to stand up and be counted. You asked for that, as a matter of fact. You didn't want to be left out of that wonderful Hall of Faith noted in Hebrews eleven. I know that you still feel that way. It might be unpleasant in the actual event, but that is for such a tiny period of time that it's insignificant. You—and Joyce too—have a wonderful future in heaven to look forward to. And I'll be with you two all the way till you get there."

"Thanks."

"And thank you, My beloved Earl. Give my heartfelt love to your darling wife." She was gone.

CHAPTER TWENTY TWO

When Jacob left her, Moira felt an instant pang of loneliness, as if half of her own body had just departed. But then the doctor and his assistant started poking around her damaged leg and her day suddenly got busier as they peered, pried, attached several umbilical hookups and used them to monitor her condition. Presently a nurse administered an anesthesia and her mind went blank.

Before she awoke from the anesthesia, Moira had another visitor. "Hi, honey," Wisdom greeted her. "Looks like things are heating up around here."

"Well, for me they are," Moira responded to the gentle beauty of the face before her. "How bad is my wound?"

"Not so terrible. Not bad enough to put you on light duty for very long," She said with a laugh. "You'll have a problem at the range with the squats for the next few weeks or so, which won't exactly endear Jesse to you, but you'll get over it. The assault on your kibbutz was a random splash out of the kettle that's starting to boil over. But since the fire's getting bigger, the kettle's just getting hotter, so the splashes will get bigger and fiercer. I thought I'd give you a heads-up on the bigger picture, so you'll know something about how you fit in. Russia has finished assembling a coalition of countries, mostly Muslim, to come against Israel. They just can't resist dominating the world in the oil market, and Israel's new oil and gas find in the Mediterranean is a tempting plum. As you know, the details of this upcoming battle are in the Book of Ezekiel. Go back and re-read Chapters 38 and 39 when you get a chance."

"Won't America stop them?"

Wisdom laughed. "You must have been too busy to be reading the news. Actually, America no longer exists as such."

"Say what?" Moira broke in, startled by this turn of events. "What happened?"

"You know from the Book of Revelation," Wisdom told her, "that in the last days of the government of man on earth, world governance would be set up. That's in the process of coming together now. Already in the Western Hemisphere, America, along with Canada and Mexico, have been integrated into a single entity called the North American Region. The world government consists of ten such regions. Actually, this structure has been in the works for a very long time. With the help of Our opposer, a number of evil dictators have come and gone in the attempt to bring it to pass earlier. Its most modern manifestation has been discussed in secret meetings of the world's most powerful people from the beginning of the twentieth century. American presidents from Bush Senior all the way to their last one have very actively supported it behind the scenes. So the State Department of the United States is now the North American State Department and, no, this North American State Department and its European counterparts are still seeking a negotiated solution to the brewing conflict over the fate of Israel. They're doing nothing of substance but simply talking, being too cowardly really to be sticking their necks out. Ezekiel alluded to that, too. While Russia is looking for domination, their Arab friends simply want to do what they've wanted all along—wipe out the nation of Israel and toss her inhabitants into the Med."

"According to Ezekiel, You're not going to let that happen."

"Not on a bet. Russia will go slinking back northward in defeat, the majority of her troops wiped out."

"I'd guess atomic warfare."

"Only partly," She said with a grin, Her white teeth gleaming in the dim light. "Mankind is so proud of its high-tech weaponry that We'll let it think for a short time that's all there is. And, to be sure, it is bad enough. At the macro level, Moira, humans have about as much maturity as those occupying a second-grade playground." Her laughter scoffed at the thought. "But We thought we'd like to take these arrogant people down a peg or two, so We've cooked up some fireworks that will make your nuclear weapons look like childrens' toys.

"What could be worse than a nuclear bomb—or several of them?"

"Oh, you'll see," She said enigmatically. "Perhaps We'll have an earthquake for starters, one like the world has never seen before. Or, how about a disease so swift and deadly it would be like a rain of poison on an anthill?"

"You'd actually do that?"

"It isn't like the world hasn't been warned. We moved Ezekiel and many other prophets to write about just that, but Ezekiel is the most important in that regard because if anyone would bother to read his book, they'd instantly see that it's all coming together exactly like he predicted, including the terrible slaughter of those who come against Israel. As for whether the devastation will be by earthquake or disease or by something else altogether, I don't want to spoil your show. You'll be witnessing the actual event soon enough. But I will tell you this: despite all their talk about going green, the world leaders are doing so much to desolate this lovely planet that We created that We simply have to put a stop to it before it goes much further. As you know, radiation poisoning is the worst. If the current leaders were allowed to continue acting like selfish little children, the nuclear warfare they would unleash, if allowed to run to its evil conclusion, would succeed in making the entire planet uninhabitable for anyone."

"I'm so very glad that You're in control, Wisdom. I'm relieved to hear that You'll be setting limits on atomic warfare. Still, if I'm going to be watching a show, it sounds scary. Other than the nukes, I can't imagine anything worse than an earthquake or disease."

"Oh, We can," She said, laughing. "How about an asteroid strike? That'll get everyone's attention. But that's all I'll say to you about it. Sleep well, My darling." She left and Moira sank back into a deep sleep.

Jacob visited her every day when he could take a break from his work. He daily grew more impatient for her to recover enough to leave the infirmary. After another week he was overjoyed to see her in their room and they clung to each other in a fierce embrace that suggested they'd been apart for much longer than the comfort range of their minds and bodies. On her own Moira returned to the firing range for a resumption of their training. As Wisdom had forewarned her, the squat position was brutal, but she insisted on working through the pain. Within a month she had recovered sufficiently to resume her regular kitchen and guard duties. Having been seasoned in combat, she carried her rifle with a new authority, and her eyes reflected an alert confidence.

During the month of Moira's recovery the commune noted an increase in movement in the surrounding area. The noise of tanks and other heavy military vehicles increased. But then the day came that the noise diminished to the point that activity seemed to have stopped and an ominous silence prevailed over the Golan Heights. After several days of like inactivity, they discussed what this might mean. Jesse reluctantly stood up in the midst of those gathered in the big room. "I didn't want to have to give you the bad news," he said, "but I think I understand what's going on. The armored force nearest us probably are digging in and waiting for the MREs and reinforcements to arrive."

"What's an MRE?" asked one young girl.

"MRE—Meal Ready to Eat. What I meant was that the combat vehicles and the troops manning them probably are waiting for their supply train to catch up, and, knowing our adversaries from past wars fought with them, also waiting until they've stacked the odds in their favor so overwhelmingly that they can't possibly lose, barring a miracle on our behalf. The real implication of what I'm trying to say is that this hunkering-in process isn't real encouraging. We can expect to see a very big army heading our way, particularly since this may well be the beginning of the war that's spelled out in Ezekiel chapters 38 and 39."

That evening when Jacob and Moira returned to their room, she closed the door and turned to him. "Speaking of which, you might want to pick up your Bible and re-read those chapters."

"Speaking of what?" he asked, bewildered. "What are you talking about?"

"Ezekiel 38 and 39. What Jesse was saying. In the context of the experience that's surrounding us, it makes for very interesting reading. Captivating, actually."

"Gee, Moira, I kind of had other plans."

"Well, now you have two things to take care of," she said, laughing. "I'm serious, Jacob. It's important."

"Oh, I get it. You had a visitor not too long ago."

"Yep. Jesse reminded me of what She'd said. I wanted to tell you about it at the time, but events seemed to intervene whenever the opportunity came up. I eventually forgot about it. Sorry. She told me to tell you 'Hi', by the way."

CHAPTER TWENTY THREE

The leaders of the numerous Muslim-dominated nations were assembled together in a meeting of unprecedented size. Despite the commonality of their religion, their immediate objective and their emotional volatility, it was precisely the latter characteristic that had maintained their separation to this point. Now the magnitude of the cause before them and its promise of the ultimate fulfillment of their most cherished dream had subdued their natural antagonism toward each other, even to the extent of creating a short-lived bonhomie among them.

But as the conference unfolded into detailed planning, it was this same characteristic of angry, hair-trigger tempers that rather quickly erupted into an ill-tempered squabbling which threatened to put an abrupt end to this particular meeting despite their common objective, which was to create the condition wherein they might observe with delight the end of the Jews as a nation and a people.

"No! No no, NO!" shouted the head of the Pakistani government, stamping his sandaled feet in anger. "I will not permit the merger of my army and my weaponry with other armies. I will embrace my brothers-in-arms in our holy war against Israel, but I insist that my army will remain mine and mine alone."

"But you do not understand, my brother," said the Yemeni leader. "We must operate as a cohesive unit if we expect to defeat the little Satan, Israel."

Enraged by the condescension of this pompous pipsqueak from the insignificant realm of Yemen, the Pakistani reached over and tugged quite hard at his well-groomed goatee, eliciting a howl of pain and a fist in the eye.

"Gentlemen, Gentlemen!" the Iranian leader shouted, clapping his hands in disapproval. "Stop this immediately!" He signaled to his bailiffs, who rushed toward the grappling men and forced them apart. It was a scene that was repeated numerous times over the three days occupied with discussions of plans to remove Israel from the face of the earth. The meeting was scheduled to last for a week, but the mutual distrust and anger among the participants was more than the Iranian leader could endure. Declaring a consensus on his tactical viewpoint at the threat of nuclear retaliation upon any dissenting nation, he outlined his plan, the timetable for its execution, and the joint order of battle. Having accomplished that, he dismissed the congregants, declared all hotels and accommodations closed, and left the assembly. That done, he telephoned the Russian leader with the news of his actions. He considered the man to be his subordinate in all things, particularly with respect to religious matters. But never to his face. And deep down, although he refused to openly acknowledge the fact even to himself, the Iranian understood the Russian to be the most powerful man in the world.

The strange, pervasive inability of brother Muslims to get along with each other had exposed the modern world to their self-willed pride and focus on hatred at the expense of love many times over, as exemplified by the Iran-Iraq conflict and the Arab treatment of the Palestinians, using their suffering as a political tool against the nation of Israel. Their behavior actually was the fulfillment of an ancient prophecy recorded by Moses almost at the beginning of Scripture, in Genesis 16:

Now Sarai, Abram's wife, bore him no children: and she had an handmaid, an Egyptian, whose name was Hagar. And Sarai said unto Abram, Behold now, the Lord hath restrained me from bearing: I pray thee, go in unto my maid; it may be that I may obtain children by her. And Abram hearkened to the voice of Sarai. And Sarai, Abram's wife, took Hagar, her maid, the Egyptian, after Abram had dwelt ten years in the land of Canaan, and gave her to her husband, Abram, to be his wife. And he went in unto Hagar, and she conceived: and when she saw that she had conceived, her mistress was despised in her eyes. And Sarai said unto Abram, The wrong done me be upon thee: I have given my maid into thy bosom; when she saw that she had conceived, I was despised in her eyes: the Lord judge between me and thee. But Abram said unto Sarai, Behold, thy maid is in thy hand; do to her what pleaseth thee. And when Sarai dealt hardly with her, she fled from her face.

And the angel of the Lord found her by a fountain of water in the wilderness, by the fountain in the way to Shur. And he said, Hagar, Sarai's maid, from where camest thou? And where wilt thou go? And she said, I flee from the face of my mistress, Sarai. And the angel of the Lord said unto her, Return to thy mistress, and submit thyself under her hands. And the angel of the Lord said unto her, I will multiply thy seed exceedingly, that it shall not be numbered for multitude. And the angel of the Lord said unto her, Behold, thou art with child, and shall bear a son, and shalt call his name Ishmael; because the Lord hath heard thy affliction.

And he will be a wild man; his hand will be against every man, and every man's hand against him; and he shall dwell in the presence of his brethren."

The only thing that had kept the world at large from calling out the most self-serving offenders was the hatred of these fanatics toward non-Muslims, which surpassed the vehemence of their discontent with each other. The consequent intimidation with the threat of violence against any individual, group or nation that spoke out about this situation was sufficient to silence their weak-kneed and fearful potential adversaries.

The Russian leader sighed to himself upon hearing from the Iranian about the necessity for his unilateral action at the conference, lamenting the childish hostility that interfered so irritatingly often with their own objective of causing the final destruction of the Jewish nation. How could one teach those idiots the wonderfully evil principles of Machiavelli when they couldn't pay attention long enough to grasp the basics? *On the other hand,* he mused, *perhaps it is far better that I, alone, understand Machiavelli's principles.*

The Russian leader had read the medieval Florentine's *The Prince* years ago in college, and had been a disciple of his ever since. He recalled the essence of how one particular passage of this deliciously dark manual on how one might obtain power over others at their own expense might be most appropriate to this present situation. Arising from his spartan chair, he went over to the far wall, which held his favorite books. After a short search he extracted a short tome bound in a black cover, and returned to his chair, where he opened the book to where his favorite passage was exposed:

> A prince should therefore disregard the reproach of being thought cruel where it enables him to keep his subjects united and obedient. For he who quells disorder by a very few signal examples will in the end be more merciful than he who from too great leniency permits things to take their course and so to result in rapine and bloodshed; for these hurt the whole State, whereas the severities of the Prince injure individuals only.

> And for a new Prince, of all others, it is impossible to escape a name for cruelty, since new States are full of dangers.

How true, the Russian said to himself, grinning at the black wisdom of the passage and the spectacular results he himself had achieved in applying it. *Am I not the king of Russia?* he gloated.

But now he had unfinished business that required some planning with the assistance of Mr. Machiavelli. He turned to the appropriate page and began reading:

> In short, with mercenaries your greatest danger is from their inertness and cowardice, with auxiliaries from their valour. Wise Princes, therefore, have always eschewed these arms, and trusted rather to their own, and have preferred defeat with the latter to victory with the former, counting that as no true victory which is gained by foreign aid.

> I shall never hesitate to cite the example of Cesare Borgia and his actions. He entered Romagna with a force of auxiliaries, all of them French men-at-arms, which whom he took Imola and Forli. But it appearing to him afterwards that these troops were not to be trusted, he had recourse to mercenaries from whom he thought there would be less danger, and took the Orsini and Vitelli into his pay. But finding these likewise while under his command to be fickle, false, and treacherous, he got rid of them, and fell back on troops of his own raising. And we may readily discern the difference between these various kinds of arms, by observing the different degrees of reputation in which the Duke stood while he depended on the French alone, when he took the Orsini and Vitelli into pay, and when he fell back on his own troops and his own resources; for we find his reputation always increasing, and that he was never so well thought of as when every one perceived him to be sole master of his own forces.

> I am unwilling to leave these examples, drawn from what has taken place in Italy and in recent

times; and yet I must not omit to notice the case of Hiero of Syracuse, who is one of those whom I have already named, He, as I have before related, being made captain of their armies by the Syracusans, saw at once that a force of mercenary soldiers, supplied by men resembling our Italian *condottieri*, was not serviceable; and as he would not retain and could not disarm them, he caused them all to be cut to pieces, and afterwards made war with native soldiers only, without other aid.

I must ensure, the Russian leader mused, closing the book and placing it on his desk, *that the Iranians, being the most noble of that ignoble lot, stay in the forefront of the battle to win some early victories but die in the process. They can be followed by the other non-Russian arms, so that they all can be decimated by the Israelis and become too weak to challenge my own ultimate leadership. Then, when they also have been cut to ribbons, I will bring my own troops into the fray for the ultimate victory over that pathetic little nation, Israel.*

The Russian, having formulated the process by which he would emerge from the clash with Israel in a position of unprecedented strength, stood and, walking back over to the bookcase, reinserted the tome back into its correct slot. But then a disturbing notion came into his mind, the thought that despite this upcoming victory, and despite the cowardly manner in which the Western powers would back off from any open confrontation with the attackers, the North American leader was still a formidable rival. Worse, judging by the actions he had taken from the beginning of his debut as American president, he also must be a disciple of the dark Florentine. This could not be allowed to persist. Jumping ahead of the imminent conflict with Israel, he began to plan the destruction of the Great Satan, which, as the North American nations merged into a yet larger entity, had become too large to continue to exist.

Eventually it was the Russian leader who traveled from country to country within the Mideast bloc of nations, personally mending the antagonism of each ruler toward the others and bringing them to an understanding that without at least a temporary unity, they could never hope to accomplish their common objective. That done, and with admirable swiftness, the Russian brought each of those nations into the grand order of battle, with a sufficient number of very minor changes as to convince them that the battle plans were his own rather than those of the heavy-handed Iranian. By this device he won their loyalty, if only temporary, so that when the battle began, he, rather than the Iranian, would be their actual commander.

The final visit of his goodwill campaign was to the Iranian. In addition to his insistent praise of the Iranian for his magnificent battle plans, he pressed on with other flatteries and culminated his visit with the promise of first entry into Jerusalem and unopposed access to the spoils therein. Then he turned firm and, with glaring eyes, demanded the Iranian's unreserved allegiance to him as chief commander. Filled with fear at the unexpected vehemence of this turnaround of disposition, the Iranian leader immediately acquiesced. Satisfied, the Russian departed for home to put the finishing touches on the plans for the impending battle.

Chapter Twenty Four

They came at night, stealthy. Earlier that evening Earl heard the sound of several helicopters. They seemed to come near enough to touch. He thought he heard them descend and idle for a while. Then the noise increased briefly and waned into the distance. After a prolonged silence he put his mind off its alert and joined the conversation the other three were having with Ron and two of his men about the prophetic Word of God and its extreme relevance to the situation they were now in. Ron and Carl seemed to accept this information, but Jack blew them off, rising up and heading for the door. "Hold on," Ron said. "I've got a bad feeling about those choppers. Gives me the willies, truth be told. If you're going out, have some protection at least." He extracted a knife from his pocket and handed it to Jack, who took it with a brief nod and exited the motor home.

He got a few hundred feet away when he saw the first trooper emerge from between two buildings. He was clothed in black and wearing SWAT gear. Spotting Jack, he raised his rifle. Jack stopped abruptly, noting with terror the red dot of the trooper's laser sight dance around his chest. The black-clad soldier spoke first. "Hey, buddy," he called. "You with the group? Or are you a Christian?"

Before Jack could answer, he saw an unruly throng of civilians heading his way. They were armed with clubs and knives, and they looked ready to kill. As they approached, they appeared to accept the presence of the armed trooper. The situation was suddenly clear. "Hey, it's all right, man," Jack told the soldier. I'm with them." He walked toward the mob with a smile plastered on his face. The soldier acknowledged his action and went over to the apparent leader. Jack overheard them discussing the most likely target for holdouts in the immediate area.

"Hey, I can help," Jack told the leader, moving alongside them. "See that trailer park over there?" he asked, pointing toward the RV park where Earl and Joyce resided along with their fellow believers. "Place is full of Christians. Every one in there is one of them." He spat in disgust. "Let's drag 'em out and give 'em what for."

The leader nodded his assent, his bulbous eyes displaying a lust for blood. He turned around toward his followers, motioning for them to be quiet. "Let's make this a real surprise, people," he told the crowd. Surround them first and then give them a taste of shock and awe. The trooper took charge and led the silent crowd slowly past the entrance to the RV park and, with hand motions, dispersed the crowd among the trailers in a cordon from which the dwellers could not possibly escape.

Eventually Ron and Carl left and the two couples turned in, unaware that the two men had gotten no further than two steps away from the door before their throats were slit and they were left on the ground to bleed out in silence. Jack wiped his knife on his pants, smiling at the men who surrounded him, reassuring himself that by his quick action there were no doubts among the others about which side he was on. Earl and Joyce, along with the two others, were asleep when a propane tank was hurled into the windshield to land hissing on the floor inside the motor home. Earl awoke with a start, sensing imminent danger. He rushed over to where the tank lay and tossed it back out the broken windshield just before a flaming jar of gasoline came out of the dark toward him. The jar collided with the propane tank and set it aflame as it went rolling back toward the crowd of thugs. This angered the mob into more direct action. One man rushed over to the door and shot out the lock with the massive .44 revolver in his hand. He rushed inside and grabbed Earl by the neck as Joyce, screaming, reached for his hair. The man backhanded her and sent her to the floor as he yanked Earl outside. In an absurd mockery of justice, he threw Earl to the pavement and, with his foot on his neck, began to interrogate him.

"Hey, dude, tell me straight. You a Christian?"

Earl gagged, attempting to speak. "Yes," he croaked when the man partially released him. "I am a Christian."

"You hear that?" the thug said to the mob behind him. "Says he's a Christian. What do we do with Christians?"

"Stomp them!" the crowd shouted in unison. The man responded by stepping down hard on Earl's neck. Joyce flew out of the trailer as if she was running on natural legs and shoved at the man, who simply smacked her on the nose and cut her down with a vicious chop on her neck. He returned his attention to Earl and smashed down on his neck with his foot, crushing his windpipe. As Earl struggled to breathe, he was forced to watch as the man, seeing the prosthetics on Joyce's legs, removed them and made her stand on her stumps. "You, too, darlin'," the man said to her. "You a Christian?"

She stood up as straight as she could, head held high and blood running out of her broken nose. She looked at her dying husband with compassion. "Yes, I am a Christian," she said, steeling herself for the inevitable blows upon her head from her right prosthetic leg. She saw Jack in the crowd, his eyes gleaming with fascination. Her surprise was cut short by a vicious blow on her head from behind. Milliseconds later, a boot connected with Earl's bloody head. The attackers lost interest in the inert forms and left them on the ground, moving on to more lively prey whose sufferings would be more visible.

Wisdom looked on, weeping at the carnage and the fallen condition of the human race that caused it. After Her lament was complete, Her mouth turned upward in a smile as She called for an angel, who came over to escort the souls within the mounting pile of bodies to a new and beautiful future. As the angel approached Earl and Joyce, She waved him off. *No,* She reflected within. *Those two are My special ones. I'll handle them Myself.* She stared down at the inert forms of Earl and Joyce, speculating. *But as to how I'll handle them,* She continued to reflect, *they really don't need to be healed. They do deserve to head up to heaven where they belong. No question. But yet—.*

CHAPTER TWENTY FIVE

Within four more days, Jesse's dire prediction was visibly, appallingly fulfilled. It was signaled by two simultaneously-appearing dust clouds, one from the distant northeast and the other from the east of where they watched in growing fear. The vast distances gave the scene an unreal, toylike appearance. The incongruity of that with what they knew to be the real situation only increased their unease.

"I'll never laugh again about Gideon's thing with the fleece," Jacob said to Moira, referring to Gideon's response to the angel about leading the people into battle against the Midianites.

"Tell me about that," Moira said, as much to get her mind off her growing terror as her interest in the story. "I'm sure that I've read about it sometime because I vaguely remember the battle and the outcome but I can't recall much about the details."

"It's in the sixth chapter of Judges. The Midianites had occupied the land of Israel with a huge, overwhelming force and they were bullying, mistreating and starving the Israelites. An angel shows up under a tree and hails Gideon, a fearful nobody, as a mighty man of valor and tells him that he'll lead the Israelites into battle against their enemy and kick them out of the land. After some preliminaries, the time comes for Gideon to gird up his loins and do the Lord's bidding. But then he stalls off and attempts to negotiate with God to make certain that the God who is calling him to action is actually God. So he bargains with a tuft of wool, a fleece. This is where I used to laugh, considering Gideon to have been displaying a shocking lack of faith. Now that we seem to be in his shoes, I'm kind of backing off from that attitude."

"Didn't he ask God to keep the wool wet with dew and the floor on which it lay stay dry?"

"The first time. But that wasn't enough. The next night he asked God to do the opposite: keep the wool dry and make the floor wet. After that, Gideon believed enough to assemble an army of thirty-two thousand men. But that was too many for God, who wanted to demonstrate to the Israelites that their salvation from the Midianites would come from Him alone. God told Gideon to release from duty all those who were afraid, of which twenty-two thousand left. Then of the remaining ten thousand, God told Gideon to separate them further by the way they drank from the brook. That really took its toll, for there were only three hundred men left to fight. With those three hundred, God routed the Midianites, who fled the country. What really happened is that God surrounded the Midianites with an army of angels. The same thing happened with Elisha. It's in Second Kings chapter 6."

"Let's just hope there's a prophetic message in that," Moira said with feeling. "We could use a few of those angels about now."

"There is. If this is the war I think it is, the outcome's in Ezekiel 39. Only a sixth part of the Russians survive, and they high-tail it back north. It takes Israel seven years to clean up the mess they leave behind. I have the feeling that my knowledge of the feedings, what I received from Earl back in the States, is only a small part of the events that bring Israel to a recognition of Jesus as their Savior. This war, I think, will force us as a people to appreciate God's hand in our affairs and bring God back into our lives as an everyday reality."

"That's extremely encouraging, Jacob. Whether or not we make it out of this alive, it's good to know that God is with us. But now that it's actually happening, I can identify with Gideon. Intimately."

They couldn't sleep that night. The darkness emphasized the noise of monster engines of war, the boom of distant guns and the crack of closer impacts. The ground shook periodically, increasing their alienation from stability. They wished for morning, but with the first pre-dawn light they began to wish for night to return as the view before them came into focus.

The twin clouds increased as off to the southeast a third cloud appeared. Over the course of the day the scene changed in apparent slow motion as the clouds increased in size and came ever closer to them. Off to their left, toward Haifa and the Mediterranean, they heard the booms of distant guns, but their view in that direction was blocked by the intervening terrain.

"Sounds like it's coming from Jezreel," Jacob said to Moira, referring to the large Jezreel valley extending southeastward from Haifa. Their limited vision in that direction was a mercy, he reckoned. Indeed it was, for surrounding the port city but hidden from their view the sea was black with the largest assembly of war ships since the allied landing at Normandy during the Second World War. While destroyers and cruisers shelled and hammered with missiles the city and surrounding enclaves of suspected Israeli soldiers, the nearer ships began a massive debarkation of troops, opening another front in the war. Farther south, an enormous movement of armor emerged out of the Sinai desert, headed for Tel Aviv and opening yet another front. The combined assault was overwhelming in size and firepower. For the first time in the battle, tactical nukes were deployed.

The inexorable movement of the armament in their direction failed to show the terrified Israeli observers the end of the massive columns. Partially obscured at times by the dust of its movement, the ponderous multi-limbed machine's forward progress simply permitted more troops and arms to march into view. Jacob and Moira ventured periodically to peek out from the sheltering rocks at the landscape below. Whenever they did this the scene evoked the same heart-stopping helplessness as a monster tidal wave coming to engulf them.

An unidentifiable hum had pervaded the air, an angry buzzing which increased in intensity as the day wore on and the armies drew closer. Eventually individual noises could be discerned out of the general clamor, that of creaking tank treads and loud, unmuffled engines. Flashes could now be seen from the nearest guns, followed by explosive impacts nearer at hand. The deep booms of the guns competed with ear-splitting cracks of explosive ordnance impacting the ground. The earth beneath them shook and trembled.

Then the warplanes came out of the horizon, swift arrows of destruction that went from black dots to enormous monsters in the blink of an eye. Other planes, Israeli fighters, shot from the left to merge with them in a frenzied battle. Some of the enemy came through and screamed overhead. Gouts of blazing napalm pocked nearby rock formations. Moira turned her head to follow their progress. "Oh, no!" she wailed. Jacob followed her eyes to see a giant fireball emerge from their kibbutz.

We're toast, Jacob breathed, holding protectively to Moira. A platoon of tanks emerged from a nearby crest to command the foreground. A turret swung in their direction.

No, a silent but familiar voice said inside his head. *Watch this.* Jacob looked around but saw nothing to shake his feeling of imminent doom. *Look up,* the voice said. He responded by lifting his eyes to the sky, and was startled to see a pinpoint of light expand rapidly until it was too brilliant to watch. An instant later a white light revealed the bones in his hands as they covered his eyes. The ground beneath them gave a mighty heave, knocking them to the earth. Jacob reached out toward Moira and resumed his hold on her body as they lay there dazed. For a brief moment an ominous silence prevailed, and then a deep moan reached their ears. It rose in pitch and volume and gathered the strength to scrape sand off the ground, then pebbles, and after that rocks. Their clothes began to flap violently and they crawled back into the cave behind them for protection against the increasing wind. The wind rose to an eerie screech that remained for several minutes and then began to diminish.

After several more minutes, Jacob ventured a peek outside the cave, seeing an enormous mushroom cloud that emerged from the valley below off to the northeast of their position in the direction of Damascus. Beyond the vertical cloud, dark, low-hanging clouds enveloped the troops in the valley and in the surrounding areas. A sympathetic earthquake shook the ground and they ran out of the cave into the open, where they saw the apron of level ground split open and swallow the tanks that had stood there.

Jacob's gaze returned to the mushroom cloud. *It is Damascus!* he said to himself. "Moira, look! That's Damascus that just went up! The world's oldest city, and now it's no more."

"That's unbelievable," she breathed. "I've read Ezekiel. He didn't say anything about that."

"No, but Isaiah did. It's in Isaiah seventeen. He said something like there'd be trouble in the evening, and before the morning, it's gone."

"Was that an atomic bomb that went off?" Moira asked him.

"No, I don't think so. The way it came down from the sky, I think it might have been an asteroid. No, I'm sure that's what it was, because it came directly from God."

"How do you know that?" Moira began, but then stopped short. "Oh. You had a conversation about it, did you?"

"Yeah," he said, laughing. "Just a short word or two, but yes. Knowing that, maybe we should stop being afraid and just watch the show."

"Do what you want," she replied, sitting down and resting her back against a boulder. "I'm going to hit the sack. Wake me when it's over." She was asleep within seconds. Jacob decided to join her. Whatever happened next, they both were content in the knowledge that they were in good Hands.

THE END...

...Except for this preview of *Home, Sweet Heaven* which is the exciting next novel in the *Buddy* series by Arthur Perkins

"Earl!" She cried, running toward him as they met in the grass. He looked entirely different, but yet she knew him as the same man that she loved so intensely. She flung her arms around him and clung to his neck, weeping with joy.

Wisdom stood behind them, observing their tear-filled reunion, which was complete now in a way that would have been impossible in the material domain. She watched as the couple reunited with Cathy and the special angel with whom Joyce had been communing. Wisdom thrilled to the anticipation of that union growing to extend to many others, and of the intimacy among them becoming a vital organic component of the spiritual Church.

A wedding was about to take place, Wisdom reflected, one that had been anticipated for ages past and which would give Her the Church as Her daughter-in-law. It would be in this grand event that the composite spiritual entity within which Earl, Joyce and Cathy would play a major role would, as a Woman of such radiant beauty as to rival Her own, come joyfully to unite with Her divine Spouse, Jesus Christ.

Wisdom's own spouse, the beloved Father, extended Himself to enter more fully into Her domain. "Hello, my darling," Wisdom whispered without words to Her cherished Partner, Her focus becoming fixed upon Him.

"And to You, My beloved Other," He returned, His love permeating Her soul. "But I am saving the pleasure of Your company for later, with much anticipation." He withdrew from the union. "Sadly, I have a request to make of You, one that won't be a happy one. But it is most necessary, and the end of it will be most wonderful, better than it would have been without the intrusion of sorrow and pain." He continued with the request, communicating the essence of it, along with His sorrow, to His divine Partner. Reluctantly, she agreed to perform a task of obvious distaste. "Yes, Boss," She replied to Her Spouse, Her gorgeous face thrust outward and Her lips pursed in a confrontational pout.

"No need for the attitude," Her Divine Spouse remarked, but His face bore a wide grin.

"Your will be done, My Lord," She acquiesced to Her Divine Lover. "But when they return, they'd better have something pretty special waiting for them, or Our own reunion after the event won't be anything to write home about."

The Father broke out into a hearty laugh. "Of course!" he affirmed. "Just please allow me to entertain the illusion that I'm running things around here."

The light-hearted exchange had softened their communication, but when Wisdom turned away to her new task She bore a heavy heart.

Wisdom had been preparing to witness Earl and Joyce commune with others of their spiritual Body. She had been anticipating with gladness their reunion with their former physical spouses, Alicia for Earl and Sam for Joyce. The four of them would have formed an initial nucleus, along with Buddy and Cathy, whose love would extend outward from there to embrace the entire feminine being of the spiritual Church. Now a frown darkened Her face as she prepared to respond to Her Spouse's request.

The frown deepened as Wisdom approached Earl and Joyce, evoking more tears from Her eyes. "I'm so very sorry," She whispered to them, "but your time has not yet come to stay. You must go back."

"What?" Earl responded in alarm "Why? Haven't we suffered enough?"

"You have indeed, and more,"Wisdom replied. "But you are needed back on earth. You will come back here, and when you do, it will be to a loving welcome of epic proportions. Come, let Me take your hands and guide you back."

ACKNOWLEDGEMENTS

I wish to extend a grateful, heartfelt thank-you to the following people who have been instrumental in the production of my books. First, to my God, whose loving character elicits my devotion and the thrill of learning and writing of His beautiful nature. Second, to my wonderful wife Carolyn, whose loving support in all matters of our happy marriage have given me added incentive and the freedom to pursue my writing endeavors. Third, to my brother Jon, whose support has been extremely helpful. Fourth, to my friend and publisher, John McClure of Signalman Publishing, for his enthusiasm and professionalism. I'm truly fortunate to be associated with him. I also wish to thank my pastor, F. David Lambert, ThD. While we don't always agree on every theological matter, we do agree on much, particularly on the divine inspiration and inerrancy of Scripture. I have learned much about God and the Church through his very thorough exposition of Scripture and Church doctrine.

Art Perkins
Eatonville, Washington

We hope you enjoyed reading *Jacob: Encounters with the Holy Spirit*
by Arthur Perkins.
For further reading including novels and non-fiction titles by
this author and others, please go to our online catalog at
http://www.signalmanpublishing.com

www.ingramcontent.com/pod-product-compliance
Lightning Source LLC
Chambersburg PA
CBHW071326250626
47159CB00004B/1485